BEVERLY LEWIS

The
Covenant

BETHANYHOUSE
a division of Baker Publishing Group
Minneapolis, Minnesota

© 2002 by Beverly Lewis

Published by Bethany House Publishers
11400 Hampshire Avenue South
Bloomington, Minnesota 55438
www.bethanyhouse.com

Bethany House Publishers is a division of
Baker Publishing Group, Grand Rapids, MI

Printed in the United States of America by
Bethany Press International, Bloomington, MN

ISBN 978–0–7642–1086–0

Library of Congress Cataloging-in-Publication Data
Lewis, Beverly.
    The covenant / by Beverly Lewis.
        p.   cm. — (Abram's daughters ; 1)
      ISBN 0–7642–2717–3 (hardcover : alk. paper) — ISBN 0-7642-2330-5 (pbk)
    — ISBN 0-7642-2718-1 (large print paperback)
      1. Lancaster County (Pa.)—Fiction. 2. Sisters—Fiction. 3. Amish—
Fiction. I. Titlle.
    PS3562.E9383   C65   2002
    813'.54—dc21   2002008665

Cover design by Dan Thornberg, Design Source Creative Services

12   13   14   15   16   17   18   7 6 5 4 3 2 1

The
Covenant

Dedication

For

three devoted sisters:

Aleta Hirschberg, Iris Jones, and Judy Verhage.

My aunties, ever dear.

By Beverly Lewis

HOME TO HICKORY HOLLOW
The Fiddler • *The Bridesmaid* • *The Guardian*

THE ROSE TRILOGY
The Thorn • *The Judgment* • *The Mercy*

SEASONS OF GRACE
The Secret • *The Missing* • *The Telling*

ABRAM'S DAUGHTERS
The Covenant • *The Betrayal* • *The Sacrifice*
The Prodigal • *The Revelation*

THE HERITAGE OF LANCASTER COUNTY
The Shunning • *The Confession* • *The Reckoning*

ANNIE'S PEOPLE
The Preacher's Daughter • *The Englisher* • *The Brethren*

THE COURTSHIP OF NELLIE FISHER
The Parting • *The Forbidden* • *The Longing*

The Postcard • *The Crossroad*
• *The Courtship of Nellie Fisher (3-in-1)*

The Redemption of Sarah Cain
October Song • *Sanctuary* (with David Lewis) • *The Sunroom*

The Beverly Lewis Amish Heritage Cookbook

Amish Prayers

www.beverlylewis.com

BEVERLY LEWIS, born in the heart of Pennsylvania Dutch country, is the *New York Times* bestselling author of more than ninety books. Her stories have been published in eleven languages worldwide. A keen interest in her mother's Plain heritage has inspired Beverly to write many Amish-related novels, beginning with *The Shunning*, which has sold more than a million copies. *The Brethren* was honored with a 2007 Christy Award.

Beverly lives with her husband, David, in Colorado.

Part One

◆ ◆ ◆ ◆

Therefore, on every morrow, are we wreathing

A flowery band to bind us to the earth.

—John Keats

Prologue

LEAH

Growing up, I drank a bitter cup. I fought hard the notion that had I been the firstborn instead of my sister Sadie, my early years might've turned out far different. Fewer thorns over the pathway of years, perhaps. But then, who is ever given control over their destiny?

When I came along my parents already had their daughter—perty, blue-eyed, and fair Sadie. *Dat* needed someone to help him outdoors, so taking one look at me, he decided I was of sturdier stock than my soft and willowy sister. Hence I became my father's shadow early on, working alongside him in the fields, driving a team of mules by the time I was eight—plowing, planting, doing yard work and barn work, too, some of it as soon as I could walk and run. Mamma needed Sadie inside, doing "women's work," after all. And my, oh my, Sadie could clean and cook like a house a-fire. Nobody around these parts, or in all of Lancaster County for that matter, could redd up a place faster or make a tastier beef stew. But those were just two of Sadie's many talents.

Truth be known, my sister was at war with the world and its pleasures . . . and the Amish church. At eighteen, she was taking classes with Preacher Yoder, along with other young people preparing to follow the Lord in holy baptism, to make the lifetime vow to almighty God and the church. Yet all the while offering up her heart and soul on the altar of forbidden love.

Still, I kept Sadie's dreadful secret to myself. *Ach*, part of me longed to see her get caught and promptly rebuked. Sometimes I hated her for the unnecessary risks she seemed too willing to take, not just foolish but ever so dangerous. I was truly worried, too, especially since I was nigh unto courting age and eager to attend Sunday night singings myself when all this treachery began. What would the boys in our church district think of *me* if word got out about shameless Sadie?

"Promise me, Leah," she whispered at night when we dressed for bed. "You daresn't ever say a word 'bout Derry. Not to anyone."

Even though I wished Dat and Mamma *did* know of Sadie's worldly beau, I was sorely embarrassed to reveal such a revolting tale. I struggled to keep the peace between Sadie and myself, but against my better judgment. Soon, I found myself wondering just how long I could keep mum about my sister's sinful ways. Truth be told, I wished I knew nothing at all about the dark-haired English boy my sister loved beyond all reason.

In those early days I was forever worrying, so afraid I'd be stuck playing second fiddle to Sadie my whole life long. Living not only under the covering of my steadfast and God-fearing father, but daily abiding in the shadow of my errant elder sister. The cross I was born to bear.

Sometimes at dusk I would slip away to the upstairs bedroom I shared with Sadie. Alone in the dim light, I gazed into a small hand mirror, looking long and hard by lantern's light, yet not seeing the beauty others saw in me. Only the reflection of a wide-eyed tomboy stared back—a necessary substitute for a father's son, though I was a young woman, after all. And as innocent as moonlight.

Abram's Leah . . .

Clear up till my early twenties, I was identified by Dat's first name. To English outsiders, the two names together might've sounded right sweet, even endearing. But any church member around here knew the truth. *Jah,* the People were clearly aware that Leah Ebersol was dragging her feet about marrying the man her father had picked out for her. So because I was stubborn, I was in danger of becoming a *maidel*—in short, a maiden lady like Aunt Lizzie Brenneman, although she was anything but glum about her state in life. For most young women, not marrying meant denying one's emotions, but not Lizzie. She was as cheerful and alive as anyone I'd ever known.

As for Abram's Leah, well, I possessed determination. "Grit . . . with a lip," Dat often said of me. And I do remember that I had a good bit of courage, too. Never could just stand by tight-mouthed, overhearing the womenfolk speculate on "Abram's rough-'n'-tumble girl"—them looking clear down their noses at me just 'cause I wasn't indoors baking pies or doing needlework. Goodness, that's how Sadie spent *her* time . . . and Hannah and Mary Ruth, and of course, Mamma.

Puh! 'Twas Dat's fault I wasn't indoors making ready for supper and whatnot. I was too busy with farm chores—milking cows twice a day, raising chickens for both egg gathering and, later, dressing them to sell. Whitewashing fences, too. Oh, and sweeping that big old barn out in nothing flat every Saturday. I wasn't one to mince words back then. I was as hardworking as the next person. Just maybe more practical than most young women, I 'spect. Sometimes I even wore work trousers under my long dress so dust from the haymow or mosquitoes from the cornfield wouldn't wander up my legs of a summer. Come to think of it, my second cousin, Jonas Mast, was the boy responsible for sneaking the britches to me—promised to keep the deed to himself, too.

Ach, I was a lot of spunk in those days. A lot of talk, too. But now I try to mind my p's and q's, make apricot jam and pear butter for English customers, and get out and weed my patch of Zenith hybrid zinnias—purple, yellow, and green—in my backyard. More often than not, I find myself saying evening prayers without fail.

'Course now, nearly all that matters in life is the memories. Dear, dear Mamma and unyielding Dat. Kindhearted Aunt Lizzie. Happy-go-lucky Mary Ruth and her too-serious twin, Hannah—competitive yet connected all the same by invisible cords of the heart. And Sadie . . . well, perty is as perty does. The four of us, Plain sisters, attempting to live out our lives under the watchful eye of the Lord God heavenly Father and the church.

Ofttimes now before twilight falls, when the sun's last rays shift slowly down over the golden meadow, if I step outside on my little front porch and let my thoughts stray back, I can hear a thousand echoes from the years. Like a field sprinkled with lightning bugs, they come one by one. Bright as a springtime morning, radiant as a pure white lily. Others come tarnished, nearly swallowed up by blackness, flickering too hastily, overzealous little lights . . . then gone.

The night air seems to call to me. And though I am a sensible grown woman, I surrender to its urging. A vast landscape in my mind seems to reach on without end as I peer across the shadows into another world. Another universe, seems now. There I see a mirrored image that I treasure above all else—the reflection of a smiling, thoughtful young man, his adoring gaze capturing my heart on the day our eyes locked across a long dinner table, when all of us spent Second Christmas with Mamma's cousins over near Grasshopper Level. 'Twas a red-letter day, though Dat soon made me want to forget I had ever smiled back.

A lifetime ago, to be sure. These days, I simply breathe silent questions to the wind: *My beloved, what things do you recall? Will you ever know that I am and always will be your Leah? . . . daughter of Abram, sister of Sadie, child of God.*

Chapter One

SUMMER 1946

Gobbler's Knob had a way of shimmering in the dappled light of deep summer, along about mid-July when the noonday sun—standing at lofty attention in a bold and blue sky—pierced through the canopy of dense woods, momentarily flinging light onto the forest floor in great golden shafts of luster and dust, causing raccoons, moles, and an occasional woodchuck to pause and squint. The knoll, where wild turkeys roamed freely, was populated with a multitude of trees—maple, white oak, and locust. Thickets of raspberry bramble had sometimes trapped unsuspecting young fowl, stunned by the heat of day or the sting of a twelve-gauge shotgun during hunting season.

"*Steer clear of the woods,*" the village children often whispered among themselves. They warned each other of tales they'd heard of folk getting lost, unable to find their way out. The rumors were repeated most often during the harvest, when nightfall seemed to sneak up and catch you unaware on the heels of a round white moon bigger than at any other season of year. About the time when all over Lancaster County, fathers came in search of plump Thanksgiving Day turkeys. But even before and after hunting season, children admonished their younger siblings. "*It's true*," they'd say, eyes wide, "*the forest can swallow you up alive.*"

Certain mothers in the small community used the superstitious hearsay as leverage when entreating their youngsters home for supper during the delirious days of vacation from books and lessons.

One particular boy and his school chums paid no attention to the warnings. Off they'd go, scouring the forest regularly, day and night, in the eternal weeks of summer, playing cowboys and Indians near an old lean-to, where hunters found shelter from bone-chilling autumn rains and reloaded their guns and drank hot coffee . . . or something stronger. The lads promptly decided the spot where the run-down shelter stood was the deepest, darkest section of woodlands, where they whispered to one another that it was indeed true—sunlight never, ever reached through the mass of branches and leaves. There, among a maze of thorny vines and nearly impenetrable underbrush, everything was its own shadow with gray-blue fringes.

The area surrounding Gobbler's Knob, on all sides, was home to a good many folk, Plain and fancy alike. Soldiers, back from the war, were streaming home to Quarryville just seven miles southwest, to the town of Strasburg about five miles northwest, and to the village of Ninepoints a short carriage ride away.

Abram and Ida Ebersol's farmland was part and parcel of Strasburg Township, according to the map. Smack-dab in the heart of Pennsylvania Dutch country, the gray stone house had been built on seven acres bordering the forest more than eighty years before by Abram's father, the revered Bishop Ebersol, who now slumbered in his grave, awaiting the trumpet's call.

The "Ebersol Cottage," as Leah liked to call her father's limestone house, stood facing the east, "toward the rising of the sun," she would often say, causing Mamma to nod her head and smile. The house was surrounded by a rolling front lawn that became an expanse of velvety grass, where family and friends could sit and lunch on picnic blankets all summer long, the slightest breeze causing deep green ripples across the grass. Behind the two-story house, a modest white clapboard barn stabled two milk cows, two field mules, and two driving horses.

Inside, the front-room windows and those in the kitchen were tall and high with dark green shades pulled up at the sash. In fact, Leah had never remembered seeing the first-floor windows ever covered at all. Mamma was partial to natural light, preferred it to any other kind, said there was no need to block out the light created by the Lord God heavenly Father, whether it be a sunlit day or moon-filled night.

The second-story dormer windows were another matter altogether. Because the family's bedrooms were located on that particular floor, window shades were carefully drawn when the rooms were occupied, especially at dawn and dusk. Abram was adamant about his and Ida's privacy, as well as that of his growing daughters.

From their west-facing windows upstairs, Abram and Ida had a splendid view of the wide backyard, vegetable gardens, the barn and outhouse, the soaring windmill that pumped well water into the house, and beyond that the dazzling forest. What intrigued Ida more than the display of trees and brushwood were the songbirds that fluttered from tree to tree and trilled the sonnets of late spring and early summer, when open windows invited the outdoors in.

Meticulously kept and weekly cleaned, the farmhouse was in remarkable condition for its age. Abram and his family, as well as all who had come before, appreciated, even cherished, the warmth of its hearth and hallways, its congenial rooms. It was a house that when you were gone from it, you were eager to return. Leah often remarked upon arriving home from a visit to one relative or another that the front door and porch seemed to smile a welcome. This, in spite of the fact that she and the entire family always entered and exited the stately dwelling by way of the back door. Still, the pleasing exterior was like a shining beacon in a sea of corn and grazing land, forest and sky.

Whenever Abram's daughters happened to take the driving horse and family buggy over to Strasburg to purchase yard goods and whatnot, the sight of the four girls turned many a head. Thirteen-year-old Hannah and Mary Ruth were not quite as tall as Leah, sixteen in a few short weeks, but they were definitely experiencing a growth spurt here lately. Hannah's facial features—the pensive beauty of her brown eyes, thick lashes, and the delicate contour of her nose and chin—resembled blue-eyed Mary Ruth to some degree, but not enough for folk to automatically assume they were twins. Due to the vivid hue of their identical strawberry blond hair, Hannah and Mary Ruth did make a striking pair when tending the orange and yellow marigolds alongside the road together or looking after Mamma's vegetable-and-fruit stand.

But more times than not it was flaxen-haired Sadie— older than Leah by three unmistakable years—who caused young men to take special notice. Leah, the only brunette of the bunch, strove in her effort not to care that Sadie was often singled out. Still, she observed quietly how boys of courting age were drawn to her enticing older sister, especially now that it appeared Sadie was preparing to offer her lifetime covenant to God and the Amish church.

Seems the closer Sadie gets to her kneeling vow, the more foolish she becomes, thought Leah one hot and humid afternoon while helping Dat bring the mules in from the field. She wasn't one to wag her tongue about any of her sisters' personal concerns. Goodness knows, enough gossip went on in the community, mostly when womenfolk got together to quilt and gab at one farmhouse or another. Family stories—past and present—ideas, recipes, the weather, and ways of looking at things came flying out into the open then to be both heard and inspected. There were some *gut* forms of chatter, but most of it was a waste of time, she'd decided early on.

Leah herself had never been to a quilting frolic. Not once in her entire life. She'd heard plenty about it, more than she cared to, really, from Sadie and the twins. Such gatherings were fertile ground for tales, factual and otherwise, seemed to her. She preferred to engage in straightforward conversation, like the kind she occasionally got to enjoy with Dat out in the cornfield, plowing or cultivating the rich soil. Leah craved the succinct words of her father, his no-nonsense approach to life. After all, Sadie had Mamma's affection, and the twins garnered adequate consideration from both parents.

Here lately, Leah had had the nerve to think that she just might have an exceptionally level head on her mature shoulders and it was time she carved out a corner of credibility for herself. Especially with Dat, even though she and her father wholeheartedly disagreed on one thing, for sure and for certain. Her father had made up his mind years ago just whom Leah should one day marry, though if asked, he wouldn't have said it was by any means an *arrangement*—quite uncommon amongst the People.

The young man was Gideon Peachey, the only son of the blacksmith the next farm over. He was known as Smithy Gid, to tell him apart from other boys with the same name in the area. Gideon's father and Dat had long tended the land that bordered each other's property even before Leah was ever born. Truth was, when they were out working the field, Dat liked to say to Leah, pointing toward the smithy's fifteen acres to the east of them, "There now, take a wonderful-*gut* look at your future . . . right over there. Nobody owns a more beautiful piece of God's green earth than the smithy."

It was a knotty problem, to be sure, since Leah wanted to please her beloved Dat in the matter of marriage. And she was well aware of the benefits for the bridegroom, as well as for the lucky girl who would become Gideon's bride, since the smithy's son was to receive the deed to his father's sprawl of grazing land upon marriage. Of course, all this had, no doubt, played a part in the matchmaking, back when Leah and Gideon were youngsters. Not only that, but the smithy Peachey and Dat considered each other the best of friends, and Gideon was the son Dat wished he'd had.

Leah had no romantic feelings whatsoever for nineteen-year-old Gideon. Oh, he was nice looking enough with wavy brown hair that nearly matched her own and fair cheeks that blushed red when he smiled too broad. He was a good boy, right kind, hardworking, sincere and all. As a conscientious objector, he'd received an agricultural deferment, to the relief of his father and the entire community, just as had many other of their boys eighteen and older.

Leah and her sisters, and Gideon and his sisters, Adah and Dorcas, had grown up swinging on the long rope in the Peachey haymow together, and ice-skating, too, out on Blackbird Pond. She knew firsthand what a good-hearted boy Gideon was. And Adah . . . one of her own dearest friends.

Yet Leah's heart belonged to Jonas Mast and there was no getting around it. Of course, no one but Sadie knew, because things of the heart were carried out in secret, the way Leah's own parents had courted and their parents before them. Now Leah eagerly awaited the day she turned sixteen. At last she would ride home from Sunday night singing with Jonas in his open buggy, slip into the house so as not to awaken the family, hear the *clip-clopping* of the horse as he sped home in the wee hours, all the while dreaming the sweet dreams of romantic love. Jah, October 2 couldn't come anytime too soon.

The hilly treed area known as Gobbler's Knob had never frightened young Derek Schwartz, second son of the town doctor. He was well at home in the vast confines of the shadowy jungle, notwithstanding his own mother's warning. As a lad he had purposely sought out frozen puddles to break through with a single stomp of his boot. He insisted on defying most every periphery set for him growing up, and he proceeded to live as though he planned never, ever to die.

When Derek met up with Sadie Ebersol that mid-August night, he was instantly intrigued. It happened in the village of Strasburg, where two Plain girls, in the midst of their *rumschpringe*—the "running-around," no-rules teen years allowed by the People prior to their children's baptism into the church—were attempting to pull the wool over several English fellows' eyes. They'd abandoned their traditional garb and prayer caps and changed into cotton skirts and short-sleeved blouses for an evening out on the town. But Derek's friend Melvin Warner, sporting a pompadour parted on the side, said right away he knew the girls were Amish. "Just look at the length of their hair . . . all one length, mind you, not a hint of a wave or bangs like *our* girls."

Derek had taken note of the girls' thick, long hair, all right. He also noticed Sadie's roving blue eyes and the curve of her full lips when she smiled. "Doesn't matter to me if a girl's Plain or not," he told Melvin quickly. "I'm telling you, the blonde belongs to me." Almost before he'd finished his pronouncement, he rose from the table where he and his cronies—newly graduated from high school—sat drinking malted milk shakes, messing around, and waiting for some action. Standing tall, he strolled over to make small talk with the wide-eyed girls. Particularly Sadie.

Sadie never would've believed it if anyone had hinted at what might happen if she kept sneaking off to Strasburg come Friday nights. No, never. She had gone and done the selfsame thing several other times before this, discarding her long cape dress and black apron, even removing her devotional *Kapp*, unwinding her hair, parting it at the side instead of in the center, letting the weight of its length flow down over one shoulder. Ach, how many times in her most secret dreams had she wished . . . no, longed for a handsome young man such as this, and an *Englischer* at that? The tall boy headed her way, across the noisy café, had the finest dark hair she thought she'd ever seen. And, glory be, he seemed to be making a beeline right for her. Jah, as she waited, Sadie knew he was intent upon *her*! The look in his dark eyes was spellbinding and deep, and she could not stray from his gaze no matter how hard she might've tried. He seemed vaguely familiar, too. Had she known him during her years at the Georgetown School, when she and her sisters and their young cousins and Plain friends all attended the one-room public schoolhouse not far from their farm? Her mouth felt almost too dry, and pressing her lips together, she hoped he wouldn't notice how awful nervous she was being here in town, this far away from her familiar surroundings.

Quickly she glanced down at herself, still not accustomed to this fancy getup she wore, including what Englishers called bobby socks and saddle shoes. She wondered how she looked to such a young man, really. Did he suspect she was Plain beneath her makeup and whatnot? Would he even care if he knew the truth? By the sparkle in his eyes, she was perty sure her Anabaptist heritage didn't matter just now, not one iota.

Sadie felt her heart thumping hard beneath the sheer cotton blouse, the one she'd slipped on *under* her customary clothes so Mamma or Leah wouldn't suspect a thing if she ever happened to get caught leaving the house after she and her sister had headed on up to bed for the night. Excitement coursed through her veins. She lifted her head and tilted it just so, the way she'd practiced a dozen or more times, and smiled demurely her first hello to the well-to-do doctor's son, who, she would soon discover, much preferred the nickname his pals had given him—Derry—over Derek, the name his parents had chosen after his devout paternal grandfather, a minister of the Gospel.

For no particular reason, Leah awakened and saw that Sadie's side of the bed was empty. On a Friday night, yet. This was not a night for a scheduled Amish singing, she knew that for sure. *Sadie's flown to the world again*, she thought, wishing Mamma and Dat might've heard their wayward daughter leave the house after they'd all gone off to bed. *Why must she be so defiant, Lord?* Leah breathed her prayer into the darkness.

Slipping out of bed, she went and stood by one of the windows and pulled the shade away. She looked out at the glaring sky, almost white with the rising moon as its light lowered itself over the barnyard below. How had Sadie made her getaway *this* time? Sadie wasn't so handy outdoors, not at all—couldn't have just hitched up one of the driving horses to the family carriage without making a ruckus on such a silent, moonlit night. Ach, it wasn't possible for Sadie. *She must've gotten a ride with someone who owns a car.* Such harsh speculating made Leah feel nearly sick to her stomach. Surely Sadie wouldn't stoop so low as to do something like that. Why, such things would not only break their parents' hearts but bring awful shame and reproach to their family. Yet Leah feared that was just what her sister had gone and done. Ach, she shouldn't let herself worry so, not about the unknown. Not about things she had no control over.

Daylight would come all too early tomorrow, she knew.

Dat would appreciate her help with the five-o'clock milking. So she needed her rest. After all, *somebody* around here had to be responsible and get a good night of sleep on weekends.

Turning away from the window, Leah let the blind block out the moonlight and tiptoed back to bed. Refusing to dwell on a host of other shameful deeds her sister might be thinking of tonight, Leah sighed. She slipped back into bed and her head found the feather pillow. She longed for sleep. Truly she did.

The café radio blared the tune "Chiquita Banana," the calypso-beat jingle: *Pepsi-Cola hits the spot, twelve full ounces, that's a lot . . .* as Derek and his pal and the two Plain girls they had picked up headed for Melvin Warner's car. Soon they were speeding down Georgetown Road, laughing and joking, toward Gobbler's Knob. He had known almost immediately that Sadie Ebersol, his unexpected date for the evening, was not accustomed to modern ways. Not in any sense of the word. "Stop here," he told the driver of the car. "Sadie and I . . . we're getting out."

"You're *walking* her home, through the woods?" Melvin said from behind the wheel.

Sadie cast a wary look at him, the first time he had sensed any hint of alarm from her all evening. "Must we go thataway?" she asked.

"Trust me. I know the forest like the back of my hand." He opened the car door and helped her out.

"Aw, Sadie, are you sure?" the other Amish girl asked, sitting next to Melvin in the front seat, leaning toward them now, seemingly very concerned. "You know what they say . . . you might never find your way out again."

Derry nodded his assurance. "We'll be fine."

"Don't worry, Naomi." Sadie flung a small knapsack bundle through the open window and into her friend's lap. "Here, take care of this for me. I'll pick it up from you tomorrow."

Once the Jeep station wagon had rumbled down the road, Derry turned and offered Sadie a hand, helping her over the ditch that ran along the roadside, then through the underbrush that led to the knoll. "So you've never gone walking out here?" he asked, turning to look at her in the moonlight.

"Not on this side of the woods," she said. "I've visited . . . uh, the woman who lives in the log house at the far edge of the forest, though. I've gone there with my sisters, by way of the dirt road, over where the foxgloves grow."

He didn't know so well the flower-strewn side of the hillock. But on several occasions he had seen the woman Sadie mentioned, as well as the No Trespassing signs posted around the perimeter to alert hunters of her five-acre property. Smiling to himself, he thought, *Sadie must think I'm thickheaded. . . . That woman is Amish.* He remembered having seen her working in the flower gardens around the log cabin. "Is the woman a friend of yours?"

"Jah . . . er, yes." Sadie frowned for a moment, then turned to look at him, smiling. "Do *you* know Lizzie Brenneman?"

He shook his head. "I haven't met her formally, if that's what you mean."

"She likes living alone, always has. Loves that side of the woods . . . and the little critters that wander 'bout the forest."

"And she can't be too old," he said.

"Thirty-four, she is," replied Sadie, though it seemed she was holding back information, that maybe the woman was in all actuality a relative, maybe even Sadie's aunt. But he didn't press the issue. He had other more important things on his mind.

We'll be sure to avoid the area of the log cabin, he thought, glad Sadie had warned him, in so many words. He knew precisely where this late-night walk should take them. Nowhere near Aunt Lizzie, he'd see to that.

Sadie's inviting smile and the false air of innocence she seemed all too eager to exude spurred him on. "Ever kiss a boy on the first date?" he asked wryly.

Her warm and exuberant giggle was his delight. He knew he'd met his match. Hand in hand they ran deep into the seclusion of the dark timberland, where the light of the moon was thwarted, obscured by age-old trees, and the night was cloudless and still.

Chapter Two

Since she was a little girl, Hannah, the older of the Ebersol twins—by twenty-three minutes—sometimes contemplated death, wondering what it would be like to leave this world behind for the next. Such thoughts stuck in her head, especially when she was alone and tending the family's fruit-and-vegetable roadside stand. That is, if the minutes lagged between customers, and rearranging the table and checking on the money box were not enough to keep her mind truly occupied.

The plight of having only a handful of customers of a morning was not so common, really, once the decorative gourds and pumpkins and whatnot started gracing the long wooden stand in nice, even rows. Their bright harvest yellows and oranges caught the eye of a good many folks who would stop and purchase produce, enjoying the encounter with a young Plain girl. But this was August, and the baby carrots, spinach, and bush string beans were the big attraction, along with heads of lettuce and rhubarb.

Shy as a shadow, Hannah could hardly wait till the

Englischers made their selection of strawberries, radishes, or tomatoes and then skedaddled on back to their cars and were on their way. Jah, that's just how she felt, nearly too bashful to tend the roadside stand by herself. She figured, though, this was probably the reason she had been chosen to watch over the myriad of fruits and vegetables, because, as Mamma would say, "The more you do something, Hannah, the better you'll get at it."

Well, that might be true for some folk, Hannah often thought, but Mamma must have never had her knees go weak on her, her breath come in short little gasps at the thought of having to make small talk, in English of all things, with outsiders . . . strangers. She felt the same way about attending the one-room public school all these years, too. Thank goodness, Mary Ruth was her constant companion; otherwise, book learning away from home wouldn't have been pleasant at all.

But looking after the produce stand was even worse, really. The sight of a car coming down the road, slowing up a bit, non-Amish folk gawking and sometimes even pointing. Were they just curious about her long cape dress and black apron . . . her prayer cap, the way she parted her hair down the middle . . . was that why they chose to stop? And then the car pulling up smack-dab in front of the stand. Ach, it wasn't so bad if her twin hadn't any chores to tend to and came along with Hannah. Working the produce stand was easily tolerated at such times, if not enjoyed.

Tonight, though, she lay in bed next to Mary Ruth, aware of the even, deep breathing of her sister, thinking once again about heaven, since sleep seemed to escape her. She wondered what it was like when their grandmother on Dat's side—*Grossmammi* Ebersol—had breathed her last, six months ago now. Dat had not been present at his mamma's bedside the night of her passing, but several of the womenfolk had been, Mamma and three aunts, Dat's sisters. The comment had been made that Mammi's passing had been a peaceful one—whatever that meant. Hannah wished she knew. She couldn't quite understand how leaving your body behind and letting go of your spirit—that part of you that's supposed to live on and on through eternity—how that could be a pleasant experience. Not when just the opposite seemed to be true at the start of one's life, when you came hollering and fussing into the world. She'd witnessed enough home births to know *that* was true, for sure and for certain.

So she didn't know if saying someone's death had been a peaceful passing was quite the best way to describe such an event. Of course, now, she hadn't attended the death of anyone, not yet anyway. "You just haven't lived long enough, daughter," Mamma had said recently, when Hannah finally got up the nerve to say just how curious she was about the whole business of dying.

"*Himmel*—heavens, Hannah," Mary Ruth had reprimanded her over a bowl of snow peas, "don'tcha believe that the Lord God sends His angels to come and carry you over River Jordan . . . when the time comes? The Good Book says so."

Hannah had kept still from then on, not bringing up the subject again. Must be not everyone thought secretly about their own deaths the way she did. Maybe she was mistaken to just assume it all along.

Now, lying in the bed she shared with Mary Ruth, she couldn't help but wonder if her twin was just too cheerful for her own good. Jah, maybe that was the big difference between the two of them. Mary Ruth was unruffled, while Hannah looked at life through serious, worry-filled eyes. For as long as she could remember, that was how it was. Of course, they shared nearly everything, sometimes even finished each other's sentences—Dat got a laugh out of that if it happened at the dinner table. Same color hair, similar hankerings for food, and some of the same boys had caught both her and Mary Ruth's eye. Even though the two of them wouldn't be expected to start showing up at Sunday night singings for another three years—it wasn't proper for nice girls to do so before age sixteen—there were plenty of cute boys at Preaching service of a Sunday morning. Especially the Stoltzfus brothers—Ezra and Elias—close enough in age to almost pass for twins, though Ezra was the older by fourteen months. She had confessed in private to Mary Ruth that she wondered if some of those boys might not be thinking some of the same romantic thoughts about her and Mary Ruth. The laughter that had spilled out of Mary Ruth at the time was ever so warm, even comforting, when she admitted that she, too, had entertained notions about some of the same young men as Hannah. Mary Ruth answered, with a twinkle in her blue eyes, "We ain't too young to start filling up our hope chests, you know."

Hannah knew that, all right. She and Mary Ruth had spent many evening hours embroidering pillowcases and crocheting doilies. Hannah especially liked to embroider—with the lazy-daisy stitch—tiny colored flowers or a butterfly in the corners of simple square handkerchiefs Mamma bought over in Strasburg. Sometimes Hannah marked them "For Sale" out on the roadside stand, but mostly she enjoyed giving them away as gifts.

Mamma would often tuck one of Hannah's perty handkerchiefs up the sleeve of her dress. It came in handy for erasing a splotch of dirt from a young child's face—any number of nephews and nieces who came to visit—or just simply nose blowing for herself. One of the handkerchiefs Hannah had embroidered featured a row of six tiny people in the corner, one for each of her immediate family. That one happened to be both Leah's and Mamma's favorite, but Mamma usually won out having it in her pocket or wherever.

Much of what was already folded away in Hannah's pine hope chest could also be found in Mary Ruth's matching trunk. What one sister created, the other usually did, too.

Just now, turning in bed, Hannah stared into the serene face of her twin. Mary Ruth's eyelids were twitching rapidly. *What sort of dream is my sister having tonight?* she wondered.

She wished she might be so relaxed as to sleep through the sound of footsteps coming up the stairs. Was it Sadie coming home after midnight again? Hannah actually thought of slipping out of bed to catch her in the act of tiptoeing back to the bedroom. But, no, best not. Who knows what handsome and interesting Amish boy might catch *her* eye someday, if she ever broke out of her timid shell, that is. Who knows what risks she might take to spend time with a beau once she turned courting age.

Restless, with a hundred thoughts of her own future and that of her dear sisters, she rolled over and stared up wide-eyed at the dim ceiling, hearing Mary Ruth sigh tenderly in her sleep, utterly free from care.

———◆———

Leah knew it was probably wrong to pretend to be asleep, when she was as wide awake as an owl and very much aware of Sadie's swift movements just now. Not to mention the loud getup her sister was wearing. Yet she trusted the dear Lord to forgive her for not sitting up right then and there, causing a scene in their quiet house.

Sadie had come silently into their room, moved quickly to the wooden chest at the base of the double bed, lifted the lid and secured it, then immediately removed her billowy, too-short skirt, then the sheer blouse and white ankle-length socks and saddle shoes.

Leah couldn't see now, and didn't try to, but she was fairly sure by the sound of it that Sadie was pushing the English clothes down into the depths of the trunk.

The rich, damp smell of the woods filled the room, that and a sprinkling of hyacinth, some cheap bottled cologne, maybe. Where on earth had Sadie found such clothes, not to mention the idea for the arrangement of her hair? It seemed that Sadie had become a frustrated artist and her golden locks, the canvas. Nearly every time she returned home late at night, her hairdo was different. Leah had no idea you could change your hair so many ways.

———◆———

Saturdays were not so different from any other choring day amongst the People. Ida did notice, though, that Sadie

36

seemed ever so sluggish this morning, lacking her usual vitality. Sadie's eyes were a watery gray. Gone the bright blue, and ach, such dark circles there were beneath her eyes. Was it possible her eldest had tossed and turned all night long? And if that was true, whatever could've plagued her dear girl's mind to torment her so? Was she ill?

"You seem all-in," she said as Sadie rolled out the pastry for pies. "Trouble sleeping maybe?"

Sadie was silent. Then she said something about maybe, jah, that could be, that she'd had herself a fitful sleep. "I'll hafta make up for it sooner or later, I 'spect."

"Anything I can do for you?" Ida replied quickly, thinking a nice warm herbal tea might help relax Sadie come bedtime tonight.

But Sadie seemed to bristle at the remark. "No need to worry, Mamma" came the unexpected retort.

"All right, then." Ida went about her kitchen work, sweeping and washing the floor. She began cooking the noon meal for Abram and the girls, knowing how awful hungry her husband, and Leah, too, would be when they came in from the barn around eleven-thirty or so, eager for a nice meal. Today it was meatball chowder, homemade bread and butter, cottage cheese salad, and chocolate revel bars, Abram's favorite dessert.

There was much work to be done in the house—plenty of weeding in the vegetable garden out back, too—more chores than Sadie seemed to have the energy for on this already muggy day. True, maybe her firstborn had merely suffered a poor night's sleep. But why on earth did she seem so nervous, almost jumpy? Didn't add up. Come to think of it, maybe Leah might know what was bothering Sadie, but Ida hadn't seen hide nor hair of the girl since Leah had gotten up with the chickens and gone out to milk cows with Abram before sunup. Besides, it was like pulling teeth to get Leah to share much of anything about Sadie or the twins. No, if Ida truly wanted to know why Sadie wore that everlasting half grin on her face, she'd have to wait till Sadie herself came confiding in her, which could be a mighty long time. Probably never.

Leah swept every inch of the barn that needed attention, whipping up a swirl of dust like never before. She couldn't help it, she simply felt like taking out her frustrations on the old broom and the barn floor. It was a good thing she'd hurried out here early this morning, so cross she was with Sadie.

An interesting discussion with Dat was about the only thing that might get her mind off her sister. She glanced over at him there in the milk house washing down the small room. He happened to catch her eye, and seeing her going about her chore with such vigor, he stopped what he was doing and hurried to her, digging deep into his trouser pockets for a clean blue kerchief. "Here, Leah, looks like you might be needin' this. It'll help keep your lungs free of grime, maybe," and he placed it over her nose and mouth, knotting it firmly behind her head.

"I'll surely scare the mules lookin' like this," she said, though awfully touched by her father's sympathetic gesture.

"Pay no mind to the animals. They've seen us both lookin' worse, ain't?"

"Guess you're right." Still, she felt awkward the way Dat's kerchief was tied around her head, pushing her devotional cap off center. So she quickened her pace, completing her job in the nick of time, just as Dat mentioned he was headed over to the welding shop. "Wouldja like to ride along? We'll be back before your mamma ever misses us," he said, already choosing his driving horse for the short trip.

"Jah, I'll go." She pulled off Dat's handkerchief. She'd much rather spend her morning with Dat than be anywhere near Sadie at the moment. No doubt in her mind! But she never let on to her father as they rode, the carriage swaying gently as the horse pulled them toward the welding shop.

"Preacher Yoder's thinking of hiring a driver to take him and his family out to Indiana for a short vacation, after the harvest is past."

"Why Indiana?"

"Well, it wouldn't surprise me if they're goin' to look for some grazing land while out there. Not for them to up and move, mind you, just to help one of his cousins who's thinking of getting married soon."

"To a girl in Indiana?"

Dat nodded. "Now don't that beat all?"

"Talk about long-distance courtship." She thought Dat might bring up Smithy Gid just then, try to blend the present topic with his ongoing anticipation of Gid marrying her; but he didn't. She was quite surprised that he refrained, especially when he easily could have slipped in a comment or two.

They rode along for a time enjoying the silence, aware of the hum of insects and chirp of birds. At last, Leah asked, "What do you think is the difference between being sorely tempted and yielding to it?"

"Well, all the difference in the world, far as the Scriptures say. We're admonished to watch and pray lest we fall into temptation."

"But how does a person avoid being tempted?"

" 'Tis by steering clear of those who may be tools of the enemy."

"You mean Englishers?"

The reins lay loosely in his lap, and he lifted his straw hat and scratched his head beneath. "Seems to me there's a time and a place to mingle with the outside world, but when it comes to making close friends or choosin' a mate, well, you know the best way is God's way."

She was trying not to think of Sadie now, afraid Dat might wisely see through her questions and suspect, maybe, why she was asking such things. They talked about the spirit being willing and the flesh awful weak at times. Dat brought up the pure conscience of the righteous and the battle that rages in every man . . . "every woman, too." He gave her a serious look. "But the most important thing 'bout temptation is knowing how to avoid it."

She fell silent then, soaking in all that Dat had said.

When Mamma wasn't looking, Sadie slipped into their large sunroom just off the kitchen, staring longingly out the windows, toward the barn and beyond to the dark woods. They'd made it through the dreadful maze—survived the denseness, the lurking shadows—just as Derry had said they would. He'd helped her find the way out, and she would tell Naomi so when she went to pick up her knapsack later on.

Why *had* she worried last night? With Derry by her side, she was safe in the forest. Safe anywhere at all, for sure and for certain.

Derry Schwartz. The most wonderful boy in the whole world. With a peculiar pang—part thrill, part anguish—she thought of his life and hers, how the two of them had seemed to collide unexpectedly, like an automobile appearing out of nowhere and hitting a horse and buggy—sort of like that. Of course, they had no business spending time together, none whatsoever. Yet they were drawn to each other, she for the sheer daring of a forbidden English boy who knew the outside world through and through and for the great love she truly believed he would soon have for her. And Derry . . . She didn't quite know yet. Maybe it was her wheat-colored hair and big blue eyes. Maybe he saw something in her other boys had missed. But find out, she must. She would fully discover what it was that the village doctor's son had appreciated in her, and in such a short time, yet . . . that he would ask to see her again, this very night! "Do you think you can meet me here in the woods? Would you be afraid?" he'd said after their joyful evening together. She'd said she didn't know—"It's ever so thick outside, confusing, too . . . with so much under-brush and all."

She had been careful not to admit to being fearful of the woods, just hoped he'd take the hint. And he had. He said he would be glad to meet her behind her father's barn at ten o'clock straight up.

"You could . . . wear your regular, uh, dress if you'd like," he'd added quickly, which took her off guard. "No need to pretend you're not Plain for my sake." So he'd known all along.

She could feel her cheeks growing warm. "You're sure?"

"Please don't risk getting caught in modern clothes that might, well, reveal that your boyfriend is modern."

Boyfriend . . . Her heart had leaped up at the thought. Derry must truly care for her already.

She decided right then that Derry was a very wise young man. For him to say outright that she didn't have to bother impressing him with fancy English clothing any longer. Jah, this was quite a burden lifted off her shoulders. She could be herself with him. Dress Plain, if he didn't mind. No more games to be played. Maybe she'd found the man of her dreams. Who knows, maybe he'd want to join church with her. Maybe he'd be asking more about life in the Plain community. Why else had he asked her to meet him for a second walk in the woods? Then again, maybe she would join *his* world and leave the Amish life behind.

She would know the answers soon enough. Now, if Mamma would just stop poking her head in the room, looking at her as if she was trying to figure out what in the world was twirling round in Sadie's head. No, she wouldn't go and spoil things by sharing her secret with either Mamma or Leah about the boy with dark wavy hair and shining brown eyes. Not just yet. Mamma would put her foot down hard about seeing a boy outside the church, heaven knows, especially when she was planning to be baptized here before too long. And Leah . . . well, she knew her sister would flat out tell her she was playing with fire. In the boundless forest, yet. Best keep all this to herself.

Mamma had often accused Mary Ruth, jokingly of course, that once she got started chattering she just didn't know when to quit. And she *had* been doing her share of talking this morning while helping Mamma cook breakfast.

I'll make a gut schoolteacher someday, she thought. *But Dat and Mamma would be alarmed if they knew.*

Her whole life, Mary Ruth had dreamed of becoming a teacher. But how could such a wonderful thing happen? Higher education—past the legal age of fifteen—was a no-no amongst the People, according to their bishop. Yet it was impossible to quiet her overwhelming desire to communicate learning skills to youngsters.

Mixing the pancake batter, she allowed her mind to wander. Tomorrow at Preaching service over at the Peachey place, there would be many little children in attendance. She hoped to spend time playing with some of them at the picnic following the church meeting. How many youngsters would the Good Lord give *her* and her future husband? And what sort of young man would share her love for books?

Eagerly, she looked forward to helping with the Lord's Day menu with Mamma and Sadie after breakfast. Unlike Sadie, she was only *slightly* interested in boys. As for Leah, well, that was the sister who captured her attention, especially when it came to Smithy Gid. He seemed to have his eye on their tomboy sister. Mary Ruth had suspected this for a year or so. Of course she hadn't, and wouldn't, utter a word to anyone. Leah was a very private sort of girl—practical, too—so there was no inkling of anything romantic in store, far as she knew.

Glancing over at Hannah setting the table, Mary Ruth could see that her twin was more curious about Sadie's glazed expression. It reminded Mary Ruth of the selfsame look in the eyes of worldly girls at the public one-room schoolhouse on Belmont Road, near Route 30, where she and Hannah attended. There, Amish, Mennonite, and English students recited their lessons together, and at recess some of the girls whispered about certain boys.

Mary Ruth didn't like the idea of comparing Sadie to worldly girls, though it was true that Sadie had attended the public high school over in the town of Paradise till she was seventeen. These days, Dat declared up and down it hadn't been such a gut idea for his eldest daughter to cultivate friendships with Englishers at school, an environment that promoted individuality so frowned on by the People. Had those years encouraged Sadie to have herself a wild rum-schpringe?

It wasn't Mary Ruth's place to judge, really. She would bide her time, wait and see how the Lord God heavenly Father worked His will and way in each of her sisters' lives.

Pouring a cup of batter on the sizzling black skillet, she shook off the annoying blue feeling. She hummed a church song, doing what she could to lift everyone's spirits, as well as her own. It was high time to rejoice, for goodness' sake. The Lord's Day was ever so near.

Chapter Three

After the noon meal Leah helped Sadie wash and dry each one of the kerosene lamp chimneys in the house. The glass tubes had been rather cloudy last evening during Bible reading and evening prayers, and Leah and Mamma had both noticed the light was too soft and misty because of it. Dat hadn't complained at all, though he did have to adjust his reading glasses repeatedly, scooting close to the lamp in the kitchen, where they'd all gathered just before twilight, the back door flung wide, along with all the windows, coaxing the slightest breeze into the warm house.

"We really oughta clean these every day," Leah said, handing one to Sadie for drying. "No sense Dat struggling to see the Good Book, jah?"

Sadie nodded halfheartedly.

"Are you going out again tonight?" Leah whispered.

Sadie's eyes gave a sharp warning. "Ach, not now..."

Glancing over her shoulder, Leah saw that Mamma was dusting the furniture in the sunroom. "*Cleanliness is next to godliness,*" Mamma liked to say constantly. Hannah and Mary

Beverly Lewis

Ruth had run outside to hose off the back porch and sidewalk.

"You'll break Mamma's heart if you're sneaking out with English boys, ya know," she said softly.

"How do you know what I'm doin'?"

"I saw you come home last night—saw what you were wearing, too." But before she could ask where on earth Sadie had gotten such a getup, Mamma returned, and that brought a quick end to their conversation.

Leah washed the rest of the chimneys, turning her thoughts to the Preaching service tomorrow. *Will Gid single me out again before the common meal?* she wondered. He had been more than forthright with his intentions toward her before, though discreetly enough. Yet she knew he was counting the weeks till she was old enough to attend Sunday singings. And so was she, but for a far different reason. "I'll be first in line to ask you to ride home with me," he'd said to her out in the barnyard two Sundays ago, when it was her family's turn to have house church.

Speechless at the time, she wished the Lord might give her something both wise and kind to say. To put him off gently. But not one word had come to mind and she just stood there, fidgeting while the smithy's only son grinned down at her.

What she was really looking forward to was *next* Sunday— the off-Sunday between church meetings—when the People spent the day visiting relatives. Mamma was awful eager to go to Grasshopper Level and see the Mast cousins again. It had been several months.

Leah remembered precisely where she was standing in the barn when Dat had given her the news of the visit. Looking

46

down, in the haymow, she'd stopped short, holding her pitch-fork just so in front of her, half leaning on it while she willed her heart to slow its pace.

She smiled, fondly recalling the first time she'd ever talked with Jonas. The two of them had nearly missed out on supper, standing out in the milk house talking about birds, especially the colorful varieties that lived on Aunt Lizzie's side of the woods, near where the wild flowers grew. She had told him her favorite was the bluebird. Jonas had wholeheart-edly agreed, his blue eyes searching hers. And for a moment, she nearly forgot he was three years older. He was Sadie's age. Yet, unlike any other boy, he seemed to know and understand her heart—who Leah truly was. Not a tomboy, but a real girl.

In all truth, she hadn't experienced such a thing with *any-one* ever in her life. Not with Sadie, for sure. And not so much with Mamma, though on rare occasions her mother had opened up a bit. Hannah and Mary Ruth had each other and were constantly whispering private conversations. Only with Aunt Lizzie and Adah Peachey, Gid's younger sister, could Leah share confidentially.

So she and Jonas had a special something between them, which was too bad. At least Mamma would think so if she knew, because young women weren't supposed to open up much to young men, unless, of course, they were being courted or were married.

Just now, Sadie glanced nervously toward the sunroom, where Mamma was still busy dusting. "Walk me to the out-house," Sadie whispered to Leah.

"What for?"

"Never mind, just come." Sadie led the way, through the utility room and enclosed porch, then down the back steps, past the twins, who laughed as they worked.

Silently they walked, till Sadie said, turning quickly, "Listen, if ya must know, I think I'm falling in love."

"In love? Ach, Sadie, who with?"

"Shh! He lives down the road a ways. His name is Derry."

"So, I'm right then, a fancy boy." Leah wanted to turn around right now and head back to the house. She didn't want to hear another filthy word. "What's happened to you? English boys are big trouble. You oughta know from going to high school and all."

"You sound too much like Dat."

"Well, somebody's got to talk sense to you! Having a wild rumschpringe's one thing, Sadie, but whatever ya do, don't go outside the boundaries of the *Ordnung*."

Sadie's eyes were ablaze. "Say whatcha want, but zip your lip."

"Maybe I *should* tell."

Their eyes locked. Sadie leaned closer. "You have a secret, too, Leah."

"Are you threatening me?"

"Call it what you will, but if Mamma finds out about me, I'll know it came from you. And if you go and tell Mamma on me, I'll tell Dat on you. And if Dat finds out you hope to marry Jonas 'stead of Smithy Gid, he'll put a stop to it."

Leah's heart sank. Sadie had her, for sure.

Glaring at her, Sadie opened the door to the outhouse and hurried inside. The second Leah heard the door latch shut, she turned and fled for home.

Sadie emerged from the outhouse, and not seeing Leah anywhere, she headed toward the mule road. The dirt path led to the outer reaches of the northwest side of the woods, where Aunt Lizzie's perty little place stood. She felt the smooth dust against her bare feet, but her throat felt tight, almost sore. She regretted having told Leah anything at all about her English boyfriend. Might be nice to visit her aunt, get her mind off things.

When she neared the white front fence, Sadie spied Aunt Lizzie opening the screen door. Her aunt came running and waving a dishrag, her long purple dress and black apron flapping in the breeze. "Well, hullo there. If it ain't you, Sadie!" Lizzie wore the biggest grin on her suntanned face.

Sadie quickened her step. "Hullo, *Aendi*—Auntie."

"Come round the back and sit a spell," Lizzie said, leading her past the tall stone wall that rimmed the cabin—high enough to keep deer and other woodland critters out of her flowers—to the back porch, where three hickory rockers spilled out all in a row.

The little four-room bungalow was tucked into the edge of the woods, "half in and half out," Mamma liked to say. One could enjoy the benefit of both sun and sky, as well as towering shade trees flanking the back of the house. And there were ample sunny spots for Lizzie's beloved roses, lavender, lilies, clematis, and a variety of herbs. Her vegetable gardens, too.

Once they were seated on the back porch, Aunt Lizzie asked, "So . . . what brings you up here and all by yourself, yet?"

"Just out for a short walk."

" 'Tis a nice day for it."

"Jah, hope it'll be nice tomorrow, too." Sadie asked about Preaching service. "Are you comin' to Peacheys'?"

"Haven't missed a single meeting for ever so long. Don't plan to start now."

Sadie nodded, aware of Lizzie's curious gaze.

"I'm mighty blessed not to be prone to illness, seems."

"Must be all those herbs you grow in your garden. Mamma says they have healing qualities."

"The foxgloves, too." Lizzie pointed to an array of snowy white, crimson, and yellow snapdragons growing wild and a golden throng of buttercups vying for attention.

"Ach, how's that?"

"Them snapdragons open their little mouths and scare the sickness away." Lizzie burst into her jovial laughter.

"Oh, Auntie, they don't really, now, do they?"

Then Lizzie said unexpectedly, "You look a bit *bleech*— sallow. Not feelin' so well?"

Sadie was sure she didn't look any more washed-out than she usually did. After all, being a blonde, her skin was rather pale most of the time, except when she had a sunburn. "A little tired is all," she replied.

Lizzie scratched her dark head, her hazel-brown eyes serious now. "Looks to me like you skipped near a whole night of sleep."

"I was out a bit late," Sadie admitted.

"Then I 'spect you'll be heading for bed bright and early tonight?"

"Maybe so."

Lizzie stopped rocking and reached a hand toward her. "Best be awful careful who you spend your time with, Sadie dear," she cautioned.

The silence hung awkward and heavy in the hot air. This

was so peculiar, Aunt Lizzie poking her nose in where it didn't belong.

She was thinking what she ought to say, when who should show up just then but Hannah, carrying a loaf of bread. Her sister had appeared round the corner, grinning for all she was worth and coming up the porch steps.

"Mamma just baked some raisin-and-nut bread." Hannah planted a kiss on Lizzie's cheek.

Since there was only one rocker vacant, Hannah wandered over and sat next to Sadie, looking like a chipmunk chasing after an elusive acorn.

Not one to jump to conclusions, Sadie watched Hannah's rapt brown eyes. Just how long had her younger sister been standing round the corner of the cabin?

Hannah found it ever so hard to sit still and listen to Aunt Lizzie chatter about her plans to dig up yet another garden plot—this time for marigolds—when the talk had been far more interesting before. So what she suspected was true.

She wanted to say something about the fun they would all have tomorrow at the picnic on the grounds at the Peachey farm, but Aunt Lizzie kept prattling on about herbs and flowers. Sadie only stared; her eyes, pale and vague, were focused on the deepest part of the woods.

"Tell your mamma I'll lend her a hand with plantin' kale and broccoli on Monday," Aunt Lizzie said.

"We're always glad for extra help," Hannah replied.

"I'll be down right after breakfast."

"Oh, but Mamma will say to come have scrambled eggs and waffles with us, won't she, Sadie?" Hannah said, turning to her sister.

"Wha-at?" Sadie stumbled over herself.

Hannah rose, eager to get home. "We'll see you for break-fast on Monday, Aunt Lizzie." She leaned down and offered her best smile, hugging her aunt's neck.

Quickly Sadie stood and said her good-byes, too, and the two girls walked home, saying not a single word between them.

Chapter Four

"Out tempting the woods again." Henry Schwartz muttered his complaint to the wind. One by one, he proceeded to pick raspberry brambles out of his son's jeans cuffs, glad to help Lorraine, his wife, whenever he could. *Derek never could stay away from that forest,* he thought, wondering why his son had lied about going to Strasburg with friends when it was clearly evident where the boy had spent the bulk of his Friday evening.

Henry held high hopes for Derek, wishing he might grow out of his aimless fascination with so many young women. Couldn't he stay home once in a while like his older brother, an ex-GI back from the war? Except now that Robert was finally here safe and sound, he slept around the clock, and when he wasn't loafing in his bathrobe, he was staring at the new television set. He also seemed to have lost any incentive for job hunting, enjoying his membership in the "52–20 Club," his unemployment pay.

"Give him more time, dear. He'll get his bearings soon enough," Lorraine had said when he voiced his concern. "He survived D day, for pete's sake."

But Henry wasn't sure it was a wise thing to let a boy coast on his wartime merits. Discharged soldier or not. After all, young Derek had the next thing to a full-time job working for Peter Mast, an Amish farmer over on Grasshopper Level, and planned to join the military once he turned eighteen in December. Robert, at twenty, needed something to get him up and going in the morning. What would be so wrong with his elder son picking up the phone and asking Peter if he had need of another hired hand?

Gathering up the dirty jeans, Henry carried them into the house and down to the cellar, where he found Lorraine piling up damp clothes into the wide wicker basket at her feet. What a hardworking, devoted wife. He knew he was lucky to have married someone like her. She had helped him through most all the years of medical school, even stayed true to him during the year their marriage was sorely tested, looking after the needs of her trio of men. One of which Henry felt he must confront with last night's walk in the woods.

◆

After lunch Mamma went off to her bedroom for a catnap, so Sadie decided now was as good a time as any to go to Naomi Kauffman's and pick up the knapsack she'd given her for safekeeping—and to cover her tracks a bit.

"Well, it's gut to see you made it out of the woods last night," Naomi said in the privacy of her bedroom. "I was so afraid you'd get swallowed up."

"I'm here, aren't I?"

"You were lucky this time. Just don't go back there again."
Naomi leaned over and pulled Sadie's pack with its bunched-
up clothing out from under the bed. "No one here suspects
where we were last night, or what we were wearing. No one
at all."

Be glad you don't have a sister named Leah, thought Sadie.
"*Denki*—thank you."

"So . . . did you let him hold your hand the whole time?"

"For pity's sake, Naomi, he's a worldly boy."

"I'm not blind! I *saw* him reach for your hand when you
got out of the car."

Sadie turned the tables. "Have I asked 'bout *your* English
friend?"

Naomi squelched a smile. "Ach, and he was ever so good-
lookin', too. Ain't so? We oughta sneak out again next Friday
night. I hear there's a doin's over at Strasburg. Wanna go?"

"Might not be such a gut idea, for us . . . well, for *me*, at
least, seein' as how I'm taking instructional classes for baptism, ya know."

"But I thought . . ."

"*Nee*—no, it's time I settled some things," Sadie insisted,
hoping her friend wouldn't suspect.

"So, then, you're finished with running round? Ready to
join church?"

That's not what she'd said exactly. Sure, she was taking
baptismal classes and all, but she was just going through the
motions so far. She hadn't decided whether or not she would
follow through with the kneeling vow when the time came.
Of course, she wouldn't be the first young person to change
her mind this close to the sacred ordinance.

Sadie sighed. "How many times do you *really* think we

could go to Strasburg dressed up—painted up, too—like fancy girls and not get caught?"

"You never seemed worried before."

"I've been thinking. You'd best be goin' to Sunday night singings from now on. Let some nice Amish boy court you, settle down some, get married in a year or so."

Naomi was indignant. "Ach, you've changed your tune, Sadie Ebersol!"

"Well now, have I?" she said, turning toward the door. Naomi followed her into the hall and down the steps.

"You said before you wanted some excitement and fun—*adventure*—out in the modern world. Wanted to see firsthand what you'd been missin'."

Sure, she'd said that. Said it with a vengeance, nearly. But now? Now she had what she wanted—a boy named Derry—but she couldn't for all the world spill the beans to Naomi. No, such a thing would spread like a grass fire, and next thing she'd know, both Dat and Mamma would be talking straight to her, in front of Preacher Yoder, maybe. Or worse, the bishop.

"Things change." She was glad her friend stayed put at the end of the lane, Naomi's bare toes curled, digging hard into the dirt.

"Are *you* goin' to start attending singings again?" Naomi asked.

"We'll see." She turned to leave.

"Sadie . . . wait!" Naomi hollered, stumbling after Sadie as if her life depended on it somehow.

She kept walking. "Mamma's expectin' me home now," Sadie said without looking back. No, she'd keep on walking alone this time, her knapsack close to her heart. No sense in prolonging Naomi's disappointment. No sense lying outright, either.

During the hottest hour of the afternoon, while Sadie went out for a walk, Leah crept up to their bedroom, closed the door behind her, wishing for a lock for the first time ever. Like a curious kitten, she hurried to Sadie's hope chest and opened the lid. All day she'd thought of nothing more than wanting to have a closer look at the modern skirt and blouse Sadie had worn last night, and even the white-and-black two-toned shoes. She couldn't imagine wearing anything on her feet at all, not till the first hard freeze, for goodness' sake. Such things as shoes, of any kind, were much too confining.

Pushing down into the depths of the trunk, Leah felt for the shoes. She moved sheets and pillowcases, enough for three beds as was customary. There were towels and wash-cloths, too, along with tablecloths, hand-hooked rugs, and cushion tops. At last her hands bumped the shoes, and she pulled first one, then the next out, peering at each one, holding them gingerly by their white shoestrings the way Dat held dead mice he found in the barn by their tails. So peculiar looking they were. Ach, she felt almost sinful just touching them, studying the fancy shoes with disdain, knowing who had walked in them, and wondering all of a sudden who might've worn them even before Sadie. The cotton blouse still smelled of cologne and the forest. The skirt was a light russet color, cut with a flair at the hem. Not so worn that she might've suspected someone else of having owned the garment before Sadie. Not the blouse, either. So then, did this mean Sadie had actually gone into an English dress shop somewhere and purchased these clothes? And if not, how had the fancy outfit landed in her possession? Through one of Sadie's former high school chums, maybe?

She thought of Sadie's Plain girlfriends, those who were testing the waters, having their one and only chance to experience the outside world before deciding whether or not to become a full-fledged member of the Amish church. There were any number of girls who might influence Sadie in such a manner. Or, then again, maybe it was Sadie who was influencing them. Come to think of it, that was probably more likely . . . Sadie being the stubborn sort she was. Sometimes Leah felt sorry for her.

Leah recalled the time when Sadie had wanted to stay home and nurse a sick puppy back to health, missing Preaching service to do so. Mamma had said *"Nothing doin',"* but in the end, Sadie got her way. Leah, at the time, wasn't at all so sure her sister was actually going to sit at home and care for their new puppy dog. She had a feeling what Sadie really wanted was to hop in the pony cart and take herself out to the far meadow, spending time gathering wild daisies on the Lord's Day, yet. And Leah was perty sure that's just what Sadie had done, too, because she found a clump of limp buttercups in Sadie's top drawer later on. Besides all that, the sick puppy died that night. Hadn't been tended to at all.

Put out with herself, Leah honestly didn't know why she was thinking such things just now. She oughta be on her knees, praying for her willful sister, she knew, asking God to spare His judgment on dear Sadie.

Stuffing the defiled clothing and shoes back into Sadie's hope chest, she sighed, breathing a prayer, knowing it would take more than a few whispers sent heavenward to save her sister from sinful pleasures. Sadly, she hadn't the slightest idea how to rescue someone from the swift undercurrent of the world, especially when there was no sign of flailing arms or calling for help. Surely Sadie wouldn't just let herself go under without a struggle.

Leah shuddered to think that by keeping her sister's secret, she just might be helping Sadie drown. *Dear Lord, am I making a terrible mistake?*

Henry Schwartz had absolutely no success talking to his youngest son. First of all, Derek had made himself unavailable for the longest time, upstairs shaving. Then when Derek telephoned his friend Melvin Warner, he was interrupted several times by Mrs. Ferguson, who wanted to gab to her newly married daughter. But Derek put her off, tying up the party line they shared with twelve other families. Once his son did finish the phone call, Lorraine was signaling them to the dining room for breakfast.

Finally Derek had come dragging to the table, where Lorraine and Robert were engaged in a lengthy conversation, discussing such heartrending topics as "friendly fire," which had killed so many Allied soldiers, two hundred at sea alone. Robert had been only eighteen at the time of his enlistment, promptly being taken off to basic training in early 1944, just as the war was heating up, during the increasing attacks on Berlin.

Sitting quietly, watching his family down their breakfast, Henry wondered if it was such a good idea to confront Derek today regarding his most recent woodland excursion. His son was in a hurry, obvious by the way he wiped his mouth on his napkin and crumpled it onto the plate, then muttered "excuse me" and exited the room with little eye contact. His footsteps on the stairs were swift, as well, and Henry assumed he was rushing off to work at the Mast farm.

Recalling that his attempts to rein in *this* son had always failed in the past, he realized anew that Derek was a boy whom he had never been able to truly influence or oversee. Not at all like conscientious and honorable Robert, but to a certain extent similar to Henry himself, who had been rather reckless in his youth. No one, not even his father, the Reverend Schwartz, could manage him in those days.

Subsequently, like father like son. For Henry to acknowledge the fact was one thing; living with it on a daily basis was quite another. So he would wait for a more opportune time to sit down with Derek. If that moment presented itself at all.

It was the custom of the People to gather for Preaching at nine o'clock sharp on a Sunday morning. The day before, the menfolk removed the partitions that divided the front room from the big kitchen, creating an enormous space, enough for as many as one hundred fifty, give or take a few. Throw rugs were removed, decorative china washed and spotless. Furniture downstairs was rearranged and stoves polished and blackened. In the barn the manure had been cleared out and, in general, the stables cleaned up. Preaching service usually lasted three hours, ending in the common meal at noon and a time of visiting afterward. A day of great anticipation, to be sure.

Ida sat on the backless bench between Lizzie on her left

and Leah on her right. Sadie and the twins sat squarely in front of them, and Ida was taken yet again by the striking beauty of the girls' hair color, so similar to her own growing up. Hannah and Mary Ruth could scarcely be told apart when viewing them from this angle; the curve of their slender necks was nearly identical. Sadie, just a bit taller, was similar in build to her twin sisters, still mighty thin for being this close to the end of her teen years. Even so, Ida admired her girls lined up all in a row, when she should've been entering into an attitude of prayer in preparation for being a hearer of the Word.

She recalled that Leah had been much quieter than usual on the walk down their long lane and out to the road. As usual, Mary Ruth had been the one doing most of the talking, though Sadie had mentioned how awful perty the clouds were this morning. "All fluttery, they are," she'd said, which made Ida wonder what was *really* on her firstborn's mind, seeing as how she'd bumped into Sadie coming in the kitchen door at nearly one o'clock this morning. Ida had gone downstairs, suffering from an upset stomach. She didn't know why, really—hadn't eaten anything out of the ordinary. She was pouring herself some milk and nearly dropped the glass, startled to hear someone opening the back door at such an hour.

When she turned to see who it was, she gasped. "Sadie, ach, is that you?"

"Jah, Mamma. I'm home" was all Sadie said.

"Out all hours," Mamma said reprovingly.

Sadie was silent.

Now was as good a time as any to remind her daughter what the Scriptures taught. " 'What fellowship hath righteousness with unrighteousness? And what communion hath light with darkness?' "

"Still . . . it's my rumschpringe," Sadie muttered, then skittered past and hurried up the steps.

A faint timberland scent mingled with a fragrance Ida couldn't quite place as Sadie nearly fled from the kitchen. Ach, if only Abram had gotten their eldest a domestic permit, keeping Sadie home from the wiles of public high school after she finished eighth grade. Both Ida and Abram had erred and were paying for it dearly, exposing Sadie to higher education, her consorting with worldly teachers and students and all. After Sadie they'd gotten wise, requesting a permit for Leah to keep Abram's farmhand separated from the world once she turned fifteen.

Though, hard as it was not to rush after willful Sadie, Ida had just let things be. Her mother heart longed to interfere, if only for Sadie's well-being. Yet it wasn't the People's way. Better for her eldest to experience a bit of the world now, before her baptism, than to be curious about it afterward. So she didn't persist on the night before Preaching. No, the house was dark and still, and should remain so, even though she'd feared Sadie had been out wandering through the woods that late at night. And not alone, more than likely.

Then, of all things, Sadie had commented on the sky and the clouds as they'd strolled to church. Ida couldn't remember having heard her eldest talk thataway, as if she had suddenly come to appreciate the handiwork of Creator-God after all these years. No, it wasn't like her Sadie to pay the heavens any mind; she never had been as conscious of nature as either Leah or Lizzie.

Since the church meeting was just next door, so to speak, she and Lizzie, along with the girls, had all walked down the road together. Ida had taken her hamper of food over to the

Peacheys last evening in the carriage, so her hands were free. Early this morning, after milking and a hearty breakfast, Abram had gone to help the smithy with last-minute details.

Here they sat, the women and young children on the left side of the room, waiting to sing the first long hymn, while upstairs the ministers counseled amongst themselves, planning who would preach the *Anfang*—the introductory sermon, *Es schwere Deel*—the main sermon, and *Zeugniss*—the testimonies.

All the while Ida couldn't keep her eyes off the back of Sadie's dear head—the strings of her white prayer cap hanging loose over her graceful shoulders. Soon, jah, *very* soon Sadie would be making her covenant with God and the church. Ida caught herself sighing audibly. Sadie was so much like Lizzie had been during her youth, it seemed—though Ida hoped and prayed her eldest would tread lightly the path of rumschpringe, not follow its fickle corridors as far as Lizzie had. Ach, there was ever so much more than met the eye to the late teen years. For some it was the devil's playground— wild parties and whatnot. "A sin and a shame," Preacher Yoder often said in his Sunday sermons, admonishing the young people to "stay in Jesus." She must see to it that Sadie finished instructional classes for baptism and obeyed the Lord in that most sacred ordinance come September.

Lizzie gave Miriam Peachey and her daughter, Adah, a hand with preparations for the picnic on the grounds. She and several other women worked in Miriam's kitchen, arranging great platters of cold cuts, cheeses, and slices of home-made bread, all the while conscious of the growing number of young people milling about the barnyard; many were coming into the age of courting and their running-round years. She was a practical woman who had learned early on to curtail any lofty expectations for the youth of the church, not put hopes too high on certain ones in particular, knowing what she did. Keenly aware of human frailty, she'd stopped focusing too much on the future, rather concentrating on the present. The here and now. After all, what you did today, you had to live with tomorrow. Ach, she knew that truth all too well.

Silently she observed girls like Sadie and that buddy of hers, Naomi Kauffman. Lizzie could tell them a thing or two if they'd but listen. Yet they would pay her no mind. Not now. They were basking in the giddy blush of youth, along with many others, delighting in their youthful heyday. Oh, how she remembered having narrowly survived those years herself. And sadly, after those disturbing days, nothing had turned out the way she'd ever hoped. Goodness knows, she'd dreamed of marrying and having at least a handful of children by this time. Instead, the prospect of her own family was fading with every passing year.

Yet, in spite of it all, Lizzie was the last person to dwell on disappointments. She tried to live cheerfully, bringing as much joy into the lives of others as she possibly could. Take Ida's quartet of girls, for instance. Now, there was a right happy group of young women, especially round the dinner table when she was invited, which she was quite often. She wouldn't think of turning down a chance to spend time at her sister's place. Oh, how they laughed and told stories on each other, Ida in particular, recalling their girlhood days, growing up with a batch of siblings—one sister over in Hickory Hollow, who at the age of thirty-eight already had ten children and another on the way.

Sometimes Lizzie wished all her siblings had settled closer to Gobbler's Knob, where—from her midteen years on—she had such wonderful-gut recollections. Memories of dewy green Aprils and gingery Octobers, though such memories soon became entwined with painful ones, the way quilting threads of jade, sapphire, and cranberry interlock with strands of ebony and ash gray.

But on such a perty day as today, what with the sky the color of Dresden blue, Lizzie pasted a smile on her face, made her way outside, down the steps, and out to the long back-yard, where picnic blankets were already being spread out in the shade of the linden tree, its thick heart-shaped leaves crackling in the heat of the day.

She refused to waste a speck more energy on feeling sorry for herself. Time to call the menfolk indoors to dish up, then the women and girls to follow soon after. She'd sit down on the large Ebersol blanket and eat lunch with Ida, Leah, and Hannah, too, while Mary Ruth ate and played with the little children, and Sadie and some of the older girls sat in a clois-tered cluster a stone's throw away, clapping out their botching game. She would enjoy the fellowship, such a merry time, sur-rounded by so many folk who managed to be happy, come what may.

Chapter Five

The train that ran between Quarryville and Atglen could rarely be heard this far away from Route 372. Occasionally, though, in the dark morning hours, before the birds began their enthusiastic refrain at first light, its rumblings along the track traveled deep through the terrain, across the miles to Leah as she rose out of bed, stepping onto the wooden floorboards. She heard the faintest whistle, ever so distant and just now almost eerie, as the air was particularly still, with nary a breeze to speak of.

Preparing to slip into her brown choring dress and apron, Leah was still aware of the far-off train whistle. Dat would be surprised if she hurried out to the barn and got busy before he did on a Monday morning, but she felt strangely compelled to get an early start. She had an urgent, almost panicky feeling, wanting to get out of bed, remove herself as quickly as possible from Sadie, who slept peacefully now after yet another late night. How her sister managed to attend to daily chores with only a few hours' sleep, Leah didn't know.

Oh, how she missed the carefree days she and Sadie had

enjoyed as little girls. Such fond memories she had of playing hopscotch on a bright summer day, spending the night at Aunt Lizzie's, and playing hide-the-thimble on cold, rainy afternoons. They enjoyed pulling little wooden wagons round the barnyard with their faceless dollies wrapped in tiny hand-made quilts no bigger than a linen napkin, extra-special things Mamma had sewn for each of them. And they'd promised one day, on a walk over to the Peachey farm, to be best friends for always; *"No matter what,"* Leah had said. And Sadie had agreed, her deep dimples showing as she smiled, taking little Leah's hand.

Leah longed for the days when they shared everything, holding nothing back. But Sadie was sadly "betwixt and between."

On Monday mornings it was customary for Mamma and Sadie to get the first load of laundry washed and hung out on the line before they even started cooking breakfast. But from the barnyard Leah could hear Mamma calling for Sadie to get up. Then, a short time later, through open bedroom windows, similar pleas for Hannah and Mary Ruth to "rise and shine" came wafting down to Leah's ears.

Returning to the kitchen, she poured some freshly squeezed orange juice for herself. Then who should appear in the kitchen, ready to go down to the cellar to lend a hand, but her twin sisters.

"Sadie's under the weather," Mary Ruth volunteered as Leah gawked, surprised to see them doing their older sister's chores.

"Either that or just awful tired," Hannah said softly, her scrubbed face still bearing the marks of sleep.

Leah wasn't too surprised to hear it. She wondered when the time would come for Sadie to simply refuse to get up of a morning. And this the day Aunt Lizzie was coming to help Mamma with gardening.

Hurrying down the cellar steps, she announced that Aunt Lizzie would probably be here for breakfast perty soon. "Did you remember, Mamma?"

Looking a bit haggard herself, Mamma nodded. "Lizzie did say something at Preaching that she'd come over and help. She also said you girls had stopped by the other day. Wasn't that nice?"

"Jah, Sadie went," Leah said.

"And I took some raisin-nut loaf up there," Hannah said rather sheepishly.

"So *that's* where my sweet bread ended up," Mamma said, getting back to work sorting the clothes but without her usual chuckle.

"It's been too long since Aunt Lizzie came for breakfast," said Leah. "I wish she'd come more often."

"Well, now, your auntie practically lives here . . . most days," Mamma replied.

That was true. Still, Leah felt right settled round Lizzie. It was like the calm sweetness after a spring rain. Jah, Lizzie was more than just an auntie to her; she was a close friend, too.

◆

Leah sat on the long wooden bench next to Aunt Lizzie at the eight-board table. Usually, their aunt, if present for a meal, would sit to Mamma's immediate left, with Dat at the head. Today Lizzie sat farther down the bench, between Leah and Mary Ruth. Sadie came dragging down the steps scarcely in time for Dat's silent blessing over the food and sat across the table, next to Hannah. Dat gave Sadie a stern sidewise glance before he bowed his head for prayer.

Such unspeakable tension in the kitchen now, and all since Sadie had come into the room. Dat and Mamma weren't totally ignorant of Sadie's behavior, Leah was fairly sure.

Not only was Leah uncomfortable, she was unfamiliar with this sort of strain, especially with someone seated at the table who wasn't part of their immediate family. Mamma's other siblings lived farther away, some over in Hickory Hollow and SummerHill, others in the Grasshopper Level area, but it was Lizzie they saw most often, since she lived just up the knoll, so near they could ring the dinner bell and she'd come running. Thankfully, Lizzie brought a joyous flavor to any gathering, and on this day Leah was more than grateful for her mother's youngest sister sharing their eggs, bacon, waffles, and conversation.

Over the years her aunt had taken time to introduce Leah, all the girls really, to God's creation, particularly the small animal kingdom. But it was Leah who had soaked up all the nature talk like a dry sponge. She recalled one summer afternoon long ago when Aunt Lizzie had shown her what squirrels could do with their tails. "Look, honey-girl," Lizzie had said when Leah was only three or four. "See how they fold them up over their little heads like an umbrella?" She was told that the umbrella-tail protected squirrels when the steady rains come, "which happens in the fall round here."

Lizzie continued as they sat in the shade of her treed

backyard. "Squirrels use their tails another way, Leah. They settle down onto their haunches and toss their tails over their backs like woolen scarves to keep them warm while they sit on the cold ground and eat."

Young Leah had found this ever so interesting, wanting her aunt to go on and on sharing such wonderful-gut secrets. So she pleaded for more while observing the many squirrels scampering here and there, up and down trees, over the stone wall.

"Well, now, have you ever felt lonely . . . in need of a hug?" Aunt Lizzie sometimes asked Leah peculiar questions, catching her off guard.

"I guess, jah, maybe I have," she'd replied, though it was hard to think of a time when she'd actually felt alone, what with three sisters in the house and more cousins than she could even begin to count.

"Squirrels get lonesome, too, don'tcha think?" And here Lizzie demonstrated with her own arms how squirrels used their tails to hug themselves, so to speak. "Ach, such a comfort it is to them."

At the time Leah wondered if her aunt was also a bit lonely. After all, she didn't have a husband to hug her, did she? She lived alone in the woods, well . . . not quite in the woods, but perty near. "You must like squirrels an awful lot, ain't so, Auntie?" Leah had said after thinking about the special things a squirrel's tail offered.

"Who *wouldn't* like such cute little animals? They look so contented with their bushy tails high over their heads or dragging behind them," Lizzie said quickly. "But the dearest thing is how their faces look like they're smilin'."

Leah had never thought of that. And every time she

spotted a squirrel from then on, she noticed not only what their tails were doing but also the humorous half smile on their furry little faces.

Just now, sitting next to Aunt Lizzie, Leah couldn't help but wonder if her aunt could use a nice hug, maybe. How long had it been since she'd spent time with her, just the two of them? Much too long it seemed. Goodness' sakes, Mamma was always one to hug her girls, and Dat and Mamma often embraced each other when Dat came in the house for supper. Surely Auntie needed hugs, too—maybe more so than all the rest of them put together. She didn't know why she would think such a thing just now, but she did. Which was why Leah decided then and there she'd take it upon herself to squeeze Aunt Lizzie's arm or hug her neck, for no particular reason today. Jah, she would.

Sadie felt her father's eyes on her throughout breakfast. And Mamma's, too. Had they heard her coming home late again last night? Did they suspect something?

Breathing in, she held the air a second or two, then exhaled, wondering if Leah had broken her word and talked to Mamma. Or maybe it was Dat who'd learned first from Leah the wicked secret they shared.

She was so tired she scarcely cared; in fact, she could hardly pick up her fork. So weak she was, nearly trembling as she sat at the table, the smell of the food turning her stomach. How many more hours before she could lie down and rest, take a quick nap? This afternoon, maybe, while Mamma, Hannah, and Mary Ruth headed down to the general store in Georgetown. Leah and Dat would be busy outside, so she'd have the house to herself, if Mamma didn't mind her staying home. She must have some time to herself here perty soon. A good solid hour or so of sleep would help a lot.

"Five more days before we visit Mamma's cousins," Mary Ruth was saying, all smiles. "Cousin Rebekah wrote me a letter, telling 'bout the Bridal Heart quilt she and the others are makin' for Anna. Seems it won't be long and there'll be a wedding on Mamma's side of the family."

The news didn't come as a surprise to anyone at the table, really. Both Sadie and Leah—probably Mamma, too—expected Mamma's cousin's oldest daughter and her beau, Nathaniel King, to be published soon in their own church district, come autumn. Of course, they'd all be invited to the November wedding.

Sadie squirmed with talk of Anna Mast and a possible wedding. According to age, she would be next in line for settling down, and rightly so. Sadie knew this, though she balked inwardly at the thought. Her attraction to Derry Schwartz was complicating things. What was she to do?

Inviting Aunt Lizzie for breakfast proved to be a mighty good idea. Leah felt nearly satisfied after Mamma's delicious eggs, scrambled up with diced cup cheese. After the bacon and toast, she had little room for waffles. She took one anyway, sipping black coffee to tone down the sweetness of the maple syrup. She observed Sadie, who wasn't herself at all, sitting nearly motionless across the table—not saying much—during the entire meal, her face pale, the color nearly gone from her eyes, too. Hannah was her usual quiet but smiling self, reddish blond hair gleaming on either side of the middle part, though she spoke occasionally, mainly to ask for second helpings of everything. Mary Ruth, bubbly and refreshed from a gut night's sleep, entered into the conversation with Mamma and Aunt Lizzie.

Dat said nary a word. Too hungry to speak, probably. As for Mamma, she looked happy to have her sister near, and she mentioned that maybe Lizzie would like to come along next Sunday "to visit Peter and Fannie and the children."

Lizzie seemed glad to be included in the outing to the Masts' orchard house and wore the delight on her bright face. "Jah, that'd be nice," she said.

"We'll be goin' to pick apples in a few weeks, soon as Fannie says they're ripe 'n' ready," Mamma said. "Why don'tcha come along then, too, Lizzie?"

"When we make applesauce—can Aunt Lizzie help us, Mamma?" asked Mary Ruth, leaning round their aunt to see Mamma's answer.

Leah hoped her aunt would agree to attend the work frolic. There was something awful nice about having Mamma's younger sister over. She was as cheerful and cordial as Sadie was sassy these days.

"The Masts grow the best McIntosh apples, jah?" Aunt Lizzie said between bites.

"Mm-m, such a gut apple for makin' applesauce," Mary Ruth spoke up.

"So's the Lodi . . . and Granny Smith apples, too," Hannah said, grinning at her twin.

Dat looked up at Sadie just then, as if all their talk had found its way to him, disrupting his thoughts. "Most folk have a preference for apples," he said. "Ain't so much the name as the quality and flavor."

Mamma continued where Dat left off. "Bruised apples, ones that fall from the trees, don't usually end up in applesauce, ya know. They're turned into cider."

Sadie frowned for a moment, her eyes blinking to beat the band. But she said nothing. It was Hannah who caught the subtle message, and when she did, her head was bobbing up and down, though she said not a word.

Aunt Lizzie must've sensed the tension and remarked that even apples used for cider could have a right sweet taste—if they were tended to carefully, spices added and whatnot. She seemed to direct her words to Sadie, because she was looking straight at her.

Leah understood what Lizzie was trying to say. In spite of falls from trees and bumps from the hard ground, your spirit—if it had been true and sweet to begin with—could be reclaimed in time and with the right kind of care.

Aunt Lizzie seemed to know what she was talking about, which was the thing most puzzling to Leah. Gathering up the dirty plates and utensils for Mamma, she thought sometime it would be nice to know something of Lizzie Brenneman's own rumschpringe, back when. Of course she wouldn't think of coming right out and asking; that wasn't something you did just out of the blue, not if you were as polite as Leah felt she was. Still, it would be nice to know.

It was midafternoon, and Sadie, stretched out on the bed, woke up from an hour-long nap. How nice to have this chance to relax before Mamma and the girls returned from the store. Leah, she knew, was out puttering in the barn or the potting shed—two of her favorite places to be, though Sadie never could understand Leah's unending attraction to the out-of-doors.

Sitting on the edge of the bed, she yawned drowsily. She

regretted having told Leah about Derry. She'd made a huge mistake in doing so and she knew it. She and Derry . . . well, their relationship was much too precious to be shared with a girl who had no idea what love was, probably, except for a smidgen of puppy love years ago. She recalled Leah's youthful account of an autumn walk with Cousin Fannie's oldest son. "Jonas says he wants to marry me someday," Leah had said with smiling eyes.

"Marry *you?*" Sadie had to snicker.

"I know, sounds silly. . . ."

"Sure does," and here she'd eyed Leah for a meddlesome moment. "You, at the ripe old age of ten, are secretly engaged to Jonas Mast?"

Leah had grinned at that, her face blushing shades of pink. "Jah, guess I am."

"You actually said you'd marry him?"

"I can't imagine loving any other boy this side of heaven," Leah had declared, her big hazel-gold eyes lighting up yet again at the mention of the Mast boy.

"Puh!" Sadie had exploded. But now she could certainly understand such romantic feeling. Back then she'd laughed out loud more than once at Leah's immaturity, so green her sister was! How could you possibly know who you wanted to spend the rest of your life with when you weren't even a woman yet? Such a big difference there was between herself and her spunky younger sister. There was not much, if anything, that could prompt Leah to ever think of straying from the fold.

Outside, she found Leah in the tidy little garden shed close to where the martin birdhouse stood ever so high, next to Mamma's bed of pink and purple petunias and blue bachelor's buttons. Near the tallest maple in the yard, where a white tree bench wrapped its white grape-and-vine motif round the base of the trunk. "Hullo," she called as she approached the entrance so as not to startle her sister. She couldn't risk getting off on the wrong foot for this conversation.

Leah turned only slightly, her fingers deep in potting soil. "Didja have a gut nap?"

Sadie nodded, bleary-eyed.

"What brings you out here?"

Sadie sensed a chuckle in Leah's voice. "Just thought we could chat, maybe. That's all," she replied.

Nodding almost knowingly, Leah smiled again. "Half expected you."

Leah's remark made it easy for Sadie to push ahead. "I hope you've kept things quiet, ya know, the way I asked you to."

"Haven't told a soul."

The pressure in her shoulders and neck began to ebb away, as if Leah's words had opened a tap in her, unlocking an inner serenity. "Not to *anyone*, then?"

"Not Aunt Lizzie; not Dat and Mamma neither."

Sadie was ever so glad. Knowing Leah as she did, she'd simply have to trust that the name Derry would forever be kept out of all family conversations from here on out. The Lord willing.

Chapter Six

Peter and Fannie Mast, walking arm in arm, strolled out to meet all of them as Leah, her mamma and aunt, and sisters stepped out of the carriage. *"Willkumm Familye!"* came the pleasant greeting. It was nearly one o'clock in the afternoon when they arrived; the blazing sun beat down, making all of them a bit droopy, though the Sunday ride had been only a half hour long.

Jonas and his seven brothers and sisters spilled out of the kitchen door into the backyard. Anna, Rebekah, Katie, and Martha Mast gathered round Sadie, Leah, and the twins, chattering in Pennsylvania Dutch, while Jonas, Eli, Isaac, and little Jeremiah Mast hung back a bit, arms conspicuously behind their backs, merely smiling.

Dat unhitched the tired horse and led him up to the barn to be watered, and Peter quickly turned and headed in that direction, too. Fannie invited everyone inside for spiced cold tea. "You children could take your glasses and sit in the shade under the willow," she said, grinning over her shoulder as they all followed her through the back door.

"Our mamma must want some quiet talk with your mamma and aunt," whispered Anna to Sadie. Leah had overheard and wondered what that was about.

"Might be cooler outside in the shade, anyways," Sadie replied. "Might catch an occasional breeze, ya know."

Leah didn't have to be coaxed. Far as she was concerned, it would be ever so nice to sit and chat with Cousin Fannie's children outdoors, though most of them were either in their teens or nearly twenty, so they were closer to being grownups than kids. Still, she hoped for an opportunity to speak with Jonas again after such a long time.

Before they left the kitchen for the backyard, Hannah passed round newly embroidered handkerchiefs to Cousin Fannie and each of her daughters. "Well, now, what a nice thing to do," said Fannie.

"*Denki*—thank you," Anna, Rebekah, Katie, and Martha said in unison.

Mamma's face was wrapped with a smile. "Hannah just loves to surprise folk with her handmade things."

" 'Tis better to give than to receive," Mary Ruth said, leaning her head on her twin's shoulder, and the twosome seemed to tilt toward each other like two birdlings in a nest.

Aunt Lizzie nodded in full agreement. Then, in spite of the white-hot air, they carried their iced-tea glasses outside, finding ample shelter beneath the towering tree in the far corner of the yard. Jonas and his younger brothers, including three-year-old Jeremiah, sat cross-legged in a jumble, off to themselves a bit but within earshot of the girls. Sadie and Anna sat together, leaving Leah, Hannah, Mary Ruth, and the four Mast girls to sit in a circle nearby.

"Won't be long and we'll all be goin' to Sunday singings,"

said Rebekah, eyes shining with expectation. "Now, ain't that something?"

Leah nodded. "How many are in your buddy group?" She asked the question of Rebekah, forgetting she was only fifteen.

"I'm not in any group just yet," Rebekah said, grinning. "Best be askin' Anna 'bout such things. Or Jonas, maybe. They go to singings all the time."

Hearing her name, Anna turned round, as did Sadie. "What didja say?" Anna asked, dark, loose strands of hair dangling below her prayer cap at her neck. She looked almost too young to be thinking of marriage this fall.

Rebekah wasn't shy and said quickly, "Leah just wanted to know how many youth go to the singings in our church district."

"More than I can count, it seems" came Anna's reply. "Just keeps growin' all the time."

Now Sadie was talking. "And you've got yourself a beau, jah?"

This brought a round of muffled laughter among the girls. Leah noticed the boys leaning back in the grass, chortling ever so hard. All except Jonas. He was staring right back at her, motioning his head just now, as if he was trying to get her attention . . . that he wanted her to go walking with him. Was that it? Or was he shooing a fly away from his sunburned face? She didn't think she ought to be looking back at him like this, no. But she couldn't help it, really. And, jah, he *was* motioning to her with his head. Of course, now, none of the others seemed to notice, so caught up in the mirth of the moment they were.

Mamma wouldn't approve, not one bit, of Leah going off

with Jonas by herself. It wasn't the time to be pairing off. Socializing was done at singings, where the church elders expected young folk to spend time talking, singing, and getting acquainted with each other—boys with girls—after sundown in one of the church member's barns. Not here, in broad daylight, with the family gathered round, and now Dat and Cousin Peter meandering back from the barn, talking slow in Amish, the way the menfolk often did, walking right past them, across the broad green lawn toward the big white farmhouse.

When Leah glanced over at Jonas again, he was busy with little Jeremiah; then he was talking to his brothers. She heard him say they should all play a game of volleyball . . . a *quiet* game, with no raising of voices, since it was the Lord's Day. The rest agreed, even though it was unbearably hot. Right there they divided up teams, under the dappled shade of the willow, and Leah wasn't surprised to be chosen on the side with Jonas, Eli, and their sister, eight-year-old Martha, along with Hannah and Mary Ruth.

"Six players on one side, five on the other. *Allrecht*—all right?" Jonas asked, and everyone nodded in agreement. "We'll play in the side yard." Smiling, he led his little brother up the back steps and into the house.

"Jeremiah must be tired," Anna remarked.

"Jah, it's time for his nap," Katie said.

Leah thought it was awful kind of Jonas, the oldest, to take time out for the youngest. *He'll make a wonderful-gut father someday*, she decided.

On the way round the house, past the well pump to the side yard, Leah hung back, walking alone. Because of that, she happened to overhear Rebekah ask Mary Ruth, "Would you and your sisters like to come over and help sew up the wedding quilt planned for Anna?"

"Sadie, Hannah, and I might," Mary Ruth replied. "But don't count on Leah comin'. She doesn't work on quilts, doesn't do much sewin' at all, really."

The look of surprise on Rebekah's face amused Leah. "Are ya sayin' Leah never quilts?"

Mary Ruth lowered her voice, but Leah considered her answer all the same. "Nee—no . . . Leah works outside with Dat."

"Doing *men's* work?"

"You didn't know?" Mary Ruth asked.

Rebekah shook her head.

"It's not like she gets callused hands—she doesn't. And Leah never lifts anything heavy. She's not built at all like a man, ya know. She just helps wherever she can, alongside Dat . . . keepin' him company. That's the way it's always been."

"Always?"

"Jah," said Mary Ruth.

Rebekah said no more, and Leah was truly glad. She felt awkward having listened in. She rather wished she'd walked on ahead, up with Anna, Sadie, and Hannah, and resisted the urge to eavesdrop. Truth be told, she felt pained—stung, really. Rebekah's startled reaction to her working with Dat made her feel less of a woman somehow. Caused her to think yet again that she was of less worth because she lent Dat a hand instead of helping Mamma with women's work. At least in Rebekah Mast's eyes, she was.

Why did she care what Rebekah, or anyone else, thought? It hadn't been her idea—not in the first place—to choose outdoor work over the chores Mamma and her sisters did. It wasn't that she couldn't cook or bake or clean house. She could easily do so, if need be. Yet, after all these years, she felt she didn't fit in at quilting frolics or canning bees. Sure, she enjoyed making apple butter or things like weeding the vegetable and flower gardens and helping Mamma with potted plants. There had been no question in her mind whether or not to consider changing ranks, so to speak. At least not till just now—this minute—listening to her sister and cousin discussing her place in life.

Still walking shoulder to shoulder with Mary Ruth, Rebekah spoke up suddenly. "I think Leah's right perty, don't you?"

Mary Ruth shrugged her shoulders. "Guess I never thought of her thataway."

"Well, she *is*," Rebekah insisted. "And I wouldn't be a bit surprised if more than one boy takes a likin' to her once she starts goin' to singings. You just wait 'n' see."

"Maybe so," Mary Ruth said softly.

Leah veered off to the right, making a beeline for the side yard, where the volleyball net was already set up and ready for play.

She preferred that neither Mary Ruth nor Rebekah know she had heard every word they'd said. What Jonas thought of her was all that really mattered. Did he find her attractive now, after all these years?

The volleyball game was not so much competitive as enjoyed for the fun of it. That, and for one another's company. Leah was especially pleased that Jonas kept setting up the ball for her to tap over the net. In fact, she found it curious just how many times that happened during the course of the afternoon. She had tried not to let Jonas distract her from playing well. For the sake of her teammates, she attempted to put aside the flutterings in her stomach, tried to ignore them so her feelings wouldn't show on her face, where just anybody might notice how much she cared for Jonas Mast.

Ida was ever so glad to have a peaceful yet short visit with Fannie, drinking ice-cold spiced tea with Lizzie, too, catching up on things here on Grasshopper Level. Abram and Peter had long since wandered into the front room, settling into a somewhat serene dialogue—voices subdued—man to man.

"Guess ya noticed all the celery we planted," Fannie said softly, leaning her chubby elbows on the trestle table.

"Can't say that I looked, really, but 'spose you're thinking of marryin' your daughter come November, jah?" She preferred not to be nosy over family matters, but Fannie had never been vague about things such as this.

"Jah, Anna's our bride-to-be, all right."

"Lizzie, the girls and I will be glad to help with whatever ya need for the wedding day," Ida offered. When her own daughters became marrying age, the favor would be returned.

"Won't be too much longer and we'll both be grandmothers, I 'spect." Fannie sighed as she fanned herself with the new handkerchief from Hannah.

"What a joyful day that'll be."

"How 'bout your Sadie . . . has she caught a young man's fancy yet?"

Ida flinched a little, though she hoped Fannie hadn't

noticed. She didn't know what to say to that, really. And Lizzie was keeping quiet—too quiet, maybe. Seemed it wasn't anybody's business that Sadie was spending far too much time outside the house come nightfall, two . . . sometimes three nights a week. She wasn't about to share that with Fannie, whose children hadn't given them a speck of trouble during their teen years. Not yet, anyways.

"Back when she turned sixteen, Sadie started goin' to singings, and she seemed to enjoy it for a time. Here lately she hasn't been going." Ida wished she might turn the topic of conversation to something else completely, talk of other relatives or recipes, anything at all.

"Well, why do you 'spose that is?" came Fannie's next question.

Lizzie rose and went to the back door, looking out.

Ida shook her head. "Can't always put much stock in some of the young people. You know how it is before they join church. They want to have their fun."

Some of the young people . . .

Why on earth had she clumped Sadie in with so many others thataway? Fannie would surely guess that something was amiss—after all, her cousin's wife wasn't so thickheaded. She was a bright woman, a few years younger than Ida, who'd seen her share of trouble amongst the young folk in the area during rumschpringe. Just probably hadn't bumped into any of her own daughters sneaking into the kitchen door in the middle of the night, carrying their fun much too far.

Ida glanced out the window, watching their youngsters playing a game of near-silent volleyball. Her gaze found Sadie—tall, slender, and beautiful. What a shame that such a girl wasn't nearly as perty on the inside. Sighing, she watched

Leah for a time. Quite the opposite was true of her tomboy girl. A lily white heart, for sure and for certain—as perty as can be, whose radiance shone through to her pleasing countenance. Ach, such an odd pair . . . complete opposites. Just the way she and Lizzie had been in their youth. Not so anymore. Life's hard knocks had a way of pushing you down on your knees. Both she and Lizzie had become prayerful women, almost like good Mennonites they were, talking silently to the Lord God heavenly Father about everybody and everything.

Fannie broke the silence. "Peter and I . . . we're gonna have us another baby next spring—end of March."

"Well, now, won't that be nice."

Lizzie turned, a grin on her face. "Ach, how nice!"

"Haven't told anyone just yet," Fannie said, eyes bright with the news. "Peter is ever so glad. And Jeremiah will have a playmate."

Ida was happy for Fannie. The new baby would be the very youngest of all her many first cousins' children. Jah, a wee one would bring joy to all, especially at their many family gatherings.

"Have you ever thought of having another baby, too—maybe a boy this time?" Fannie asked unexpectedly.

"Why, no, guess I haven't, really." She was a bit taken aback by Fannie's bluntness. "I'm movin' past childbearing years, I 'spect."

"After four girls, wouldn't it be awful nice for Abram to finally get his son?" came Fannie's too-quick reply. "To carry on the family name."

Ida thought it but didn't say that Leah had always been considered Abram's son. That was fairly common knowledge amongst the People. Of course, Leah was blossoming more and more as a young woman here lately. Chances were that someday Leah would get weary of the outdoor work and start wanting to prepare for marriage . . . learning to quilt and sew at long last.

She found it awkward that Fannie would talk so. The truth was, neither she nor Abram had ever worried their heads over the Ebersol name not being passed on. "We've always trusted the Lord for our children," she said. "If God wanted us to birth boys, well . . . I do believe we'd have some by now."

That silenced Fannie right quick, and Ida was more than relieved.

Sadie was startled when a car drove into the dirt lane, and she wouldn't have known who the driver was if she hadn't looked just then between plays. Her side of the volleyball net was rotating positions, getting ready for young Isaac to serve the ball, when a shiny gray car pulled up next to the house.

Once she realized who the driver was, she had to will herself to turn her attention back to the game. But she only half succeeded and watched Derry Schwartz get out of the car and hurry to the back door—as if he was family or something. His boldness further shocked her. Nobody but relatives and friends would knock at the back door of a Plain house. Anyone else used the front door. But Derry hadn't knocked on the door at all; he'd gone immediately inside, as though Peter or Fannie had been expecting him.

How odd, she thought. *Does Derry know Mamma's cousins?*

It wasn't but a few minutes and he came back out again, carrying a large basket.

That's when Jonas called to him from the server's position, "Hullo, Derek! Did you finally pick up the strawberry jam for your mamma?"

Derry paused before getting into the car. "I was out this way, so thought I'd drop by," he said, his hand on the door. "Need to make some brownie points at home."

Sadie had no inkling what Derry meant by that. And she was trying her best not to call attention to herself, when Jonas invited Derry to set the basket down and come meet some of his father's kin.

Derry still hadn't noticed her there; otherwise, she doubted he would have put the basket of preserves in the backseat of the car and come over to meet them at all. She was afraid she might breathe too quickly and pass out, so nervous she was.

When Jonas brought him over to her, Derry only smiled and said, "Nice to meet you, Sadie." Just as he had before when meeting Leah, Hannah, and Mary Ruth. He'd treated her the same, as if she wasn't his sweetheart-girl at all. Just a distant relative to Jonas Mast and his family, playing a game of volleyball on a hot Sunday afternoon.

She could hardly stand there and keep herself in the game, especially when Derry seemed to catch her eye for an instant as he turned the car round in the lane, slowing some as he waved out the window at all of them, heading for the road. Jonas had introduced her English beau to them as one of his father's hired help. So Derry was working for Mamma's cousin, Peter Mast. Doing what? And why hadn't he ever told her on their many woodland walks that he worked for an Amish farmer?

Her thoughts flew ahead to the next time she was to see Derry. Would he explain why he'd pretended not to know her today? Why he acted as if he was meeting her for the first time?

Leah collided midplay with Mary Ruth, both of them reaching high for the ball. Her sister wasn't hurt at all, but when Leah lost her balance and fell, she wrenched her ankle and lay there in the grass, unable to move her foot. Jonas rushed to her side first, asking whether or not she could walk. Then, while moaning and holding her foot—the pain was unbearable—she bravely tried to get up and see if she could take a step.

But before she could, Jonas reached down and scooped her up in his arms, carrying her across the yard toward the house. "I've got you, Leah," he said softly again and again. "You'll be all right."

She nestled her head against his blue shirt, embarrassed to have fallen, and feeling nearly as light as a pigeon feather the way Jonas was carrying her so confidently.

"I'm sorry . . ." she muttered.

"Ach, 'twas an accident, Leah."

The steady throbbing from her ankle may have clouded her ability to hear, but she almost thought Jonas had said *"my Leah"* as he strolled up the back steps with her and into the kitchen. So maybe he *hadn't* forgotten their childish secret engagement!

Ida, Fannie, and Lizzie all turned and looked at Jonas bringing Leah into the kitchen, carrying her, of all things, their conversation abruptly interrupted. Ida was rather relieved to have a diversion from the direction their talk was taking. But, goodness' sakes, she was sad to see Leah in so much pain. What on earth had she done to herself? And what was that odd look of triumph on Jonas's face?

"Leah's hurt her ankle," Jonas announced, still holding her.

Fannie fairly flew to Jonas, instructing him to put Leah there in the straight-backed chair near the wood stove. "Now . . . careful, that's right . . . don't jostle her too much."

Ida and Lizzie were close behind, kneeling quickly to tend to Leah's bruised ankle. "Best to get the pained foot iced," Ida said.

"And elevated above your heart, so the swelling can go down," Lizzie broke in.

"Jonas, go get some cold packs down cellar," said Fannie. Once he was out of earshot, she mumbled, "And make yourself useful, for pity's sake."

Ida frowned. Wasn't it clear that Jonas *had* done his part by bringing Leah inside? Holding Leah's swollen left foot in her right hand, she touched it lightly where black and blue streaks marked the painful area. Silently she prayed—for two things: that Leah's ankle was not broken, and that Jonas's intentions were simply helpful ones.

Yet, bristling at the memory, she recalled the snowy January day—nearly six years ago—when Abram and she had brought their young brood here to Peter and Fannie's for dinner to celebrate "Old Christmas," or Epiphany. Leah had been only ten at the time, and Jonas thirteen—a new teenager. She'd noticed them looking at each other across the table off and on during the meal, grinning to beat the band. But then later in the afternoon, she'd happened upon them outside in the milk house. Of course, they were only talking, but it was that rapt gaze in Jonas's azure eyes that worried her enough to mention something to Abram later after they returned home. Her husband, who had already decided that Leah should fall in love with the smithy's boy, was mighty quick to give the poor girl a tongue-lashing. Much later, in the privacy of their bedroom, Abram told Ida, "Nothin's getting in the way of Gideon Peachey becoming Leah's husband. Not even your cousin's eldest."

She shuddered, remembering the fury in Abram's voice and eyes. He had paced like a mad dog, back and forth across their upstairs room, stopping only to stare out the window for a moment, then turning, had paced some more, his hands pulling on his brown bushy beard, gray eyes flashing. "I'll be fleabit if Leah doesn't end up with Smithy Gid!" he'd said.

But, ach, this wasn't the time to dwell on such a day. Best to keep her attention on her dear girl's painful ankle, get Leah into the main-floor bedroom, have her recline so her wounded foot could be propped up higher than her heart, as Lizzie had said to.

Chapter Seven

After Bible reading and evening prayers that night, Leah hobbled up the stairs before anyone could offer to help her. She wanted to be alone—needed a reprieve from the events of the day. The one pleasant thing that still made her heart flutter was Jonas being concerned enough to carry her into the house thataway. She thought again of her face against his shirt, his strong arms holding her safe, his words of comfort and reassurance. Why hadn't he waited to see if she could walk after she'd stumbled to the ground? Thinking back on the accident, she felt she might've been able to limp to the house, given half a chance. But Jonas had been so impulsive, eager to help her himself.

In the stillness of the shared bedroom, she stood on one foot—her good one—and peered into the hand mirror, trying to find the beauty Rebekah had seen in her. But the reflection staring back just now wasn't near as perty as Sadie's or even Anna's face, not the way *she* thought of a girl being attractive. Maybe it was because her sisters had such light hair; could that be it? But no, she knew within her soul—made no difference that her hair was brown, she just didn't feel perty. Tomboys weren't supposed to be attractive. The truth came home to her yet again, pounding its way into her temples, causing pain in her head as well as her wounded ankle.

Mamma and Aunt Lizzie were mighty kind to her during the next few days, insisting she remain indoors, keep her left foot elevated either while in bed or on the downstairs couch. They brought her breakfast, dinner, and supper on a wooden tray, coaxing her to eat more than she needed, probably, but it was their way of demonstrating their love. Dat was short-handed outside, what with early potato digging and the second alfalfa cutting coming on real soon. But there wasn't anything she could do about it. Smithy Peachey and son Gid came over several times to help out during the week, but other than that, the work fell entirely on Dat's shoulders.

Aunt Lizzie said she was willing to walk to a nearby doctor, have him come take a look at Leah's ankle, tell whether or not it was broken. But Mamma didn't think it was, especially since Leah could move her foot—wiggle her toes, too—without causing her additional pain. So it was mutually decided that the ankle was just sprained. "Which," Lizzie reminded her, "can be as painful or worse than a break."

After the first few days Leah yearned for the outdoors, in spite of Hannah and Mary Ruth showing her how to embroider, Mamma giving her pointers on mending clothes by hand, and Sadie and Aunt Lizzie teaching her how to make the tiniest quilting stitches—things she might've never learned till now, since she was rather laid up. So, in some ways, her sprained ankle was turning out to be a blessing. Providential, she began to think, and she was more determined than ever to become a real woman. The kind of woman Jonas would be proud to have stand alongside him.

She enjoyed a good many unexpected visitors throughout that week. Two being Fannie and Rebekah Mast, which was awful nice of them to come all this way.

The next day Jonas Mast surprised her by dropping by with two blueberry pies and a burnt sugar cake for the family. While he was delivering the desserts from his mamma, Leah, who was reclining in the front room, happened to see him just where he stood in the kitchen. Of course, Mamma put her foot down about him going any farther than the doorway, only allowing him to call to her—"Hullo, Leah . . . hope your ankle's healing quickly"—before he was herded out the back way.

Adah Peachey stopped in one afternoon and stayed for two hours, reading the Bible and some of her own writings— she called them "personal essays on life and other things." Leah found her dear friend's sharing so interesting, even lovely, and told her so. "Mamma just won't let me do hardly anything till my ankle's better," she explained. "I'm ever so glad you came to visit."

They were upstairs in Leah's room, where Adah sat on the chair next to Leah, who was perched on top of the yellow-and-green quilted coverlet. "There's something else I'd like to read to you before I go," Adah said, her sea green eyes soft and glistening. She opened an envelope and removed the folded letter. "Well, on second thought, I 'spose you could read it for yourself."

Leah accepted the letter, and when she spied Gid's hand-writing she knew Adah's brother, still sweet on her, had sent it.

"Go ahead, open it. My brother has a nice way with words," Adah encouraged her.

Honestly, she was tempted to push the letter back in the envelope.

"Aw, Leah, for goodness' sake, read the note."

Lest she hurt Adah's feelings, or worse—how would Gid feel if Adah recounted this moment to him later?—Leah opened the letter from the young man her father seemed to admire above all others. She began to read.

> *My dear friend Leah,*
>
> Greetings to you in the name of the Lord Jesus.
>
> I happened to hear that you are under the weather, suffering an injured ankle. My sister Adah promised she'd deliver this letter to you in person, and I hope you will accept this heartfelt gesture as one of great concern and friendship. Please take care to stay off your bad foot and know that our family's prayers follow you daily.
>
> Very soon, you will be up and around, going to the Sunday night singings—you, Adah, and I will be. Mend your foot quickly.
>
> Da Herr sei mit du—May the Lord be with you.
>
> Most sincerely,
> Gideon Peachey

She was touched momentarily by the tender tone of the letter, but she knew she ought not to reveal this to Adah. No, she knew she must be very careful not to lead Adah to think her brother had a courting chance. "Denki," she said softly. "Tell Gid the letter was right thoughtful of him."

Adah's face shone with delight. "Jah, I'll be sure 'n' tell him."

Her heart sank just a bit seeing the look of near glee on Adah's face. So then, no matter what nice thing she might've said about Gid's note, his sister would have probably misunderstood, so hopeful Adah was. Ach, Leah felt she couldn't win for losing.

◆

The afternoon could've easily been mistaken for early evening, so gray it was outside, with drenching rain coming down like Noah's flood. Not even the hearty fork-tailed martins who resided in the four-sided birdhouse next to the barn attempted to take flight this day. They preened their white torso feathers, waiting not so patiently for the sun to shine again.

Leah sat in the front room, her foot still propped up with cold packs, listening to the boisterous music of the rain on the roof. She didn't mind being alone, sitting there embroidering yellow and lavender pansies on a new pillowcase. Actually, she was beginning to enjoy the domestic "indoor" work of womenfolk and wondered what Dat might think if she joined ranks with Mamma, Sadie, and the twins. She knew she'd miss the infrequent yet meaningful chats with her father, would miss them terribly. Still, she couldn't help but feel she'd purposely been kept away from her mother and sisters all these years. Besides being the "sturdy girl" of the family, she didn't know, nor did she care to speculate, on the reasoning behind Dat's initial plan to keep her busy outdoors . . . except for the farm permit, so she wouldn't fall prey to higher education, as Sadie had.

Just as soon as her ankle was strong again, she'd be right back outside helping in the chicken house and elsewhere. Meanwhile, she found she rather liked the glide of the needle and thread weaving a path through the fabric. She hoped she might have more opportunities to sew and quilt, though not with a bum foot for company.

Aunt Lizzie surprised her by coming for another visit the next day. Leah was pleased, hoping for some quiet time with her favorite aunt. With eight years between Lizzie and Mamma, Leah had often marveled that the two seemed closer than Mamma and her other siblings, though some were only a couple of years or so younger or older. Goodness, how the two of them loved to joke and laugh together while out gardening in either Mamma's or Lizzie's vegetable patches!

There had also been a few times when Leah, as a young girl, had happened upon them and they'd startled her a bit by ceasing their talk when they saw her—embarrassed her, really—acting as if they were still youngsters themselves . . . secretive little sisters playing house. Made her wonder, though she had no idea, really, just what they were whispering. Probably nothing at all about her. Yet such things had been going on for years, for as long as Leah could remember.

"Didja have a very long rumschpringe?" she asked when Lizzie and she were alone in the front room at last.

"Well, I wouldn't say *long* really." Her aunt offered her a plump strawberry from the bowl she held. "I can tell ya one thing . . . I'm not proud of those years. Not a bit."

"Oh? Didja tempt the devil?" The words flew out before she thought to stop them. "Like some young people do, I mean."

Aunt Lizzie sighed loudly and turned her face toward the window. The rain was still coming down hard, hammering against the roof. "I wish I could say I led a godly life during that time. Truth is, I went the way of the world for too long. I should've put my trust in the Lord instead of . . ." She stopped then, looking at Leah. "You're comin' into that time of your life, too, honey-girl."

Leah was surprised to hear her aunt use the nickname. How long had it been since Lizzie had called her that? She sighed. "Well, I don't want to make the mistakes many young folk do," she told her aunt.

" 'Tis a gut thing to wholly follow the Lord no matter what age you are. My prayer for you is that one of our own boys will court you when it's God's will."

One of our own . . . The way Lizzie said it had Leah thinking, wondering if Lizzie knew something about Sadie. But no, how could she? As for the Lord God having anything to do with her courting days, well, she wondered if Aunt Lizzie had forgotten about Dat's plans—that Smithy Gid would be asking for Leah's hand in marriage sooner or later. How could the Lord God heavenly Father have any say in that?

She felt she had to ask, wanted to know more. "Did *you* fall in love with a Plain boy back then?"

A faraway look found its way into Lizzie's big eyes again. "Oh, there were plenty of church boys in my day, jah, there were. One was 'specially fond of me, but he ended up marryin' someone else when all was said and done. Can't blame him, really. *En schmaerder Buh!*—a smart fellow he was."

"To miss out on marryin' you, Aunt Lizzie? Why, how on earth could that be? I say he was *dumm*—stupid—if you ask me."

"No . . . no, I dawdled, sad to say. Fooled round too long. He had every right not to wait for me."

Leah wasn't so curious about the boy as she was annoyed that her aunt thought so little of herself. "I think you're ever so perty, Auntie," she said suddenly. "Honest, I do."

Eyes alight, Lizzie touched her hand. "Keep as sweet as you are now, Leah, will ya?"

She wanted to say right out that she'd never think of hurting Mamma and Dat—nor Aunt Lizzie either—the way Sadie was bound to if she kept on rubbing shoulders with the world. But she said none of what she was thinking, only reached over and covered Aunt Lizzie's hand with her own, nodding her head, holding back tears that threatened to choke her.

When the day was through, long after Aunt Lizzie had gone back up the hill to her own little house, Leah lay on her bed in the darkness. Positioning her still-painful ankle just so beneath the cotton sheet, she thought of her newfound joy— needlework and mending with her sisters and Mamma. Of course, she didn't dare tell Dat she thought she might prefer to work inside, where she rightfully belonged. No, she wouldn't just come right out and say something like that to him. She'd have to bide her time . . . wait for the right moment, then feel her way through, just the way she carefully gathered eggs of a morning, so the fragile shells wouldn't shatter in her gentle hands.

———————◆———————

Leah sat out in the potting shed, glad the afternoon shower had held off till just a few minutes ago. After returning home from school, Hannah and Mary Ruth had helped her hobble out to help Mamma redd up the place a bit before it rained.

"This place has never been so filthy," Mamma said, using a dustpan and brush to clean off the counter that lined one complete wall. Several antique birdhouses sat there, waiting for spring. A collection of tools—hand rakes, gardener's trowels, hoes, and suchlike—and a bag of fertilizer were arranged neatly at the far end, along with the family croquet set and a box of quoits on the highest shelf. And the shared work apron, hanging on a hook.

"I'll wash the inside of the windows," she volunteered, happy to be of help. Today had been her first day outdoors in nearly two weeks. She'd gathered eggs in the chicken house and later scattered feed to a crowd of clucking hens and one rooster, who, come to think of it, had treated her like a stranger. She'd never considered her interaction with the chickens before and burst out laughing as she sat washing the dusty streaks off the shed window.

"Well, what's so funny?" Mamma asked.

Just now, looking at her mother, Leah noticed yet again that gleam of contentment. Mamma was always lovely to look at.

She began telling how the hens especially had behaved oddly, backing away from her as if they didn't know her.

"Hens are temperamental, that's all. Don't make anything of it, dear."

"It's funny, ain't so?"

Mamma seemed to agree, her blue eyes twinkling as she smiled. "They ate the feed, though, didn't they?"

That brought another round of laughter. "Jah, they did."

Still smiling, Leah was happy to share the amusement of the moment. Seemed to her that she and Mamma had made some special connection in the last couple of weeks. "Mamma, what would you think if I told Dat I want to sew and cook and clean, like you and Sadie do?" she asked.

An unexpected burst of sunlight streamed in through the newly washed window, merging with the dust Mamma was sweeping up. "Sounds like you've been thinking hard 'bout this."

"I have" was all she said, and she found herself nearly holding her breath, waiting to see what Mamma's answer might be.

"Jah, I think it's time you learned the womanly skills. It's all right with me."

She felt more than relieved with Mamma's response. After all, wouldn't be too many more years and she'd be married, keeping house for her husband, sewing clothes for her children. It was high time she caught up on her hope chest, which was fairly empty at the moment, except for the few quilts and linens Mamma, Aunt Lizzie, and several other relatives had given as gifts over the years.

"Wouldja like me to talk to your father?" asked Mamma.

Leah felt she wanted to do it herself. "Denki . . . but no.

Best for me to see how Dat takes to the notion. All right?"

Mamma shrugged her shoulders, going back to her sweeping. Leah felt some of the burden lift. Jah, in a few more days
she'd get up the nerve to talk things over with Dat.

Chapter Eight

Leah's ankle had improved so much by now she was able to wash down the walls and floor of the milk house. She had to be mindful about where to place each step, hesitant to ask for help from the twins anymore, though her family was more than willing to rush to her beck and call. Stopping only to catch her breath, she gingerly climbed up the ladder to go sit high in the haymow. There she coaxed a golden kitten out of hiding and was stroking its soft fur, rubbing her hand gently down its back, when Dat opened the upstairs door and stood there with a serious look on his sweaty face. "Hullo, Leah," he said.

"Mind if we talk, Dat?"

He came and crouched in the hay, eyeing the kitten in her lap. Then slowly he removed his straw hat and wiped his forehead with the back of his arm. "Glad to have you back, Leah. Missed ya."

"Me too. I was just thinking . . ."

"I was hopin', now that your ankle's all healed up, that I could still count on you."

She waited patiently for him to go on, wondering now if Mamma had said something, even though Leah had made it clear she wanted to be the one to break the news to her dear father.

His eyes were flat, his ruddy face deadpan. "Truth is, Leah, as much as you want to help your mamma and sisters, that's how much I need your help out here in the barn . . . in the yard, and with the harvest."

Am I stuck doing men's work forever? she wondered, though she didn't dare speak up.

"If I thought you were going to marry in, say, a year or two, well then, I might think otherwise," Dat explained.

She was ever so glad he hadn't put Gid's name in the middle of things. "I don't even have my hope chest filled yet." The kitten's purr turned to a soft rumble in her lap. "What sort of wife would I be with no table linens or bed quilts? How could I keep a husband happy with no cookin' skills, not knowing how to make chowchow, put up green beans, or make grape jelly?"

"This you've been thinkin' through, jah?" A hint of a chuckle wrapped round Dat's words.

"Just since I hurt my ankle. Before then I was downright ignorant to what I was missing in the house." She filled her lungs for courage, smelling the sweet hay and the hot lather of the animals in the stalls below. "Now that I know how to stitch and mend, make Chilly Day stew, and bake date-and-nut bread—all the things Mamma enjoys—well, I'd like to have a chance to practice . . . be as skilled at keepin' house as every other girl in Gobbler's Knob."

Dat's jaw twitched a bit, but he looked straight at her, his honest eyes filled with understanding. "Are ya tellin' me that you're ready to be a daughter, too, 'stead of just a son?" A twinkle appeared in his eye.

"Aw, Dat . . . I—"

"What do ya say we make ourselves a deal?" He was more serious again.

She was all ears. After all these years, what would he tell her?

"What if you do the milkin' twice each day, gather the eggs, and if Dawdi Brenneman comes to live with us—and he needs help feeding and waterin' the barn animals—well, you could do that, too?"

Ach, she could think of a gut many things he'd failed to mention. Things like mowing and fertilizing the front, side, and back yards, shoveling manure out of the barn, washing the milking equipment, and much more. Did he mean to tell her that Dawdi might be up to doing all of that? Sure, what Dat had suggested was a place to start, so she spouted off what she thought he was getting to really. "Then, I 'spose the rest of the day I can work helpin' Mamma?"

Dat smiled weakly, nodding his head one slow time. He lifted his hat to his oily head and stood up, still looking her full in the face.

The kitten in her lap was not one bit interested in being moved or set free. Not when the sun's rays had found both Leah and the cat there in the haymow, where Dat had spoken some mighty important words, letting her know that *he* knew she was no longer a tomboy but a young woman. Truly, she was.

Goodness, she felt like jumping up and running round the barn. *Glory be!* she thought, grinning for all she was worth. Such gut news.

At sunset Gobbler's Knob was one of the pertiest places in all of Lancaster County, Sadie felt sure, with its view of the farmland below, dotting the landscape, shadowed in the gray-blue dusk.

She had become braver in her visits to the knoll, not waiting for Derry behind the barn any longer. She didn't feel the need to be led into the depths of the woods. After so many weeks, she knew the way to the hunters' shanty. Sometimes she arrived a half hour or so before Derry did, perched on the wooden ledge hewn into the wall. Or she might move to the windowsill, where she sat silently, peering out of the tiny square window, waiting for her beloved as darkness gathered over the forest. Often she remembered Derry's cautious yet compassionate remarks, told to her on one of the first nights they'd walked together amidst the brambles and undergrowth, all the things in the knoll that were dangerous, even deadly. Things like poison oak, wild orange mushrooms, a certain genus of herbs . . . and if you weren't careful, the way the darkness could creep up suddenly, almost out of nowhere, catch you unawares. "You can easily get turned around in here," he'd said, looking up at the dense trees, "or even lose your way completely." At the time she thought it was ever so kind of Derry to point out such things. She still did. It was as if he was looking after her, caring for her in a way that other boys wouldn't think to.

Oh, how she cherished everything he was to her, living for the hour when they—each of them—left their individual societies behind and sneaked away to the woods. To their secret place against an unforgiving world. They shared an unspoken pact now, a lovers' promise that she belonged to him and he to her. There was no one else for Sadie in all the world. And she was more certain than ever that Derry felt the same way.

Not even the coming rain, the wind high in the trees, disturbed her eagerness for the arrival of her beau tonight. When she and Derry Schwartz were together, she was able to forget who she was, really—to play a trick on herself and dismiss the truth that she was Abram and Ida Ebersol's firstborn, that sooner or later she would join church, marry within the confines of the Amish community, give birth to numerous children, carry on amidst countless work frolics with fifty or so other women, dress Plain forever, and live a life with strict rules and regulations set down by a bishop she scarcely knew.

Yet the reality of her future faded when she was with Derry. Then, and only then, was she free to be herself. Someone her own mamma would never even recognize, probably . . . a seething yet fragile spirit that knew no bounds. And when it came time for Derry and her to part, she attempted to grasp each precious moment, wishing she could lengthen the span of time, resenting the walk home alone, knowing she would gladly do anything he said, even run away with him, never looking back, she was convinced. She was frustrated at what she might have to face if Leah happened to be awake again when she tiptoed past their bed, slipped into her long white cotton nightgown, her beloved Derry long since having returned to his own separate world, his "I love you" still resounding deep within her heart.

You could lose your way. . . .

With trembling fingers, she traced the embroidered butterfly on the corner of her handkerchief, made by Hannah. She wished she might one day be like this butterfly and fly away, to just where, she didn't know. A place called freedom, maybe.

Counting the seconds now, she wondered how much longer before she'd see Derry running through the drenched woodlands, fast as can be, to her side. Would he ask her about her Plain life and heritage this time? Whisper of his anticipation for their future together? With all her heart, she truly hoped that maybe tonight he would.

The next day was a shining afternoon, and what a good opportunity to visit Leah's dear friend, once all the barn chores were finished. It felt wonderful-gut to have some mobility back, though her ankle was still tender certain ways she walked. Together she and Adah walked slowly through the moving meadow grass toward Blackbird Pond, out behind the Peachey barn and stables.

Leah shared her newfound joy of sewing and quilting, talking up a blue streak about all she'd learned in the last few weeks. Of course, she didn't share a thing of her hopes and dreams concerning Jonas, not with Adah thinking she might like to have her best friend for a sister-in-law and all.

"Wouldn't it be ever so much fun to live like real sisters?" Adah said. "Then I wouldn't feel so much like I'm the middle child, sandwiched in between Gid and Dorcas."

"I know how that feels," Leah replied, bypassing the real question. "Sometimes I think I'm nearly invisible in my own family."

"Ach, *you*, Leah?"

"Oh jah. I've always felt a bit lonely somehow. I don't rightly know how to explain it, really. Maybe it's . . . well, a little like the way Aunt Lizzie must surely feel."

"Seems to me middle children don't have any idea how important they are to their families," Adah said.

Leah bent down to pick a white snapdragon, growing wild in the expanse of grassland and flora, where meadow-foam grew to be five feet tall, striking the sky with pink cotton-candy-like blossoms in June. "Children comin' along behind the firstborn have their opinions, too, but seldom are heard . . . or understood," she said softly, unsure why she'd said such a thing.

" 'Tis awful sad to feel lost," Adah replied, reaching for Leah's hand. "You don't feel that way *now*, do ya?"

"Well, no . . . not when we're together." And this was ever so true. Leah and Adah were as close as any two sisters could hope to be. Sometimes she even wished Adah was a real sister to her. The *only* reason to even consider marrying Gideon, maybe.

Hand in hand, they came upon the glassy pond, where many a happy winter day had been spent skating and playing with the Peachey children. Even now, as teenagers, they would all be out sledding and skating here once winter's first hard December freeze came and stayed through February. Wouldn't be safe to skate on Blackbird Pond otherwise, since the water was mighty deep. Leah knew this was true, because Gid had held his breath for forty-five long seconds just so he could dive to the bottom and touch the muddy pond bed one summer when they all were little. "It's spring fed, for sure," he'd told them after a huge gasp of air, his face raspberry red from holding his breath longer than he ever had in his young life.

"We'll be together at our first singing soon," Adah spoke up.

"Jah, won't be long now."

Adah brightened. "We could ride to the local singing with Gid, in his open buggy."

"Best not."

"Well, now, what're you saying?" Adah demanded, letting go of Leah's hand.

"Just that I thought . . . well, that I'd like to go to a different one."

"Not *our* church district?"

"No, guess not."

"Well, we could still all ride together. Gid will take us wherever we want." Adah paused a moment. "Who you end up with after the singing . . . well, that's your business."

Still, Leah was worried Gid might think she would simply ride home with him, too. But that wasn't the way she'd planned things in her head. She must have a semblance of freedom, in case Jonas was in attendance, and she thought he would be, remembering how they'd talked together a week or so ago, when Dat and Mamma took all of them over to pick apples.

The morning spent in the orchard had started out ever so murky, she recalled, but by the time the Mast children and Cousin Fannie, along with Leah, her sisters, Mamma, and Aunt Lizzie had gone out to the apple trees with bushel baskets in hand, the fog had begun to lift slowly, allowing the sun to peek through. Leah had never had such a pleasant time picking apples, though they went to Grasshopper Level to do so every single year. She guessed her happiness had more to do with Jonas and his faithful observing of her all the while. Jah, that surely was the reason. Even now, as she remembered the day, her cheeks were warm with the memory.

Jonas had come right out and asked which of the October Sundays was she going to singing for her first time. And where? She had been at ease enough with him to tell him that the very first singing "after my birthday, I'll go. Prob'ly near Grasshopper Level." To this, Jonas had grinned, nodding his head, as if to say that was ever so fine with him. She'd taken his response as a not-so-subtle indication he'd be there himself, and if so, maybe he would ask her to ride home with him in *his* buggy. Well, if that happened, the way she thought it might, Smithy Gid would be out in the cold. Which, in her mind, was right where he'd been all along. Unknown to Dat, of course.

Sighing just now, she told Adah, "Denki for asking me, but I'll ride to singing with Sadie, prob'ly."

"So Sadie's goin' back to singings, then?" Adah seemed too eager to know.

Leah wasn't sure what was going to happen in the next weeks. Hoping against hope that Sadie might surprise everyone and follow through with joining church, Leah had thought of asking Sadie about Sunday singing here perty soon. Maybe she would tonight if Sadie stayed home for a change.

"I think you're gonna see a lot more of my big sister from now on." She said what she herself hoped might be true.

"Oh, at singings, you mean?"

"I have a feeling Sadie misses goin'. Honest, I do."

"Then, why'd she ever quit?"

Leah kept walking, didn't want to stop just because they'd come to the giant willow on the north side of the pond where she and Adah always liked to stand in its shade and skip pebbles, watching the ripples swell out across the blue-gray water. "Sadie's got her own opinions, same as we do" was all she said.

"I 'spect so," Adah answered. "It's all part of growing up, Mamma says."

"Ain't that the truth." With that, Leah tossed away the snapdragon she'd picked and sat down in the dirt beneath the willow tree.

"What're ya doin'?" Adah eyed her sitting there.

"Just come sit beside me . . . 'fore we grow up too quick."

Adah was nodding her head. "Jah, lest we forget who we are, who we *always* were."

Leah smiled, lifting her face to the sweet sunshine. Sitting here with Adah, she felt wonderful-gut all of a sudden, the cares of life falling off her back, tumbling into the plentiful grazing grass under the crooked willow and a wide blue sky.

◆

At the corn-husking frolic that afternoon, Ida brushed off the remark made by Preacher Yoder's wife, Eunice, that Sadie had missed the next-to-last baptismal class. Seemed Ida's daughter's forgetfulness or downright apathy had caused more than one eyebrow to rise askance. Lest the gossip focus too much on her family, Ida quickly turned the women's attention to her most recent visit to Grasshopper Level. "Abram and I took all the girls—and Lizzie, too—over to pick apples at my cousins' orchard here lately. You should've seen us make quick work of 'em trees."

"What kind of apples?" asked one.

"McIntosh. Wonderful-gut for applesauce-makin', ya know." She went on, talking too much about the sweetness and texture of the apples found over at Peter Mast's orchard and felt downright peculiar going on so. Especially with all eyes on her, waiting . . . wanting a response to the preacher's wife's comment.

Their gaze was on her, boring ever so deep with unanswered questions. Why would a girl continue in her rumschpringe at the same time she was preparing for church baptism? Made no sense. Preacher Yoder—the bishop, too— would have every right to confront Sadie with simple laziness or even worse, indifference, if this wasn't nipped in the bud. The brethren might exclude her from baptism altogether. Ida knew that shoddy behavior and tendencies were to be reported, and goodness' sake, folk were already beginning to talk. She'd have to confide in Abram about this as soon as possible. Sadie's future in the community was in jeopardy.

Frightened, even distraught by her daughter's seeming lack of concern, Ida felt ever so lonely just now, yearning for Sadie to acknowledge her as a sounding board for whatever was ailing the girl spiritually. Not looking up at the women at all, she kept on husking ears of early sweet corn, hoping and praying there was some way to divert the conversation away from her *ferhoodled* and defiant daughter.

Chapter Nine

Leah couldn't help but recall the conversation she'd over-heard between her cousin Rebekah Mast and her sister Mary Ruth that hot Sunday afternoon back toward the end of August. Seemed downright ironic that here she was driving horse and buggy over to help Anna Mast put together a wedding quilt on a Saturday, and both Mamma and Sadie sick in bed with stomach flu. It wasn't that she was filling in for either of them. She would've come along today, no matter. She was truly looking forward to her first quilting frolic.

A hint of fall was in the air. The horse snorted and *clip-clopped* along, and boastful blue jays shrieked at sunflowers growing near the road. Enjoying the short ride to Grasshopper Level, Leah was mindful of how this horse had been a balker back when Dat first bought him from Uncle Noah Brenneman. The steed had been doing fairly well the past year, especially when the reins were in Leah's able hands. Seemed he liked knowing Leah was in charge, which was a gut sign that her confident yet gentle ways with the animals hadn't been lost during the time she'd been laid up.

Leah was also very much aware of the quiet giggling of Hannah and Mary Ruth in the seat just behind her. "C'mon, now, isn't it 'bout time you two shared the joke with me?" Leah said, looking over her shoulder.

"Well . . . guess it ain't so funny, really," Mary Ruth spoke up.

"What's not?" Leah asked, thinking she knew now what had tickled the younger girls so.

"You sittin' up there in the driver's seat like Dat usually does," Hannah said at last.

Leah smiled. "So then, you're thinkin' you've got your very own driver?"

"Well, jah, could be." Mary Ruth leaped over the front seat and sat there next to Leah, still laughing. "There now, how's that?"

"What 'bout me?" Hannah leaned over Mary Ruth's shoulder playfully.

"There's room, if you want to squeeze in a bit," Leah replied.

"Jah, we'll make space for one more." And with that, Mary Ruth scooted over so close to Leah she could scarcely sit.

"Let's make ourselves right skinny," Leah said, holding the reins just so . . . holding her breath, too.

That brought another round of sniggers, and off they went—the three of them smushed together, but mighty happy about it—heading off to a daylong quilting bee.

"Too bad Mamma's under the weather," Hannah said as they made the turn off the main road. "Ain't like her to go back to bed after breakfast."

"Not Sadie, neither," Mary Ruth offered.

"Guess they must have the same bug. Or something they ate made 'em sick," Leah said, yet she wondered why the rest of the family were healthy as horses.

◆

Going to the quilting bee turned out to be a wonderful-gut idea. Leah surprised herself, really, at how much she enjoyed sewing quilting stitches into Anna's Diamond-in-the-Square quilt. Come winter, the happy bride and groom would snuggle beneath its colorful woolen squares, cozy and warm. It made Leah wonder how much longer before Mamma might be saying they ought to start thinking about the number of quilts and coverlets Leah should have in her hope chest by year's end.

It was an exceptionally sunny day, which made for plenty of light shining in the front-room windows, the shades high at the sashes, as twelve women sat in short intervals round the large frame. Three of the quilters were Leah's first cousins from SummerHill—triplets, Nancy Mae, Sally Anne, and Linda Fay. Two of the older women, Priscilla and Ruth Mast, were also close cousins, by marriage, to Fannie Mast. Old acquaintances, longtime cousins, and friends all mixed together. Leah sat between her sisters, Hannah and Mary Ruth, near Cousin Fannie's three oldest girls, including Anna, who seemed to wear a constant smile these days, while eight-year-old Martha entertained little brother Jeremiah outdoors.

Still a bit unaccustomed to a sewing needle between her fingers, Leah was grateful to be here. Though nary a word was said about the fact that here she was on the brink of her six-teenth birthday, and yet this was her first-ever quilting frolic. She wondered if one of the older women might not mention something in passing as the hours ticked by. But the women were good-natured, seeing as how she was nearly a stranger to them—not by blood nor church ties, no. Only in respect to never having spent time at their frequent frolics and work bees.

Leah found herself settling into her usual comfortable silence, like the tiny green stitches she made that seemed to disappear into the jade background.

"Since America's war, ain't it harder to get nice material and dyestuff?" Fannie Mast said, across the frame from Leah. She asked this of Priscilla and Ruth.

"Jah, and the fabrics just don't hold up so well, neither," replied Priscilla.

Ruth nodded her head. "Colors just fade out in the wash."

"The sun fades 'em, too," Fannie added.

"I have seven quilts that are nearly wore out in just a few years," Priscilla agreed.

"Well, and such a shame, too, since some of my best stitchin's in them quilts of yours," Ruth said. This brought a peal of laughter all round.

When it was finished, Anna's new quilt would measure seventy-five by seventy-six inches. The border was nice and wide, and the corner blocks were big and bold. But what Leah liked best was the color contrast—green and scarlet against plum-purple. Such gay colors reminded her of a joyous cele-bration. Jah, that's what a wedding—a lifelong uniting of two cheerful souls—ought to be.

She was nudged out of her contemplation by Fannie's

cousin Ruth, who must've been talking about the fact that Ida was down sick with the selfsame illness as Sadie, "for goodness' sake." Then came the peculiar reference to Leah herself—"But we're awful glad to have Abram's Leah with us today."

All eyes met hers. *Abram's Leah* . . . Surely Ruth Mast hadn't meant that Leah was headed for a life of singleness, like Aunt Lizzie. She didn't see how they could be thinking such a thing today, now, would they? Not when she'd come to quilt with her sisters on her own accord and having such a wonderful-gut time of it, too. Till this moment.

———————◆———————

The September day dawned breezy and a bit nippy, accompanied by a flat white sky. By midafternoon the heavens had turned indigo, a telltale sign that colder weather was on the way. Lizzie had gotten up at six o'clock, unable to stay in bed a second longer. An uneasy feeling had settled in round her, yet she couldn't put her finger on just why.

After a breakfast of fresh fruit, black coffee, and fried eggs, she set about cleaning her little house, going from the front-room parlor to the kitchen and back to her bedroom—redding up, dusting, sweeping, and changing the bedclothes on her big feather bed, bequeathed to her by her mamma. So grateful she was for the hand-me-down bed, glad for anything at all from her childhood home. Thinking on the goodness of the Lord, she returned to the kitchen and took a loaf of bread out of the oven, surprised at how quickly she was completing her chores this day.

"I'll have myself a nice long walk," she said, going to the pantry, which also doubled as a utility room. Finding her woolen shawl on the peg near the back door, she took it down and slipped it over her shoulders. Then she headed outdoors.

Large red-winged blackbirds fluttered from tree to tree, following her as she made her way toward the deepest part of the woods. Walking briskly now as she often did, Lizzie was conscious of scurrying animals, especially the graceful brown-red squirrels flitting up and down the trunks of flaming yellow oaks, playing hidey-seek with each other. In a couple of months, hunters would be up here combing through these woods, hoping for a nice plump turkey to take home for a Thanksgiving feast, and she'd have to find another spot to do her walking till all the shooting was done.

This time of year brought with it plenty of wistfulness, almost a feeling of homesickness. Her sisters, especially Ida, never seemed to pay much attention to the turning of the seasons the way Lizzie did. She actually looked forward to it, particularly the autumn when leaves danced and crackled, showing off their daring new colors. So she walked often through the woods—winter, spring, summer, and a scant few weeks in early fall, bundled up against the cold, somewhat sheltered by ancient trees that had become her constant companions.

She followed an unmarked path, one she sometimes took up to a little lean-to where turkey hunters rested and ate ham-and-cheese sandwiches sent along by their wives and sweethearts. A place where some of the men smoked cigars. She'd find the remnants discarded carelessly on the simple wood floor long after hunting season was over, having gone there to redd up the place a bit, even taking her own broom and dustpan sometimes. She liked things to be clean, even if the shanty was over a half mile from her own house.

Today she'd had no intention of sweeping out the old shelter, and she wouldn't have bothered to stop there at all if she hadn't heard what sounded like a raccoon or maybe a sick dog inside, whining to beat the band.

Pulling hard on the old door, she went in to see what all the racket was. And then she spied the most pitiful sight—a baby raccoon, tiny as can be, coming toward her as if it hadn't eaten for days, trapped in here away from its mamma. "Go on, s'okay, little one. Go home now." With that he scuttled past her, out the door, making a beeline for the woods. "Your family will be mighty glad to see you," she called after the downy, black-masked critter, wondering how on earth the poor thing had ended up inside instead of out in the forest where he belonged.

Standing in the doorway, she gazed after him till she could no longer see his bushy ringed tail. "Lord, please be ever mindful of your smallest creatures this day," she prayed softly.

Leaning against the door, she closed it behind her, knowing full well it would stick tight due to the current dampness, and soon she'd be prying it open with all her might when she was ready to leave. Still, she wanted to shut out the cold air and the sound of those raucous blackbirds high in the trees, no doubt waiting for her to walk home.

Suddenly overcome with fatigue, she went to sit on one of the wide wooden benches, noticing just how clean the place was since her last visit here. Noticing, too, how few human trappings littered the place. Usually she would find refuse in the corners—old newspapers, bottles of soda pop and beer, wadded-up paper bags and Baby Ruth candy bar wrappers, and the ever-present cigar stumps, smoked out. Looking round the small room, she had the feeling someone had taken extra care to redd up. It was uncommon for the place to be this free of rubbish. Someone *had* to have been here, taken their personal belongings, trash and all. Seemed ever so peculiar.

Not fully rested but ready to get home, knowing she had a long walk back to her cabin, she rose and straightened her shawl. As she did she noticed a white handkerchief lying on the floor beneath the bench, a delicate hemstitch round the edges. Leaning down, she picked it up, the cutwork embroidered butterfly catching her eye.

"Well, for goodness' sake," she whispered, recognizing Sadie's favorite hankie.

A metallic taste sprang into her mouth, the taste of fear. Slowly she brought the handkerchief to her heart, blinking back tears.

Lizzie took the short way home, through the thickest brambles; though, if she wasn't mistaken, there seemed to be a slight path cut through the wild brushwood, ever so subtle, as if a tall and willowy young woman had come this way on more than a handful of occasions. So then had her eyes *not* deceived her back several weeks ago? That half-moon night when she'd gotten up in the wee hours, too warm and restless to sleep. She'd thought she had seen someone running through the woods, past the foxgloves, past the high stone wall . . . a wispy likeness of a girl, lantern in hand. Though at the time Lizzie had wondered if she was just too sleepy eyed to put much faith in what she thought she saw.

Why must history repeat itself? she wondered, sorrowfully

making her way to the back porch of her house. *Why, oh why, dear Lord?*

The *caw-cawing* of the blackbirds was loud, if not merciless and grating. A swarm of them were so bold as to perch near her flower beds. But their heckling was not the answer she sought.

Sadie searched everywhere she could think of for her lost handkerchief. Unable to find it in any of her bureau drawers, she wondered if it might not be clinging to the inside sleeve of the dress she'd worn yesterday. But when she slipped her hand into the blue dress hanging on the wooden peg in her bedroom, she felt nothing. *Where'd I lose it* this *time?* she wondered, retracing her steps in her mind.

Then suddenly she knew. Sure as anything, she must've dropped it on the way up the knoll to the little hunters' shack, where she'd waited and waited for Derry last night. But he hadn't ever arrived, and she just assumed he had to work late for Peter Mast. Either that or something else important had come up. She didn't know for sure, though.

Now that she really thought on it, she was certain she'd taken the butterfly handkerchief along. And she worried that if she'd dropped it in the lean-to itself, someone might recognize her sister's stitching, so well known was Hannah's handiwork on tiny handkerchiefs amongst the People. If found, a body might put two and two together and know that one of the Ebersol girls had spent time there in the hunters' shack . . . and just why would that be? Especially since the drafty old place was supposed to be for grown men—Englishers—in need of a haven against the elements. A place to sit and drink a steaming hot cocoa or coffee. She'd noticed two abandoned thermoses on separate occasions recently.

To her the little shanty—*their* shanty—was a paradise of sorts. A home away from home; for when she was in Derry's arms, the world stopped spinning round, seemed to stand still just for them.

Now, in the dim light of the bedroom, she lay very still, awaiting Leah's steady, deep breathing that was sure to come. She stared across the room at the nearest window, where the tiniest crack of light from the moon had sifted beneath the shade like a silver splinter at the sill. She thought back to the night Leah had tearfully confided in her, telling of Dat's "arrangement" with Smithy Peachey. Gentle Leah was so close to her own rumschpringe. Just how would *she* handle her courting years? Would she submissively bend to Dat's wishes . . . be courted by the blacksmith's son—marry him and bear his children?

Sighing, Sadie wished she didn't have to change out of her nightclothes and scurry into the darkness. The evening breeze might chill her further. She'd felt so queasy and dizzy earlier. She stared at Leah next to her, almost asleep if not already. No need to have Leah wonder again where she was going at this late hour. No need to have more pointed questions asked of her. Not after the way Leah had lashed out earlier tonight.

Here, in the privacy of their shared room, her usually calm sister had gone much too far in her quest, asking . . . no, demanding that Sadie start going again to Sunday singings, spending more time with the church young people. "Why must you run off to the world for your fellowship?" Leah wanted to know, her eyes probing deep into Sadie's heart. Then her voice had softened suddenly, and she'd said,

"Won'tcha come along with me to my first singing, Sadie? *Sei so gut*—please?"

Sadie hadn't known what to say, so she'd said nothing. She was befuddled, torn between Leah's angry, accusing words, followed by the unexpected question, spoken with such tenderness. Oh, she wanted to be the kind of older sister Leah needed. She wished they might be as close as they had been in childhood. But now . . . *now* she was caught up in a world of her own making. She couldn't let go, even if she tried. She even struggled to breathe sometimes if she didn't see Derry every few days, wondering if this was how a girl felt when she'd met the boy of her life. A boy the Lord God surely intended to become her husband.

What seemed like an hour later, Sadie lifted herself silently out of bed, pulled on her choring dress and apron, and hurried outside, lantern in hand. Searching along the thin woodland path she'd carved out over the weeks, Sadie hunted for her hankie. *I must be more careful,* she told herself, mindful of a single oil lamp still burning in the back bedroom of Aunt Lizzie's cabin as she crept barefooted but a few yards away, through the soggy underbrush of Gobbler's Knob.

Out of breath, she finally arrived at the shanty, having not found the handkerchief along the way. She pushed hard on the door. Stuck! Turning, she set the lantern on the ground, then pressed her full weight on the door, leaning on it with all her might. When it gave way, she rushed inside, tripping over her long skirt. Brushing herself off, she went to retrieve the lantern and began to look for her handkerchief, hoping it might be somewhere near . . . where she might've accidentally dropped it.

She was beginning to think she'd made a wasted trip

when she spied something white over on the window ledge. The very spot where she'd sat and daydreamed, watching the rain drizzle down the windowpane, waiting for Derry. Hurrying to the wide sill, she found the butterfly hankie, folded ever so neatly, placed there for all to see . . . for *her* to see.

Someone else knows, she thought, her heart sinking. There was only one who would dare set out so far, past the clearing and into the depths of the knoll. Only one other person felt as comfortable in these dark woods as Derry Schwartz.

Part Two

◆ ◆ ◆ ◆

Their heart is divided; now shall they be found faulty. . . .

They have spoken words, swearing falsely in making a covenant:

thus judgment springeth up as hemlock in the furrows of the field.

—Hosea 10:2, 4

Chapter Ten

Sadie spent part of Saturday morning refilling the lamps and lanterns in the house with kerosene, in spite of her ongoing nausea. Mamma, who was still a bit pale, and Hannah and Mary Ruth were busy redding up the *Dawdi Haus*, the smaller addition connected to the main house, built on years ago when Dat's parents were still alive. But now Dawdi Brenneman was coming to live next door so Mamma could keep an eye on her widower father. It wasn't that Dawdi was being asked to leave his eldest son's place over in Hickory Hollow. The decision had come since Uncle Noah and Aunt Becky Brenneman were themselves getting up in years, and their youngest son and his wife were ready to take over the dairy farm.

So it was time for Dawdi John to come live in Gobbler's Knob. And all well and gut, for Sadie was fond of Mamma's father. At age seventy-seven, Dawdi wasn't the least bit ailing, and she felt sure he had many pleasant years ahead. Not even a trace of arthritis. Truth was, Dawdi seemed almost as spry as Dat on some days. Sadie hadn't thought of this before, but now she wondered if Leah had gone and pleaded with Dat to let her do less of the barn and field work and come inside to help Mamma. Jah, she thought that was probably true, though she didn't know just yet. Maybe that was even the reason why Mamma and Dat had eagerly agreed to have Dawdi come live here. Seeing as how he could help with the easy barn chores and whatnot in Leah's stead. Come to think of it, what better way for her sister to finally get her wish.

Sadie had to smile thinking of Leah's sudden interest in sewing and quilting, baking, cooking, canning, cleaning, all the many things the women were expected to do. Made her wonder if Leah might not be looking ahead to courting days and marriage here before too much longer. If so, she'd be attending baptism classes next year, from May to August, beginning after the spring communion, just as Sadie had.

As for the prospects of her own baptism, she'd suffered the embarrassing situation of having Dat quote to her Romans chapter twelve, verse two, all because Eunice Yoder had tattled that Sadie had missed meeting with the preacher for the next-to-last class.

A deep line of a frown marked Dat's suntanned face, and his gray eyes were as solemn as she'd ever seen them. " 'Be not conformed to this world: but be ye transformed by the renewing of your mind, that ye may prove what is that good, and acceptable, and perfect, will of God,' " he'd quoted. Out of the blue, he'd sat her down in the kitchen—with Mamma near—reminding her that the good and acceptable thing for her to do was to follow the Lord in holy baptism into the church, "as you planned to do." He went on to say that if she ever hoped for his and Mamma's blessing on her marriage, "whenever the time came," or on the *Haush-dier*—the house furnishings that fathers were expected to provide—then she'd best to *die Gemee nooch geh*—follow the church.

Humiliated and irked, she hardened her heart as Dat continued to lay down the law to her, and unbeknownst to her parents, she made a decision. Outwardly, she would meekly apologize to Preacher Yoder and attend the final Saturday session prior to baptism—where the articles were read to the members. The young candidates would then receive the consent and blessing of the membership into fellowship. The following day, Sunday—after the second sermon—Sadie would make her covenant to God, false as it was.

Wearing the weight of the world on her shoulders, she returned each of the oil lamps to their spots in the bedrooms, the front room, and kitchen. Back near the door in the utility room, she set down the big lantern on the floor for use if one of them made a quick trip to the outhouse after bedtime. Of course, Mamma preferred they used the chamber buckets; they were much handier than the outhouse when your eyes were groggy with sleep. And she would put lye soap shavings into each one, which kept the odor down but made for plenty of suds in the night.

Before heading over to the Dawdi Haus to see if her help was needed, Sadie sat down at the kitchen table and jotted a note to Derry. She didn't know when she'd be seeing him again, since he was working longer hours for Peter Mast, he'd said. Ach, how she hated the thought of missing him so. Why couldn't he simply meet her down at the end of their lane on the weekend, pick her up in his car, take her for a sandwich somewhere—spend just a little money on her? Or why wouldn't he think of taking her to the Strasburg café, where they'd first met? After all, it was coming up on one whole month since that wonderful-gut night of nights.

She wrote a quick note to send through the mail, hoping that just maybe he'd take the hint and return the favor. Oh, how she would treasure having a letter or card, something tangible from him. Something she could look at and be reminded of his love for her.

Dear Derry,

How are you? I'm doing fine here, helping round the house and looking after the roadside stand during the afternoons. I help Mamma get quilting squares ready for a quilting bee, coming up soon over at Grasshopper Level. That and fall housecleaning, which is always a busy time of washing down the walls, shining windows, and whatnot. My mother's father is coming to live on the other side of our house in two days—Monday afternoon. I'm looking forward to that.

Well, I must close now. But I miss you something awful. Thought I'd just say so and drop this in the mail to surprise you.

All my love,

Sadie

P.S. If you happen to have the time, would you like to drive over while I'm tending the produce stand next Wednesday? We could talk then while you pretend to be a customer. All right with you?

She didn't bother to read what she'd written. She was so eager to get the note folded and into the envelope, addressed and stamped. In the telephone book, she looked up Derry's home address, not knowing just where he lived. It was under the name Dr. Henry Schwartz that she located the correct mailing address, which was but half a mile away, up Georgetown Road to the northwest, then over on Belmont Road just a bit. Within walking distance, really.

Honestly, she felt she might do most anything to see

Derry again. Wanting to be alone with her beloved, she longed to be told yet again that she was the only girl for him, delight in his whispered adoration and his promise that "somehow, someday" they'd be together. Oh, she would willingly run the risk of losing her parents' blessing, even all that was rightfully hers, to spend time with the boy whose deep brown eyes held an irresistible sway over her, tugging at the core of her Anabaptist beliefs . . . at the underpinnings of her very soul.

Jah, she knew now what it was Derry had seen in her that first night. She wasn't just a perty face to him, no. They were cut from the same mold, sharing a common bond, in spite of their contrary cultures. In all truth, she was the murky, irreverent replica of him. He'd met his match, so to speak, and so had she.

Hurrying outside, she deposited the envelope in the mailbox at the far end of the lane. Come Monday, her beloved would hold her written words in his hands. What would he think of her invitation to drop by? Would he be pleased rather than put out with her being so *vorwitzich*—forward? Mamma would be ashamed of her if she knew. But Mamma *didn't* know, and if Leah even so much as hinted at taking back her word, well, Sadie would threaten her sister with spilling the beans to Dat—that Leah and Jonas Mast had made a silly childish pact between them. Jah, that would take care of that.

So Sadie had nothing to worry about, nothing at all, till Dat spied her and called to her, "Get your tail feathers over 'n' help your mamma and sisters!"

She didn't quite get why her father was so short with her just now, but she picked up her pace all the same and headed straightaway to the Dawdi Haus.

The chickens behaved much better this morning, the way they always had before Leah hurt her ankle. Jah, even the lone rooster was mighty pleased with her soft clucking as she stood there in the pen. Sometimes she actually liked to chatter to them, always quietly with a smile on her face. "Eat gut, now," she would coo at them. "Enjoy your dinner."

As soon as she finished her outdoor chores—less than half the farm duties she'd been used to—she planned to dash across the backyard to the Dawdi Haus and help Mamma and the twins, and Sadie, too, with the dusting and sweeping, washing down the walls and windows, getting the little house ready for Dawdi Brenneman. Ach, how Sadie's eyes had lit up at Dat's announcement yesterday that Dawdi was moving in. Far as Leah was concerned, it was a wonderful-gut thing he was coming to live so close. Because Sadie was in need of some wise counsel. Someone to take her under his sensible wing, since she didn't seem to heed Dat's admonition much anymore. Sadie did as she pleased these days. Take last night, when she must've thought Leah was deep in sleep, waiting ever so long to leave for the woods. Yet Leah had felt the bed heave, heard her sister shuffle across the room for her clothes, then head for the hallway and tiptoe all the way down the stairs. Listening for the creak of the back screen door, Leah must've fallen asleep before Sadie leaned low to pick up the lantern at the back door, stealing out of the house yet again. Headed to who knows where.

Mamma greeted Leah with a welcoming smile, though she looked rather tired and probably should've taken a nap instead of cleaning out the Dawdi Haus in a single day. "We can use your help, Leah. Why don'tcha go and strip the bed, then take all the rugs outside and beat them with a broom."

Hannah and Mary Ruth were cleaning the old wood stove in the center of the medium-sized kitchen, using plenty of elbow grease, though from where Leah stood, the stove didn't look dirty at all. The kitchen wasn't nearly as big as Mamma's. Still, it would serve Dawdi well if ever he wanted to take his meals separate from the family, though she'd be surprised if Mamma would hear of such a thing. There might well be times when Aunt Lizzie would come over and cook up a pot of oyster stew or Yankee bean soup. Jah, she was perty sure Lizzie would spell off Mamma a bit, take over some of the Dawdi Haus chores, probably. And here was yet another opportunity for Leah to practice her cooking and baking skills on someone who'd be happy, more than likely, to eat most anything she fixed. She had to smile, almost laughed out loud, and could hardly wait till Dawdi was just a hop, skip, and jump from their own back door.

Carrying the throw rugs down the steps, she saw Sadie coming up the sidewalk, looking for all the world as if she'd lost her only friend. "What'sa matter?" Leah asked, dropping the rugs in a heap on the grass.

"Nothin', really" came the hollow reply.

"Nothin', then?"

" 'S'what I said."

Leah bristled. "You sound miffed . . . are ya?"

Sadie shook her head. Leah picked up the first rug and went to hang it on the clothesline so she could beat it free of dust. "Sounds to me like you need a gut Sunday meeting."

"I'm gonna join church next Sunday," said Sadie.

"Didn't know you were thinkin' otherwise," Leah spouted, secretly thrilled.

"No . . . guess I wasn't."

"So, then, why're ya tellin' me this?"

Sadie shrugged. "Just thought I'd tell someone."

Someone . . . so is that what she'd become to Sadie? Just a someone, not the closest sister and best friend Sadie had ever had, before rumschpringe came along. "What's gotten into you anyhow?" she blurted without thinking. "What's *wrong* with you, Sadie?"

Sadie's eyes flashed anger. "I don't know what you're talking 'bout!"

"You most certainly do so!" Leah shouted back.

"Girls . . . girls, no need to raise your voices," Mamma rebuked them from the doorway.

Sadie turned and marched right past Leah, up the steps, and into the Dawdi Haus. Leah was left there, the mound of rugs at her feet.

"Didja think a yelling match was best, Leah dear?" Mamma said, walking toward her.

"Sorry, Mamma." She kept her eyes lowered, truly sad about what had just happened, though she didn't understand the extreme tension between herself and Sadie. Didn't like it one iota. Then, raising her head, she could see that Mamma didn't, either.

"Come along now . . . we'll have us a nice walk over to Blackbird Pond."

"But, Mamma . . ."

"I've waited long enough. It's time you told me what you know 'bout Sadie."

Leah's heart sank as sure as the clods of grass she, Adah, and Smithy Gid used to toss and let sink into Peacheys' pond. "Sadie's well into courtin' age, ain't so, Mamma?" She didn't have to remind her mother of the People's secretive courting tradition. What went on under the covering of night was always kept quiet till the last minute; then the second Sunday after fall communion in October, couples who planned to marry in November were "published" by the bishop. That's how it had always been in their Old Order circles, the way it had been nigh unto two hundred fifty years.

"Won'tcha consider confiding in me, Leah? I'm ever so worried."

"Well, I can tell you this . . . Sadie said she's joining church one week from tomorrow."

Such joyous news brought a flush of color to Mamma's cheeks, and she stopped walking and kissed Leah's face. "Denki for tellin' me. Oh, Leah!" With that, she promptly headed across the meadow.

Leah watched Mamma's skirt tail flapping in the breeze. *Sadie oughta be mighty glad I kept her secret all this time*, she thought.

Turning back toward the pond, she walked more slowly than before. She contemplated her mother's words to both her and Sadie a few years ago as they hung out the wash together. *"Remember, girls . . . purity at all costs,"* Mamma had said. *"May be old-fashioned, but it's God's way . . . and the best way."* Mamma also said that a person with a pure heart could draw strength from prayer. The mention of God in such a personal way was odd, really, Leah had thought at the time.

Oh, she knew her mother prayed more than most womenfolk, probably. But talk of the Lord God heavenly Father wasn't something many of the People felt comfortable doing. Sacred things weren't discussed so much, except at church from the lips of Preacher Yoder and the deacon's Scripture readings.

Reaching the old willow tree, she sat down and watched dragonflies skim over the surface of the gray-blue pond, ever so glad she'd had something good to tell Mamma. What if Sadie and she hadn't exchanged heated words earlier? What if she hadn't known her sister was headed for the kneeling altar? But now Sadie would be making her covenant to the church, so surely Derry was out of the picture.

Thankful for that, Leah breathed a sigh of relief. Keeping Sadie's secret had tuckered her out but good, knowing that if something bad had happened to her sister, Leah herself would've borne the responsibility. Things were changing for the better, after all.

Chapter Eleven

Wednesday at the noon meal, Sadie volunteered to tend the vegetable stand by the road, "so Leah can help Mamma if need be," she'd said. Dat nodded his head, looking a mite bewildered at her eagerness. Mamma said that was all right with her, since Leah and the twins—once Hannah and Mary Ruth returned home from school—had other chores to see to later this afternoon. Mary Ruth had offered at breakfast to go out round four o'clock, "spell you off some," she'd said, but Sadie insisted she could easily look after things without any help. She didn't want sympathy just because she wasn't feeling so well these days.

So she was on her own, just the way she'd planned to be, having taken extra care to comb her hair back smoothly on the sides, tucking the loose strands tightly into the low bun at the nape of her neck. She'd worn Derry's favorite color, too. "The color of your eyes," he had said early on, after one of their first meetings. Now she sometimes wondered if he even noticed how closely the blue fabric matched her eyes on the sunniest days, as today definitely was. Temperatures had dropped slightly in the night, so she wore her clean white sweater over her cape dress, and though she'd come out to the roadside barefooted, she thought about returning to the house to pull on her high-top black shoes, first time the idea had crossed her mind since clear last spring. During the night there had been a trace of frost on the ground, maybe a bit soon for this early in September. Still, she remembered looking out the bedroom window this morning and seeing Dat's and Leah's footprints left behind on the thick green lawn. Now the sun stood high in the blue sky and there wasn't a breath of wind. The day had turned out much warmer than anyone might've expected. Who would've guessed the pre-dawn hours had been so cold?

Farmers were in full swing, busy filling silos. Vegetable gardens were slowly emptying out and the corn was turning fast. "Buddies Day" came round perty often, when cookie-baking frolics and canning bees were plentiful, well attended by the younger women, especially. Sadie didn't mind so much making chowchow. Actually, she preferred cooking and canning bees over quilting, maybe because she sensed such scrutiny the past few times she'd been. She was glad Leah had gone in her stead recently to Anna Mast's quilting. Not that she was happy to be under the weather, no. Just hadn't felt like putting up with raised eyebrows and the unspoken questions that were surely being thought as she sat and stitched amidst a dozen or more women in fairly close proximity.

The last time she and Mamma had gone over to Hickory Hollow for an all-day frolic, *two* big quilts were in frames— the Sunshine-and-Shadow pattern for Mamma's friend Ella Mae Zook, the other the Log Cabin pattern for Ella Mae's twin sister, Essie King, both women distant cousins of Fannie

Mast. On another day the same group of women had gotten together at Ella Mae's to make a batch of fruit mush. Sadie's mouth watered at the memory just now, and she recalled that she and Mamma had returned home to find Leah turning the handle on the butter churn and feeling awful tired doing so . . . the closest thing to cooking she'd ever come.

Not so today. *This* morning, of all things, Leah had insisted on making breakfast for the family. *Erschtaunlich*— astonishing, really. Sadie had squelched a smirk, observing the look of delight on Mamma's face, the pleasant smiles from Hannah and Mary Ruth. But the fried eggs had turned out a lot harder than Mamma's usual "over easy," the way Dat liked his. As for the bacon, the long strips had gotten much too crisp, almost too hard to eat. Yet the family was as polite as could be and ate what was set before them, chewing longer and harder than they had in many a year.

Sadie was thankful for this time to be alone, out here near the road, wondering if Derry would come by or not . . . hoping he'd received her note. Going round to the front of the stand, she eyed the arrangement of long wooden shelves she and Leah had constructed late in the spring when early peas and head lettuce were first coming in. All told, there were three levels—bushel baskets of sweet potatoes and red beets on the first; bicolored pear-shaped gourds, as well as lime green, yellow, orange, and dark green gourds shaped like miniature bottles, eggs, and apples on the second shelf, along with acorn squash and butternut squash, late raspberries, strawberries, and blackberries. Turnips and tomatoes lined the third shelf. Occasionally, Hannah brought out a flat basket with embroidered handkerchiefs, offering them to the regular customers if they purchased more than a dollar's worth of produce. Of course, there were always the favorites—usually nearby neighbors—who insisted on purchasing the dainty hankies no matter how much produce they bought. Here lately, Mary Ruth had been baking a whole lot of pumpkin-nut loaf, which was selling out nearly as fast as she could bake it.

Just as her first customers for the afternoon drove up, Sadie moved back to the side of the produce stand. It was Mrs. Sauder and Mrs. Kraybill, two of their most frequent visitors, just down the road about a mile and a half to the southeast. Mrs. Sauder was always headed somewhere, like Strasburg, running errands with two preschool-age children in the backseat, "before my hubby gets home from work," she would say. Mrs. Kraybill was the Mennonite neighbor who drove Hannah and Mary Ruth to school three days a week. Dat, on the other two days, took the twins to school in his market wagon on his way up to Bird-in-Hand.

"What'll it be today?" Sadie asked, folding her hands and waiting while the women looked things over.

"Oh, I think I'll have several pints of strawberries and blackberries," said Mrs. Sauder.

"Makin' some pies, then?" asked Sadie.

"My husband loves his fruit pies. So do the children." Here, Mrs. Sauder motioned toward little Jimmy and Dottie, who were grinning up at Sadie from the car.

After Mrs. Kraybill chose her fresh vegetables for the week, a steady stream of folk began to stop by. It seemed to Sadie that the gourds and squash were in greatest demand, and by two o'clock, once she'd sold what was left of them, the berries and tomatoes were almost gone, too.

Standing there, reshuffling the remaining items, Sadie was

a bit surprised, yet very pleased, to look up and see Derry's gray automobile pulling onto the shoulder of the road. At once she noticed his plaid wool jacket and cuffed blue jeans as he strolled toward her. Usually when she saw him he was wearing a short-sleeved shirt and sometimes a nicer pair of trousers. But today he'd dressed as if he had made the trip just to see her instead of having come straight from work.

She looked at him and smiled, waiting for him to speak first.

"Hi, Sadie," he said.

"Hullo." Her eyes searched his.

"I almost didn't drop by today."

Was it the note she'd sent? Was he displeased?

"Well, I'm glad you did," she said. "Care for some sweet potatoes or turnips for your mother?"

Nodding his head, he dug his hand in his pocket, pulling out some change. "Here, take whatever you're asking for them."

"No . . . no, I didn't mean it thataway. I meant for you to take something home for supper, to your family, from me . . . to them."

He broke into a big smile then, warming her heart. "Thanks, but I can pay." He chose a turnip and a handful of yams.

"You'll enjoy a tasty meal tonight." She felt odd making small talk, aware of the awkward strain between them.

"I received your letter." His voice had turned suddenly flat. "My mother saw it first, in the mailbox."

"Oh . . . I'm sorry if—"

"From now on, it would be best if you didn't send anything through the mail. Wait until I contact *you*."

So she had been too bold. But with no telephone, no other way to keep in touch with him except the mail, how were they to communicate? Seemed to her the last couple of times they'd talked, it had been too easy to offend him, though she didn't know why . . . and it was much harder to make amends.

He turned to leave, heading back to his car, carrying turnips and sweet potatoes in the brown bag she'd given him. Should she say again that she was ever so sorry? Plead with him? Mamma would say no, plain and simple. It wasn't a gut thing to be *schandlos*—shameless—with a young man. Yet Sadie would like to hear him say good-bye to her at least. Anything at all. But something in her knew that if she dared to call out, she might not see him again. And she could never live with that. So she remained silent, the lump in her throat crowding out her very breath.

Please come back, she thought, fighting tears.

He started up the engine and drove slowly to the front of the stand, stopped, leaned his head down, and called to her through the open window on the passenger side, "Hop in, Sadie. Let's go for a spin."

A ride in his car? Ach, he still loved her!

She wanted to abandon her post and go with him, wherever he was headed. Yet what would her sisters think if she turned up missing? And worse, what would Mamma say if she left the remaining vegetables unattended? Then she knew what she could do. It was the clever thing Miriam and Adah Peachey did many a time when they were too busy with house or garden chores to just wait for customers. They made a sign, which was exactly what she did, too.

"I best be pricing the produce," she told him, overjoyed

that he wanted her with him. This day was turning out far better than she would've ever dreamed.

Reaching over, he opened the glove compartment of his car and took out a tablet of paper and a pen. "Here, price away."

She propped up one of the homemade signs against the turnips. It read, *Self-service today. Pay on the honor system.*

Suddenly she felt ever so merry. More than she had for quite some time. The afternoon would be wonderful-gut, she could just tell now by the glow in Derry's eyes. Jah, already the landscape looked brighter round them, as if someone had sprinkled golden sunbeams all over the cornstalks.

The school day was over promptly at three-thirty, and Hannah and her twin rode home with their Mennonite neighbors, whose children also attended the Georgetown School. As they made the turn off the road into their lane, Hannah noticed that the produce stand wasn't being looked after. *That's odd,* she thought.

The twins thanked Mrs. Kraybill for the ride, then headed into the house, kissed Mamma, and placed their school books on the kitchen table.

"How was your day at school?" Mamma asked in the midst of stirring up a chocolate dessert.

"Oh, we spent most of the day reviewing simple algebra," Mary Ruth said.

"Was it easy for *you,* Hannah?" asked Mamma.

"Not so much, no," Hannah answered. "Mary Ruth's much better at numbers, you know."

Mamma raised her eyebrows. "Algebra sounds like school to me."

"It's required, is what the teacher says," Mary Ruth spo up, and Hannah wished her sister would just leave it be Mamma didn't need to know how awful exciting such hard problems were to Mary Ruth.

"Well, all I'll say is do your best . . . but don't be lookin' to go past the eighth grade. That's enough book learnin' for Plain girls." Mamma motioned to Hannah right then. "Run out and tell Sadie to come inside, will ya? I'm baking a triple batch of fudge meltaways, and I don't recall the creamy filling part."

"Does Sadie know?" Hannah asked.

Mary Ruth was nodding her head that jah, their big sister would definitely recall the ingredients for the filling.

"I'll see if I can fetch her, then," Hannah said, heading out the kitchen door.

So intent was she on finding Sadie, Hannah almost missed seeing the handwritten note propped against the turnips at the produce stand. "What's this?" she whispered, wondering where her sister might've gone, leaving a note for their frequent and loyal customers of all things. This wasn't satisfactory, not the way they were taught to do. Dat would be displeased, even though they knew of others who didn't bother to oversee a roadside stand for hours on end. But that just didn't seem considerate, somehow. Now what was she to tell Mamma, who'd sent her out here to trade off with Sadie?

Looking up and down the road, even going out on the hot pavement barefooted, she strained to see if her sister might've taken herself off for a short walk in either direction. But there were only acres and acres of corn, the golden brown tassels floating in the gentle breeze. And up the way, farmers threshing their golden wheat.

"Where could she have gone?" she said aloud. "Where?"

She shuddered to think that she'd have to tell Mamma about this. Turning, she ran back to the house to first tell Mary Ruth, who was raking the side yard, that Sadie had plumb disappeared. Then, realizing the seriousness of what this might mean, and having received an alarming reaction from her twin, the two of them rushed into the kitchen. There they found Mamma reciting the old recipe by heart, as if saying the ingredients out loud might help her remember every part.

"Mamma! Hannah says Sadie's gone—left the produce stand without tellin' a soul," Mary Ruth exclaimed.

Mamma's frown was hard against her forehead. "Hannah?" she said, looking right at her, all ears.

"Jah, Sadie left a sign for the customers." Hannah nodded her head. "I looked all round, but she's nowhere to be seen."

Mamma's shoulders slumped about two inches. "Well, she's gotta be *somewhere*, ain't so?"

But then and there, the plight of missing Sadie was dropped. Almost faster than Hannah could grasp, really. She was promptly sent back out to the road to remove the sign and stand there to greet folk and make change and whatnot. And Mary Ruth was the one chosen to help Mamma with the chocolaty coconut recipe. All the while Hannah kept thinking Leah didn't know about Sadie's being gone. Dat, neither. What would they think? Would they worry as Hannah was doing now? And as Mamma was, too, though trying to hide her concern. Surely Sadie hadn't been forced to leave against her will. Or had she?

Something truly peculiar had been happening the last full month; Hannah knew that for sure. Her big sister was off somewhere else, at least in her head she was, and most all the time. Maybe that was about to change, though, because from what Mamma had said recently, Sadie was headed for church membership in just four days. Jah, she'd be in the line for baptism come this Sunday, which made Hannah feel ever so much better now, thinking on it . . . even with Sadie gone from where she usually stood behind the hearty turnips and juicy red tomatoes.

Derry drove Sadie all the way out to Pinnacle Overlook, near Holtwood, where they stood high on a cliff and gazed out at the Susquehanna River, an expanse of greenish gray water beneath a robin-egg blue sky. He took her by surprise, whispering in her ear that he loved her and was sorry about what he'd said earlier . . . about his mother discovering the note in the mailbox and all. He seemed to want to make up for his hasty words and kissed her softly on the cheek when tears in her eyes threatened to spill down her face. He held her hand as they strolled along. All was forgiven again.

"Uncle Sam wants me after Christmas," he said when they were back in the car, speeding down the highway.

"Your uncle?"

He pursed his lips and motioned her over next to him. And she did. She slid across the front seat and sat right beside him, snuggling close when he put his arm round her shoulders. She listened carefully to his curious explanation that Uncle Sam actually stood for the United States—"Understand now, Sadie?" Ach, he could be so dear when he wanted to be.

But what he said next left her completely shaken. "You're gonna join up with the soldiers?" she said.

"That's right. I'm enlisting into the United States Army the minute I turn eighteen."

"But I thought—you and I . . ."

"Aw, Sadie, it won't be forever. You'll see."

"So, then, are you sayin' I'll know where you'll be?"

He turned toward her then, his breath sweet on her face. "Sure, I'll write to you twice a day."

His tender promise touched her deeply, so much so she nearly forgot his plans with the American uncle. She was more than willing to remove her prayer cap as they rode along, letting down her waist-length hair just for him. She took pleasure in the warm breeze coming in through the car windows, blowing her long locks back away from her face, breathing in the spicy scent of early autumn.

Derry was a fast driver but awful gut at it as he steered with one hand on the wheel, the other caressing her shoulder. If today he asked her to be his wife, she'd say she would marry him, let the chips fall where they may. Truth was, come Sunday she was joining church, so if she ran off and married him after that, she'd be shunned for sure. Even still, she had to go ahead with baptism for Dat's and Mamma's sake, if nothing else.

Such worry faded quickly with his kisses. She knew once again, in her heart of hearts, Derry was her one and only love, for always.

Chapter Twelve

The night of Leah's sixteenth birthday she dreamed of her hope chest, newly filled with birthday treasures, though still rather bare compared to Sadie's. In the dream, the daring sun peeked its golden head into each of the bedroom windows, shining forth a brilliant shaft at the foot of the double bed, where both girls' pine chests stood, side by side. Glancing at Sadie's, she found herself eager to look inside. She wanted to compare her gifts with the many items Sadie had made and received over the years. Leaning down, she opened the heavy wood lid, and there before her eyes were the beautiful contents of Sadie's years of hard work.

Still dreaming, Leah dug even deeper, suddenly startled to see all of her *own* perty birthday remembrances, each and every one . . . inside *Sadie's* hope chest. She lifted out the lovely hand-sewn pillow tops, crocheted doilies, and other linens she'd just received from Aunt Lizzie, Aunt Becky, and other aunts on both sides of the family, as well as from Fannie Mast and Miriam Peachey. She was especially delighted with Adah Peachey's embroidered floral pillowcases and the yellow

quilted potholders and matching mitts from Mary Ruth and
Sadie. Hannah had her own surprise for Leah. Seven perty
handkerchiefs, one for every day of the week. Mamma, too,
gave a useful gift—a complete set of sheets, with pillowcases
to match, a woolen blanket, and a quilted coverlet. Here they
were, all neatly folded inside her sister's chest.

"Ach, Sadie . . . what have you done?" She began to cry.
Her sister had somehow taken away her few cherished gifts.
The sky was a sudden gray, and she was terribly afraid.

Awakening, she sat straight up in bed, breathing ever so
hard and looking round the dark room. It was nighttime, not
noonday at all. And Sadie was next to her, sleeping quietly.
Tempted to slip out of bed and investigate the two wooden
chests, she was aware of the beating of her heart. But the
longer she sat there, the more she realized the dream had only
seemed real—the result of having a second helping of
Mamma's dessert surprise. A wonderful-gut pineapple upside-
down cake with fresh whipped cream. No need to think twice
about such a dream. She turned on her side, facing away from
Sadie, and hugged herself. *May my dreams be sweet now,
Father God,* she breathed a prayer and closed her eyes, falling
asleep once again.

◆

The morning of Sadie's baptism was as gloomy and rainy
a Sunday as any she ever recalled. Seemed to her the heavens
were already unleashing divine wrath upon her as she stood
in the line, waiting with five other girls to take their places
in the center section over near the minister's bench. Just now

she felt an overwhelming need to *rutsche*—squirm—but her memory served her all too well. During many a Sunday Preaching service, when she was little and not able to sit as perfectly still as Mamma would expect her to, Sadie had received Mamma's firm pinch on her leg. She could almost feel the smarting pain even now, a bleak reminder of her indifference to those things her parents deemed sacred.

A holy hush came over the room. The applicants for baptism prepared to turn their backs on the world and all its pleasures, saying a resounding "Jah" to the Lord Jesus and the Ordnung—the unwritten rules for holy living.

Preacher Yoder had literally pounded away at the aspects of covenant making, as stated in the Old Testament, teaching them that a vow made had lifelong consequences if broken. "To disobey the church would mean death to the soul."

Obey or die. . . .

There had been exhortation from Dat, too, Sadie recalled. He'd sat her down just yesterday and read aloud from Genesis chapter fifteen, where Jehovah God made a covenant with Abram of old. The blood of a young heifer, goat, and ram, along with a dove and a pigeon, had been spilt. Then a blazing torch, representing the Holy One, had appeared and passed through the blood path, sealing the covenant. "Making a covenant with the Lord God heavenly Father is a very serious matter," Dat had said. Yet she had remained silent.

Kneeling before the bishop and his wife, Sadie battled in her spirit, caught betwixt right and wrong, good and evil. But she went ahead with her baptism, making good on her parents' hopes and wishes for her—paying merely lip service, so unable was she to deny her desperate love for Derry Schwartz.

◆

A few weeks later Gideon Peachey and his father worked together, chopping and stacking wood, a backbreaking chore. Keeping his eye on the log, Gid swung the ax down hard in one mighty blow, splitting the log apart at the center, the way his pop had taught him to do.

Close to one o'clock Gid happened to look up and see Abram Ebersol coming across the pastureland, cutting through the side meadow and round the barnyard to where they worked, a long stone's throw from the barn. "Will-kumm!" he and his father called at once.

Abram moseyed over and offered to lend a hand. Gid was glad for the extra help, since there was more wood to hew than he and Dat could possibly split in three hours' time, and the afternoon milking would be rolling round here before too long.

Nodding, Abram smiled stiffly. "Thought I could make myself useful."

Gid cheerfully gave Abram a spare ax, and the two of them worked on the pile of wood while Dat went to stacking. They kept at it for an hour and a half before Mam brought tall glasses of sweetened iced tea for each of them. Mopping his brow, Gid glanced at the man who might be his father-in-law someday. If Leah Ebersol would have him, that is. From the moment his father's and Abram's plan had been revealed to Gid, marrying Leah had appealed to him. He hadn't let on to either Dat or Abram that long before his school days he'd had his eye on the perty brunette girl who lived just across their grazing land. Of the four Ebersol sisters, Leah was the

one who'd most caught his attention. Same thing once they
started attending school together. Leah had been the kindest,
most pleasant of all the girls in his class, which wasn't taking
into account whatsoever that he thought she was downright
beautiful—inside and out. Adah and Dorcas, his younger sisters, must've thought so, too, because the girls, especially
Adah and Leah, had struck up an instant friendship back
when they were just little.

Truth was, everyone who knew her spoke well of Abram's
Leah. Gid could only hope he would be worthy of courting
her. That she might allow him to accompany her home in his
black open buggy come this Sunday night. Evidently Adah
had already talked to Leah about driving to the singing
together, the three of them. But Adah had said that Leah
wanted to go a little farther away—over to the Grasshopper
Level singing—which was right fine with him. It was the
returning home part of the evening he cared most about.

According to Adah, she hadn't been able to pin Leah
down about riding over with them. Seemed Leah preferred to
go with Sadie. If so, would Leah meet up with Adah later?
Did Leah mean to say she might give Gid a chance at being
the young man to drive her home? The question had nagged
him ever since Adah reported back about her quiet conversation with Leah out near the pond some days ago.

And what of the note he'd sent, delivered by Adah, where
he offered his sympathy for Leah's hurting ankle? He would've
gladly done more than simply pen a get-well message. If things
weren't so downright awkward, what with both Dat and Abram
plotting to set things up between himself and Leah, well, he
might've gone over there to visit her awhile. Maybe even
played a tune for her on his harmonica, having learned another

new melody from Dawdi Mathias Byler. He and Dawdi Mathias liked to spend their evening hours practicing the mouth organ whenever they could. Dawdi would play his while Gid stumbled along, letting his ear tell him whether to slide up or down on the notes. Of course, the bishops wouldn't approve of their playing hoedown music at singings or whatnot, encouraging dancing and all. Still, it was all right for them to play in their homes, for their own enjoyment—"or our amazement," Dawdi Mathias would say with a chuckle and a twinkle in his eyes. Both Dawdi and Mammi Mattie Sue enjoyed having their grandchildren come for visits. "Come over whenever you like," Mammi always said, coaxing the three of them to spend the night on the Byler dairy farm, where they'd fall asleep to Dawdi's rhythmic serenade.

Thinking back to Leah, Gid was more than certain that Dawdi and Mammi would wholeheartedly approve of her, though he hadn't breathed a word of his affection to a soul, except to Adah, though ever so subtly, asking her to be a messenger girl just that once.

From now on, though, he planned to handle things on *his* terms. Very simply, he would have to draw Leah into conversation quickly at her first singing, be the only one to win her consent to see her home in his carriage. If not, he might lose his chance to court lovely Leah at all. With her winning smile and ways, she would be a magnet for any number of young men.

On the other hand, Sadie Ebersol—if she was to accompany Leah to the singing—was downright difficult to figure out. He honestly hoped Sadie might have other plans or be too busy at home to go along with Leah, which would give him a better prospect. Sadie just didn't seem to care much for him. Not romantically, of course, but just in general. She had looked down her nose at Gideon on several occasions lately, though he didn't know why. This struck him as odd, since both Hannah and Mary Ruth—and Abram and Ida, too— were as friendly and nice as Leah had always been. There was just something different about Sadie. Though she was ever so fair and had the most unusually blue eyes, well . . . he could almost surely put his finger on the root of the problem. Leah's older sister was plumb full of herself. She seemed to think rules were made to be broken, too. He'd heard tell from some of the youth; it was rumored that Sadie might be seeing someone outside the fold of the People. This was hard for him to accept, what with Sadie having bowed her knee before the bishop and the whole church membership after the Preaching service over at Moses Stolzfus's house several weeks ago. The sacred act firmly signaled the end of her rumschpringe. But none of this added up, not if Sadie was being untrue to her vows immediately after making them. But time would tell.

Secretly he had watched Leah while her sister was standing in line, ready to kneel and make her promises to God. Leah's perty face had twitched uncontrollably, as if she were fighting back tears. But why should she be sad at her sister's baptism? Were they tears of joy, maybe? He would never pry, wasn't his place, yet he did wonder sometimes what Sadie was thinking joining church when she seemed to lack the genuine goodness and spirit of honesty so evident in her sister Leah and others. Maybe someday dear Leah would share her feelings on all this. Then again, maybe not.

Sadie insisted to Leah that she was much too weary to attend singing on the following Sunday afternoon.

"Are ya sure?" Leah asked.

But Sadie only shook her head. No amount of pleading was going to change her mind. She said she planned to retire early this evening—a new twist for certain, Leah thought. And something Sadie ought to do more often, seeing as how she was awfully worn out. Yet she was staying home all the time, hadn't sneaked out of the house once lately. Leah was relieved and wondered if joining church *had* changed things for the better. Could it be?

Yet one thing still troubled Leah. She found it peculiar that she'd never heard an explanation for Sadie's disappearance that one afternoon, just days before her baptism. Where *had* her sister gone when she was supposed to be looking after the produce stand? No one—not even Dat and Mamma—seemed to know, or care. And if they did, they were keeping it hush-hush.

Well, all of that aside, the most important and blessed thing had happened at last. Sadie was an official member of the Old Order Amish church. Baptized and set apart.

Struggling not to be put out with Sadie for refusing to go to singing with her, Leah was determined to have some good fellowship, with or without her sister. Finished with both indoor and outdoor chores, she told Mamma where she was headed.

Then Leah hurried over to visit Adah round three o'clock, taking the shortcut through the meadow. She would have to find out from Adah if Gid really *would* drive them over to the Grasshopper Level singing.

But Adah seemed overjoyed at the idea that Leah should ride with them. "Such wonderful-gut news!" Adah said, beaming. "And don't worry about the little bit of distance. I'm sure Gid won't mind at all."

Giggling, they grabbed each other's hands and pranced round the bedroom Adah shared with Dorcas. And praise be, young Dorcas was nowhere in sight. Which was a very good thing, too. Leah surely didn't want to stir up any mistaken notions that she was soon to be courted by their only brother, who, just now, was out past the barnyard splitting logs with her own father and the smithy.

It turned out Leah and Adah rode in the second seat in the courting buggy, behind Gid, who wore a euphoric grin, reins in hand. She and Adah whispered to each other nearly all the way there. Gid was silent for the most part, joining in the conversation only occasionally to inquire of a particular male youth who might also have turned the appropriate age for the singings . . . but not a young *woman*, which Leah found interesting. It was as though Smithy Gid was bent on avoiding any talk of another girl having caught his fancy.

Of course, she kept her thoughts to herself about what Gid might be thinking. Wasn't her business to second-guess. He had every right to pursue any of the girls who might be in attendance tonight. She wouldn't stand in his way; that was certain.

Young people from several church districts were already gathering at the big barn when Leah and Adah stepped down from Smithy Gid's buggy. Almost immediately, Gideon unhitched the horse and led him up to the barn. Later, Adah told her, he would head off in the direction of a group of boys, playing the part of older brother not only for his sister Adah's benefit, but also for Leah's, since she had no brother to accompany her to the singing. There was the unspoken agreement that just because she had consented to ride with Gid and Adah didn't mean she was obligated to return home in the same buggy.

Leah's dearest hope was that Jonas Mast might show up tonight. She would be heartbroken if he didn't. Yet something within her assured her he *would* be here. And with a smile on his handsome face, just for her.

Ach, it was ever so nice to see so many young folk all in one place. And the boys, well, if they didn't look spiffy! It was as if they were attending preaching service, with hair clean and brushed, straw hats in hand, wearing long-sleeved white shirts, tan suspenders and black ties, and such fine black suits free of the slightest wrinkles or dust.

On the way up the lane, she'd taken special notice of the buggies lined up on the side yard, all shiny and neat. Some of the horses, she'd seen on the ride over, had too many reflectors on the bridles, just for show.

The girls were equally well-groomed for the occasion, many of them wearing their *for gut* blue or purple cape dresses, including a clean, long black apron. She had chosen her purple dress, just as Adah had.

"C'mon," Adah whispered to her, "let's gather round the table. It's time to begin, looks like."

Leah, feeling suddenly timid, followed her friend to a long table set up on the barn floor, swept clean for the evening.

The boys were expected to sit on one side and the girls on the other. So far, the girls were getting seated first. The boys were straggling over, three and four at a time, as if they might be sizing up the situation—seeing what new girls were here.

She felt prickly all of a sudden, a tingle of anticipation going up her spine. She still hadn't spotted Jonas, but Sadie, of all people, had cautioned her not to appear too eager for a particular boy. "If Jonas comes, you'll know he's lookin' to take *you* home and no other," Sadie explained. Leah assumed her sister was probably right.

The singing began almost before Leah realized what was happening. Several girls announced the first hymn, blew a pitch pipe, and got the melody going. They seemed to sing only the faster ones, and sometimes words were put to different songs than they sang at Preaching service. This was all new to Leah, but she caught on quickly and found herself joining in, singing heartily, just as Mamma always did in church, singing right in Leah's ear. Ever so joyful Mamma was at such times. Just as Leah was now, especially because Jonas Mast had just caught her eye, a long ways down the table.

Jonas is here! she thought, her heart gladdened. But she was careful not to look his way too often, lest both Adah, next to her, and Smithy Gid, directly across from her, might know there was really no chance she'd be riding home with the village blacksmith's son. None whatsoever. Yet she would be cautious not to hurt their feelings—his and her best friend's, both.

Between the selection of songs, there was enough time to talk to the boys across the table or, in Leah's case, to Adah and two other girls nearby. By the time ten o'clock rolled around, there were enormous bowls of popcorn brought in and soda pop and lemonade. Another whole hour would pass, with plenty of visiting and joking—and boys already doing their best to line up a girl to take home.

"If we instruct our children well, they won't forsake the truth." Mamma's words rang in Leah's ears as she sat there observing over a hundred young people, some moving away from the table, already pairing up.

Getting up, she looked around for Adah, who had disappeared. She was mindful of Gideon, but didn't want to be found standing alone, didn't want to be too available for Gid to approach her. Then she spied Adah way over on the other side of the barn, talking to a boy from their church district, of all things. So Adah had abandoned her for a boy on the first singing. But she didn't much care. Because, in the end, she was rather glad to be standing there alone, under the rafters where two cooing pigeons had perched high overhead.

Jonas sneaked up behind her and said in her ear, "Hullo, Leah."

She spun round and greeted him. "Nice to see you again," she said, grinning and wishing she might say more, but hoping they had the rest of the night to talk together.

"Saw you rode over with Adah Peachey and her brother," he said.

"Jah . . .'cause Sadie's not feelin' so well."

He showed some concern. "Is it the flu, then?"

"Must be. Both she and Mamma have it something awful."

Then he touched her elbow gently, guiding her to a more private spot under the haymow where they could talk without being overheard. "Leah, I was hoping . . ." His blue eyes were blinking fast. "What I mean is . . . would you like to . . . uh, will you allow me to see you home after a bit?"

Smiling, she gave her answer. "Jah, that'd be awful nice. Denki for asking."

His face lit up as if he wouldn't mind asking her the self-same question for a good many singings to come. As if he was right now ready to leave and go driving with her. Of course, he shared with her what was expected. They would stand round and visit together, munch on popcorn and other snacks, watch some of the boys pull practical jokes on each other and other antics. Then, close to eleven o'clock, couples would pair off and head outside to the buggies for a nice, slow ride home under the stars.

Hearing from his lips how the evening was supposed to be, she could hardly wait for the rest of it. Yet it would be unthinkable to wish to rush the next full hour, knowing she had Jonas's full attention, and him right here by her side. Jah, her best dreams were coming true this very night.

Chapter Thirteen

In the morning Leah took charge of cooking breakfast, since both Mamma and Sadie were resting quietly, a rare thing for Mamma, at least. Sure was taking a long time for both of them to get back on their feet, Leah thought. But she was more than happy to help, to have another practice run at frying up the eggs and bacon, especially after the last time. Her family had been oh so polite, not saying a word about how awful bad the food tasted, sinking like a stone in the stomach. Come to think of it, maybe her sorry cooking had added to Mamma's and Sadie's digestive miseries. Could be. But today would be different. Maybe she would try her hand at poaching eggs for Sadie and Mamma instead of frying them. For Dawdi Brenneman, too. Might be more soothing. That and a bit of oatmeal.

She was setting the table, thinking back to last night's singing . . . and dear Jonas, when here came Aunt Lizzie, wanting to help. "Mamma's upstairs," she told her, "still not so gut."

"Ach, and Sadie?" asked Lizzie.

"Sadie, too. But this flu bug hasn't traveled through the house yet."

"Well, now, that's something to be thankful for, jah?" With that, her aunt headed up the steps, calling out softly, "Ida . . . are you presentable? It's your sister Lizzie."

Leah smiled, thinking how dear and close Mamma and Aunt Lizzie had always been. Sometimes Lizzie would show up clear out of the blue, without warning . . . no one telling her she was desperately needed or that something was up. No, she just seemed to know when to wander on down to them. And to tell the truth, Leah was awful glad to have Mamma's sister around this morning, because Leah was beginning to be stumped at what could be ailing her mother. As for Sadie, it was fairly obvious. She'd worn herself out running off to see her English boyfriend, Derry somebody. But, praise be, all that seemed to be a thing of the past. Now Sadie was merely catching up from all the nights she hadn't gotten a speck of sleep, probably.

When the poached eggs looked firm enough, she tested them with a fork. Sure enough, the yolk was only a little runny, the way Mamma liked hers. Leah found the wooden "sick" tray in the pantry and arranged it with a plate of eggs and buttered toast, a small bowl of warm oatmeal, and a cup of raspberry tea, awful gut for settling the stomach.

"Knock, knock," she called through the closed door at the top of the stairs, aware that Mamma and Aunt Lizzie were having themselves a quiet chat.

"C'mon in." Lizzie opened the door, her eyes wide when she spied the tray in Leah's hands. "Well, lookee here who's cooked up a right healthy-lookin' breakfast for you, Ida."

Ever so slowly, Mamma pushed herself up in bed at the

mention of food. Aunt Lizzie went over and helped prop her up with several more pillows. "How nice of you, Leah dear," her mother said.

"I trust this meal is tastier than the last one." She set the tray down on top of the covers over Mamma's lap once she was situated. "Is there anything else I can get you?"

"Well, why don'tcha look in on your sister Sadie, if you don't mind," Mamma said. Her face had a pasty look to it and her hair was still in a single long braid down her back.

"I'll check and see if she's feelin' hungry yet." But Leah wasn't really so keen on the idea of tending to her big sister. More and more, she felt it best they keep their distance. That way Sadie could work through whatever was bothering her here lately. Just maybe giving up her fancy man for the church was starting to sink in some. Jah, probably was, because Sadie wasn't nearly as cheerful as Leah had expected her to be after offering up her life and all her days to almighty God.

"Denki, Leah," said Mamma softly.

"Just tell Aunt Lizzie if there's anything else you need or want. Have her call it down to me, and I'll bring it on up for you." She felt almost like a short-order cook. A right nice feeling, really.

"Sure, I'll let Lizzie know," Mamma said, motioning to her sister to come sit on the bed. "You're awful gut to your old mamma, Leah."

Leah smiled. There was nothing old about her mother. Maybe she was just all tuckered out for some reason. Pulling the door nearly shut, she left it open a crack, then hurried down the hall to see about Sadie. She poked her head in the door. Her sister was stirring a bit but still in her nightclothes, stretched out in bed. "Will you be wanting anything to eat?" Leah asked softly.

Sadie, her hair in two thick, long braids, turned in bed and looked at Leah. "Maybe some tea, but that's all for now. Denki."

"You sure you wouldn't like some oatmeal? I made more than enough for Mamma."

"Later on, maybe." Sadie groaned a little, pulling the sheet up round her neck. "So Mamma's still under the weather, too?"

"Seems so."

"I wonder what *she's* got."

Leah shook her head. "Don't know."

"Well, whatever it is, I'm exhausted. Is Mamma, too?"

Leah recalled their mother's pale cheeks. They were usually a healthy, rosy hue. "Mam looks all washed out, same as you."

"Maybe after I eat a bite I'll feel better . . . like yesterday."

And the day before that, thought Leah.

She was on her way back down the hall when she heard what sounded like someone weeping softly. Stopping in her tracks, she heard Mamma talking, trying to tell Aunt Lizzie she thought she must surely be coming into the change of life.

"Well, if that's all 'tis, no need to fret so, Ida. If you ask me, I was wonderin' if you might not be in the family way."

Mamma laughed out loud. "Ach, don't be silly."

"Well, if you're right, then some raspberry tea oughta do the trick," said Lizzie.

Goodness' sakes, Leah had heard more than she cared to. Mamma going through the change at forty-two? She knew of other women getting teary eyed and sluggish come their mid-forties. It was just awful hard to think of her mother slowing down, when she'd always been one of the first to finish a chore at home or at a work frolic. Just couldn't be, could it?

Jonas Mast and his brothers, Eli and Isaac, found their father at the northernmost corner of the apple orchard just after breakfast. Mam had sent the three of them out with a thermos of hot coffee, "for later, if Dat gets chilled," and she shooed them out the back door. Jonas and thirteen-year-old Eli planned to help Dat gather up all the many apples that had fallen to the ground. Bruised apples made for gut cider, they knew. Isaac, who'd just turned eleven, said he'd stay for only a couple of hours, then he must return to his yard chores. That way, according to Mam, they could all sit down together for the noontime dinner.

Dat agreed. "You best work fast. No shirkin' today, son." To which Isaac nodded and set to work.

Picking up the fallen apples, Jonas's thoughts flew back to last night, where the sweetest girl of all had consented to ride home with him from singing. And what a buggy ride they'd had. Why, they had talked a blue streak, covering nearly every subject under the sun, too. The moon, really. Yet he had never tired of the lively conversation with his agreeable second cousin. On the contrary, she was one of the most interesting girls he thought he'd ever known, including his four sisters, and some of their first cousins, not to mention a whole bunch of girls in his church district—some had made it clear with either their enticing eyes or words that they wouldn't mind being courted by him.

The topic of their childhood promise had come up, but

neither of them was able to recall exactly what they'd said to each other years ago. Still, he knew he loved Leah *now* more than anyone else on God's green earth. And Lord willing, he would marry her one fine day.

Oh, what have I done? Sadie thought, pulling herself up to a sitting position in the bed. Tucking a pillow behind her, she let her tears fall freely. That thing she'd greatly feared had come upon her.

Thoughts of shunning filled her mind; ach, the sin and the shame of it all. Holding herself together, she was worried sick about Mamma's reaction once Sadie told her wicked secret. Dat might want to send her away, force her to give the baby up for adoption . . . she didn't know any of this for sure, but she fretted what would happen to her and the baby. As far as the church was concerned, she was an immoral young woman, an out-and-out lawbreaker. Unless she offered a kneeling repentance before the membership, she would be kicked out, forced to live separate from the community of believers.

Any joy she might've had, even for a moment—had she been a young bride instead of the way things were—faded quickly. Truly she was panic-stricken, unsure of just what she should do now. Or in due time. What would happen when her birth pangs began? Just who on earth would help deliver her baby? She couldn't think of contacting the Plain midwife; then for sure the word would get out.

Ach, a whole multitude of troubling questions clouded her mind.

Worst of all, she was alone, having to bear the blackness of sin's consequences. "Be sure your sin will find you out" was written in the Good Book, along with "The wages of sin is death."

And Dat wouldn't hesitate to remind her, no doubt. Soon as he knew.

By the noon meal Leah thought Mamma seemed to be feeling somewhat better. Aunt Lizzie had stayed through the morning to help redd up the house; then she'd peeled a pile of new potatoes for a big pan of scalloped potatoes. Hannah helped, too, since school was out for the English observance of Columbus Day. Mary Ruth was outside checking on the wash hanging on the line, seeing if some of the things might not be dry already. Soon she was bringing in an armload of clothes and had them all folded before Aunt Lizzie ever set the table.

Meanwhile, Leah's morning had been awful busy, too. She'd gathered the eggs from the chicken house, as well as emptied all the chamber buckets from each bedroom. Washing her hands now at the sink, she was glad *that* chore was completed. Of all her indoor responsibilities, it was the worst job of all. Mamma could never get Mary Ruth to help Leah with it, even if Leah pleaded and offered to do one of Mary Ruth's chores for her. Some things just had to be done . . . like it or not.

On her way out to call both Dat and Dawdi to dinner, she caught herself looking across the fields toward the smithy's farmhouse. Ach, she still felt a little sad inside—for Smithy Gid and what had happened last night. She hadn't known, really, how to tell him that she'd already been asked to ride home with Jonas when he came over to her, all red-faced and shy. Oh, she had tried to let him down ever so gently, even though she'd never promised or led him on in any way. Adah, thankfully, had been talking with a boy she liked; otherwise, it would've been even more awkward, Leah was sure. And poor Gid—she'd heard through the grapevine—had ended up driving his buggy home all alone. Hadn't bothered to ask another girl at all.

What could she do? Both boys were awful nice. And she could say, if asked, that she truly liked Gid. Such a friendly fella he was. Ever so loyal, it seemed. Which made her wonder just how faithful Jonas might've been if *he* hadn't asked her first. Would Jonas have ridden home alone, the way Smithy Gid had? She assumed so but didn't know. Not for sure.

Still, she felt blessed to have enjoyed the very best first singing a girl could ever hope to have. And she already had another date with Jonas to look forward to—in two weeks. The Saturday night before their off-Sunday, he wanted to take her riding again. This time their meeting was to be kept secret. So they were truly a courting couple. Glory be!

Chapter Fourteen

Hannah was anxious for a visit with Dawdi John, no school today and all. She knew he'd spent several hours working with Dat in the barn earlier, so he was sure to be tuckered out. An hour or so after the noon meal, she wandered over next door to find him waking from a nap.

Stretching a bit, he was sitting in his favorite wing-backed chair, all smiles. "Well, hullo, Hannah," he said, a light in his gray-blue eyes at the prospect of some company.

"Didn't mean to wake ya." She sat on the deacon's bench near the front-room window.

"Glad you come over."

Glancing out the window, she could see her father hurrying about the barnyard from where she sat. "Is Dat expecting you outside again?" she asked.

Dawdi laughed softly. "I 'spect your pop's had 'bout as much of me as he can stand in one day."

She didn't have the slightest notion what her grandfather meant by that. Sighing, she waited for him to say more. When he didn't, she asked if he wanted some hot coffee, because he was pulling his gray sweater closed just now, a bit chilly maybe.

"I'll have me some coffee, denki. Make it black."

"Jah, Dawdi, I remember," she called over her shoulder, heading out to his small kitchen. Next thing she knew, here he came, ambling out to sit at the little square table. Seemed he was as eager for a nice visit as she was.

One thing led to another—talk of the harvest, of upcoming doings over at Hickory Hollow, Dawdi reminiscing of days spent at Uncle Noah's place—and perty soon their chatter was focused on Gobbler's Knob. Hannah talked of growing up on this farm, having been the only place she'd ever known.

"Well, now, this here's the third house I've lived in," he said with a wry smile.

"That's right. First, 'twas your own farm . . . then Uncle Noah's, and now this Dawdi Haus."

He nodded. "Guess I'm tryin' to keep up with your aunt Lizzie."

"Oh, has she lived in several different places, too?"

"Three. Same as me."

Hannah clicked off in her head the places Aunt Lizzie had lived. "Hm-m, guess I only come up with two. Your house with Mammi when Lizzie and Mamma and their siblings were growin' up in Hickory Hollow, and later the log cabin. Was there another?" Far as she knew, Lizzie had gone directly from her parents' farmhouse to the log cabin, once she was considered a maidel.

Dawdi was nodding his head. "Didn'tcha know Lizzie lived right here in this little house?"

"Here, really?" Such peculiar news, though she didn't know what to make of it.

"Jah, for a time . . . shortly after her rumschpringe. Lizzie joined church here in Gobbler's Knob, coming to live near your mamma and pop."

"Aunt Lizzie and Mamma were always close, ain't so?" she said, knowing it was true.

Dawdi smiled at that. "Guess you could say Ida—your mamma—was Lizzie's second mother back then."

"That wonders me, what you said," Hannah spoke up. "Why should my aunt need a second mother if she was grown up enough to join church? And why didn't she ever marry, perty as she still is?"

Things got ever so quiet. In fact, Hannah thought she could hear the murmuring of a housefly's wings as it flew past her just now.

When Dawdi finally did speak, it was in a whisper. "Might not want to be askin' too many questions."

She was feeling more befuddled by the second. "But if Aunt Lizzie lived here once she was baptized, just when did she move to the cabin on the hill?"

"I 'spect once the place was built." Dawdi sighed, as if he was becoming restless. "Your pop and his brothers set to buildin' it for her."

"So she could live near Mamma?"

Dawdi rubbed his long gray beard. "Most maidels want a bit of independence, I 'spect. As I recall, Lizzie wanted that, jah. Yet here she could still be close enough for family activities and whatnot."

She thought on this. Aunt Lizzie *was* awful fond of them, which was mighty nice. And they loved her, too, same as all their aunts and uncles. "I'm glad Lizzie lives near us."

"Well, now, I am too," Dawdi declared.

His coffee needed warming up, so she got up from the table and poured some more for him without asking. "It's nice *you've* come to live here," she said.

"This way I can get to know my granddaughters better over in this part of the world."

She had to smile at that. Surely Dawdi must feel as if his children and grandchildren were scattered all round Lancaster County. And they were, come to think of it. Which was the reason Dat and Mamma hardly ever made the trip over to see Aunt Becky and Uncle Noah and all those cousins. Such a long way it was.

Suddenly she said, "You're the last of my *Grosseldere*—grandparents." Oh my! She hadn't meant to say it out in the open thataway. Still, she'd been thinking—pondering, really—the fact that both Dawdi and Mammi Ebersol had gone to heaven, and Mammi Brenneman, too. "So you're all I have left."

Dawdi smiled the kindest smile and reached out his hand to her. "Don't fret over such things or I'll hafta name you a worrywart. I've got lots of living to do yet, Lord willing."

Right away, she felt bad. "Mamma says I worry over things that will never come true."

Dawdi nodded. "Guess we all do, to some degree or 'nother."

"Still, we oughta enjoy every single day the Good Lord gives us, ain't so?" she replied.

Still holding her hand in his, Dawdi chuckled. "Don't be feeling sorry for me, Hannah. Living here is gonna be right fine. Already 'tis." There was a twinkle in his eyes. " 'Specially with so many interesting folk to talk to."

She felt better now. So Dawdi found her to be an interesting granddaughter. He didn't consider her to be a chatter-box, which he'd remarked in jest about Mary Ruth at the sup-per table last night. "We'll have us another chat here perty soon," she said, hearing Mamma calling to her from the other side of the house.

"Jah, I'd like that." He grinned up at her.

With that, she leaned down and kissed Dawdi's crinkly forehead.

Mary Ruth was glad for the near ceaseless flow of custom-ers at the roadside stand all afternoon. She enjoyed selling a basketful of decorative gourds to Mrs. Ferguson, one of their many faithful customers. Then Mrs. Esbenshade arrived, almost before Mrs. Ferguson could get her spanking new green Nash sedan out of the way.

"I hear there's to be a wedding coming up soon in your family," Mrs. Esbenshade said.

The only family wedding she knew of was the Masts', and she mentioned Anna's name to the woman. "Do you know my second cousin, then?"

"Oh my, yes. I buy apples every year from Fannie and her girls." The woman's plump face brightened. "My neighbors' second son works for Peter Mast, doing odd jobs."

"We pick all our apples over there," Mary Ruth said, mak-ing small talk, what she loved doing best.

"When *is* Anna's wedding?"

"Third Tuesday in November. Anna and her beau were published in church right after the fall communion. That's our custom."

"So Amish weddings occur only in November and December?"

"Around Lancaster, jah . . . and once in a while late October or early January, if need be. There are only so many Tuesdays and Thursdays in a two-month period, ya know."

Mrs. Esbenshade smiled. "Well, I can't pretend to know much about your ways, Mary Ruth. I suppose I'll wait for a written invitation from Anna."

"A gut idea, I'd say." And with that, she tried to interest the English woman in some pumpkins, which were coming on real gut now.

"Oh, I'll come back tomorrow and pick out a nice big one for my nephew. He's seven this year and wants to carve a jack-o'-lantern all by himself."

"Tomorrow, then. Either Leah or Sadie will be here tending the stand, for sure." Mary Ruth knew nothing much about Halloween, only that it was a night English children went from door to door begging for candy. It wasn't a holiday the People had ever observed. The best thing about October was selling so many pumpkins, except the ones Mamma had already set aside to make pumpkin-nut cookies, pumpkin-spice cake, and pumpkin-chiffon pie, her specialty. So pumpkins were awful gut for business, and it seemed the more they planted each year, the more they sold.

A few minutes after Mrs. Esbenshade drove away, young Elias Stoltzfus rode up in his father's market wagon. He pulled off the road a bit and gave the horse a sugar cube before walking over to the produce stand. "Hullo there, Mary Ruth," he called to her, taking his straw hat off his head and completely ignoring the lineup of fruits and vegetables. Seemed he had a talk on, and that was right fine with her. "My pop says we might be goin' over to the Mast wedding next month. Now, what do you think of that?"

She liked the sound of it, sure did. And, so as not to be forward, she nodded her head slowly and smiled at the red-headed boy named for his father, a long-standing deacon in their church.

"What I'm getting to, Mary Ruth, is when it's time to sit down for the wedding feast, I hope you'll sit 'cross from me at the table."

"Jah, I'd like that, Elias." Her heart filled with joy at his invitation.

"I'll do all I can to make sure I'm lined up just right 'fore we sit down. Don'tcha worry none. We'll have us a wonderful-gut time."

Even though she was far from courting age—Elias surely knew that, and so was he—she liked the idea of being friendly anyways. Of course, she would be right sensible about boys, just as Leah had always been . . . and Mamma most surely had been back when. She wouldn't think of behaving the way Sadie had here the last year or so. Thank goodness her big sister had settled down and joined church. All for the better.

Elias didn't bother to purchase anything, just grinned, showing his teeth a little too much, and waved to her as he turned to go. "See ya tomorrow at school, jah?"

"Jah, at *recess*," she said, hoping he'd remember and come say hello to her maybe.

Running back to his horse and wagon, Elias got himself seated, then whistled loudly to alert the Belgian steed to pull out quickly. And he was on his way. Ach, and what a fast driver he was, Dat would surely say if he'd seen the way Elias handled the horse. But the Stoltzfus boy had always been like that, young and spirited, like his stallion. Yet there was something gentle and sweet about him, too, Mary Ruth knew. There was no getting round that.

She was mentally counting the years till her rumschpringe when another customer came calling. This time a fancy Englisher with the darkest hair and eyes she'd ever seen. A right handsome young man, really, as fancy boys go. His hair was groomed neatly and he wore pressed black trousers and a long-sleeved white shirt with a woolen red vest and black bow tie, as if he might be a Fuller Brush salesman. "How can I help you today?" she said, greeting him, thinking he'd surely have plenty of money to clean out the stand if he wanted to.

"I'm not interested in buying anything," he said bluntly. "I'm here to deliver a message to your sister. I assume you're related." He handed her an envelope.

"That depends on who you mean. I have three sisters, sir."

He smiled at her just then. "Please, you don't have to call me 'sir' . . . I'm not much older than you are."

She wasn't sure if he winked at her or not, but he was truly flirtatious. Glancing down at the letter in her hand, she saw it was addressed to Sadie Ebersol. "Jah, Sadie's my sister. I'll give it to her."

"I'd appreciate that." He nodded slightly, behaving again like a proper gentleman all of a sudden.

She slipped the letter into her pocket. "I'll see that Sadie gets it by suppertime, if that's all right with you."

"No hurry," he said. "So long." He turned and rushed back to his shiny gray car, then sped away like nobody's business.

She found it ever so curious that both boys had wanted to show off for her, one with a heavy hand on the reins, the other with a lead foot. Feeling for the letter in her dress pocket, she reminded herself to find Sadie as soon as she went inside, come suppertime.

It was well past dusk when they all sat down together for Bible reading and evening prayers in the kitchen. Sadie was glad to be keeping the glass chimneys on the oil lamps consistently clean; so much better it was for Dat when he read long passages from the Scriptures, which he did this night.

He read aloud in Pennsylvania Dutch from Luke chapter nine, beginning at verse twenty-three. " 'And he said to them all, If any man will come after me, let him deny himself, and take up his cross daily, and follow me. For whosoever will save his life shall lose it: but whosoever will lose his life for my sake, the same shall save it.' "

Dat continued to read, but Sadie's thoughts got stuck on the words "whosoever will save his life shall lose it." She wondered, was that what she'd done by making her kneeling vow before the bishop and the membership last month? Had she attempted to save her life . . . her very soul?

But what of the tiny life growing within her now? What was to become of Derry's baby once it was born into the Plain community? Would he love Sadie enough to marry her? She had no idea. She only knew that she was terrified and wished she might see Derry again very soon. She had to tell him that what she'd suspected for several weeks was absolutely true. And best she could calculate, by mid-June she'd be giving birth.

She could only imagine how hurt Dat and Mamma would be if they knew. Yet she couldn't bear to tell them today, not this week either. She didn't rightly know just when she could bring herself to reveal such a disgraceful thing as this. She recalled the church community's stand—and the consequences for the sinner—when a young girl had become pregnant back two years ago. Such a time that had been. And now here she was in the same jam! How? How could such a thing have happened to her?

Her thoughts continued to whirl as Dat's voice droned on. More and more she was thinking that if she weren't in danger of being shunned—would the bishop make an exception?—she could marry Derry and go fancy if he refused to join the community of the People. Save her family from *some* embarrassment, maybe. Though such ideas were truly hogwash, she knew. There was no getting round the *Ordnung*. It would be craziness to think otherwise. All she really knew, without a doubt, was that she had to share her startling news with her beloved. She could only guess what he would say or do. Surely he'd convinced her of his love—she could rely on that, couldn't she? He'd declared it outright so many times she dared not try and count. Truth was, her revelation might put them on dangerous ground. He could become angry at the least little thing.

She scarcely knew what to do first. Best keep this to herself for a while longer.

Mary Ruth rushed into the bedroom where Sadie and Leah were both in long cotton nightgowns, brushing their waist-length hair. "Ach, I forgot to tell you, Sadie," she exclaimed. "A young man—all dressed up—dropped by the roadside stand this afternoon. He asked me to give you this."

Sadie wondered what on earth Mary Ruth was talking about, and so excitedly at that. She saw her name printed on the envelope and her heart leaped up. Was this a letter from Derry? One of the very things she'd longed to see . . . to keep in her treasured things. Could it be?

Well, now that Mary Ruth had made her delivery, she wasn't leaving the room, wasn't leaving Sadie alone with this precious letter from her dearest one. "May I have some privacy?" she said at last.

Both Leah and Mary Ruth took the hint and left together, closing the door behind them. Moving to the small oil lamp atop the dresser, she stood there, fingers trembling, and opened the envelope.

> *Dear Sadie,*
>
> *I hope you are well.*
>
> *This may come as a surprise, but I hope you'll agree that the time has come for us to part. You are a baptized member of your church now, and I am preparing to enlist in the army, which will undoubtedly take me far away from Lancaster County. I realize we've discussed this already, that I promised to keep in constant touch with you during my military duty.*
>
> *However, thinking about the potential problems of such a long-distance relationship, I have second thoughts about tying you down with no promise of marriage. I should not expect loyalty like that from you, and even if I did, it wouldn't be fair to either of us, would it?*
>
> *I hope you have a happy life.*
>
> *Sincerely,*
> *Derek Schwartz*

Sadie felt as though she'd been punched in the stomach. Was Derry saying good-bye to her for good? But how could that be? She couldn't begin to comprehend, after all they'd meant to each other. After *everything*. And now such a horrid letter when she needed him more than ever. Oh, she felt so ill . . . as if she might lose all her supper.

The time has come for us to part. . . .

Staggering to the bed, she clutched the letter, not caring to repress her sobs. Not realizing that now, as she buried her head in the pillow, Leah had slipped into the room, closed the door silently, and was leaning over her. "Aw, Sadie . . . my dear sister . . ." And then she felt Leah beside her, lying ever so near, wrapping her arms around her, holding her as if she were a little child. "There, there," Leah whispered. "Weep if you must."

"Ach, I loved him so," she cried. "I truly loved him. . . ."

Leah said no more, and somewhere between the blackness of night and the veil of bitter tears, Sadie slept.

Leah was torn between her sister's obvious grief and her own curiosity over the letter still clasped in sleeping Sadie's hand. So . . . Sadie *hadn't* ended her relationship with the English beau earlier, as Leah had hoped. No matter, it was over now. And though she felt terribly sorry for Sadie, she was mighty glad that Derry was gone once and for all. He'd broken things off in such a spineless manner! Well, the boy wasn't worthy of anyone's affections, let alone her sister's.

Leah purposely stayed awake, shifting her thoughts to Jonas. She had no reason to ever expect a coward's letter from *him*, now that she had proof of his keen interest in her, in his plan to court her. One year from now their wedding plans would be published in church, and by Thanksgiving Day they would be wed, probably. Jah, the year ahead would be the best one of her whole life . . . if Dat came to see the light, that is. Smithy Gid, too.

Sighing, she rose to pull up a lightweight quilt over her sister. Leah hoped and prayed that Sadie might enjoy the same depth of happiness she herself had found in dearest Jonas, only this time with a nice Plain boy.

But she worried, unable to sleep. Had Sadie's reputation been tarnished by the grapevine amongst the community of the People?

Chapter Fifteen

Derek Schwartz talked his brother into going out for a night on the town, to Harrisburg, thirty-eight miles away. Robert was a wet blanket when it came to having fun, particularly this Friday night, and Derek accused him in so many words as they drove to a downtown soda shop called The Niche.

After a near-silent supper they headed to the YMCA, where a bevy of girls were eager to dance to a live local band, and a Sinatra wannabe was crooning onstage and making time with the microphone. Derek was more than happy to oblige and danced with four different blondes before noticing Robert sitting over on the sidelines. This annoyed him, but he decided to keep his yap shut this time. Poor, miserable big brother, suffering the aftershock of war. Shouldn't he be content having survived Normandy's invasion with all his limbs and mental faculties? Some of the young guys his age had come back with a hook for a hand—or worse, in body bags. His father had told Derek in a whisper one night in the hallway connecting the small medical clinic to the house, "Your brother will need patience from all of us . . . time to adjust to civilian life again."

Even so, Derek could not muster up a trace of sympathy for Robert tonight. Why should he waste his dance-floor energy having to twist Robert's arm when the atmosphere was charged with pure exhilaration, perfumed and coiffed girls, and great music? Didn't the ex-GI know it was time to celebrate? He was alive, for pete's sake!

By the time they were back in the car and driving home, Derek was proud to have collected four phone numbers, all from blue-eyed blondes. One, a deep-dimpled girl, could have easily passed herself off as Helen O'Connell, sweet canary of Jimmy Dorsey's swing band. Yeah, the phone numbers were long-distance ones, but he didn't have to dial up all of them within the space of a week . . . or even a month. One thing was settled in his mind—he was ready for a new girl. Harrisburg, York, Reading, he didn't care. The fling with Sadie Ebersol had gone on way too long. He could kick himself for leading her on as he had, letting her believe he would keep in touch with her as an enlisted man. Or that he loved her at all. What got his goat was how innocent she had been . . . too trusting, too. He bristled now, recalling their furtive trysts in the woods. Memories of the past two months haunted him—the risks he'd taken—dragging off to work, too tired to pull his fair share.

Wisely, and in the nick of time, he had rid himself of Sadie with a tidy and to-the-point letter, which her cute—

and quite cheerful—younger sister had promised to deliver. By now, knowing Sadie as he did, she would have cried herself to sleep more than two nights in a row. Soon, though, she would be out flirting again, finding herself a good-looking but rowdy Plain boy, most likely, now that she was a bona fide member of that back-woodsy church. He made a mental note to be more discreet with his sugarcoated doublespeak in the future, having made empty promises repeatedly. His best move so far had been cutting things off before something happened to tie him down to her.

Robert broke the silence, intruding into Derek's reverie. "How can they do it?"

"Huh?"

"People act like things are fine. Don't those girls at the 'Y' know there's been a war? Our guys were blown to smithereens and they—you . . . *everyone*—acts like nothing happened."

Derek turned and looked at his brother. Robert was gripping the steering wheel with both hands, at ten o'clock and two, just as their father had taught them.

"How can things be the same here at home?"

In the four months since his brother's return, Derek had never heard him speak of his war experiences. He hadn't heard the edge of frustration, the intense anger in Robert's voice. "Maybe it's because some of us weren't there to see people get blown to kingdom come . . . that's how," Derek shot back, not sure why he felt so angry now himself.

Robert fell suddenly silent again, which made Derek uneasy. His brother's face was often as white as the sheets their father used to drape over a corpse from time to time. Robert proudly wore the mask of unwitting demise, which bothered Derek. It was as if this young war veteran had to experience death vicariously, here and now—after the fact— to somehow justify what his slaughtered best buddies had faced and lost. And now Robert was driving much too slowly on the highway as the turn-off for Strasburg came into view. What was really wrong? Derek wondered. Why was Robert driving like there was no need to get somewhere? Ever? Like he was in no hurry to arrive home, to crawl into bed and sleep in the safety of their father's home instead of a foxhole. Was he afraid he might endure the nightmarish dreams of the Normandy beaches all over again?

When the good doctor heard the knocking on the side door, he was slow to get up out of his comfortable chair to see who it was. The boys should be back soon, was his first thought. Maybe they'd forgotten the house key. But, no, when he opened the door he was met by the tear-streaked face of a young Amishwoman. "I'm ever so sorry to bother you," she said softly. "I was wonderin' . . . is Derry home?"

"Derek? You wish to see *my* son?"

"Jah, if that's all right."

He glanced around her, expecting to see a horse and buggy parked in the lane. "Did you come on foot?"

She nodded. " 'Tis important."

"Well, Derek isn't home," he said quickly, aware of her eyes in the porch light. Lovely, sad, faded blue eyes. "I wouldn't know when to expect him."

"I'd be willin' to wait."

Raking his hand through his hair, he wondered what he ought to say or do, wondering what was best for Derek. "Let

me run you home. I can't say how late it might be before
he—"

"Denki, but no. I must see Derry tonight."

*She knows his nickname? What sort of relationship does this
girl have with my boy?* he worried.

Suddenly, he felt he must encourage her to visit tomorrow, or another day. But no amount of persuading could
convince the girl that she should *not* sit outside on the porch
step waiting, and she insisted on doing so. And now here
was Lorraine, in her bathrobe, coming to see what all the
commotion was, asking why Henry hadn't invited the poor
dear inside.

"No . . . no, I can't do that," the girl said. "I wouldn't
think of imposin' on you."

"But it's nothing," his wife insisted. "Please, do come in."

The girl, who gave her name simply as Sadie, was more
stubborn than the two of them. She turned and planted herself on the second step of the side porch, determined to wait
for Derek.

At last Henry closed the door on the girl, turning to
Lorraine. "Why must you be so hospitable at this hour, when
we don't even know the young woman?" he said, checking
himself. It wouldn't do to protest . . . to make a mountain out
of a simple molehill, most likely.

"She's surely a neighbor, Henry," his kind and compassionate wife said. "We have lots of Plain folk living up and
down the road; you know that."

"But . . . an Amish girl asking for Derry?" He forced a
chuckle. "How ordinary is that?"

The tension was ultimately diffused by their laughter,
though he found himself checking out the window every

fifteen minutes to see if the girl was still there, hoping for Derek's sake she might change her mind and walk back home. Where she belonged.

The highway was dark, the headlights the only source of light on the narrow road hemmed in by cornfields on all sides. Robert surprised Derry by breaking the silence. "Did Dad ever warn you about women?" Robert asked.

"Nope."

"Before I left for the war . . . at the train station, Dad said certain things."

Derek shook his head. "What're you getting at?"

" 'Stick to your own kind'—that's just what Dad said, slapping my back while the train chugged into view. And he seemed to feel strongly about it . . . even wrote letters warning me to keep my nose clean when it came to European girls. Dad said women were trouble."

"Not *all* women," Derry said. "Dad got lucky with Mom."

"Well, I didn't listen to him. I fell for a German girl named Verena." Robert stopped talking, having to cough several times.

"What happened?"

"She died in an explosion." His brother paused again. "Thank God she was asleep . . . it happened in the middle of the night . . . she never knew what hit her." Robert signaled and pulled over, then turned off the ignition and opened the window.

"Yeah? That's rough."

They sat there for the longest time, listening to the motor ticking.

Soon Derry was the one coughing. "Are we ever going home?"

Then Robert turned to face him, as if he were going to whine about the war some more. "This might sound weird to you, but I made a promise to God over there. When everyone around me was drowning or getting blown to bits . . . I prayed that if I got out of that hellish place alive, I'd give my life to Christ somehow. Do something big for Him."

"Like what?"

Breathing in audibly, Robert leaned his arm on the open window. "What would you think if I became a minister, like Grandpa Schwartz?"

Derry felt like laughing, but this wasn't the time or place. "Hey, it's your life. Mess it up if you want to."

"But . . . you didn't see how bloody—how unspeakably brutal the war was. Don't you understand I shouldn't be alive today? You should have a brother buried six feet under. . . ." Robert's voice trailed off to nothing.

"Well, don't let me be the one to tell you how stupid it could be to break a vow, or whatever, to God." Derry was sick and tired of all this talk from his big brother. All this religious talk . . .

It was time for Robert to quit spilling his guts and drive home. That's what. And when Derry said so, Robert stared back at him for a moment, then straightened and turned on the ignition, saying no more.

Sitting on the porch, having just met Derry's parents— Dr. Henry Schwartz and his friendly wife—Sadie waited for their son, thinking back to her childhood years here in Gobbler's Knob. For the longest time, she'd had a carefree, happy life . . . obeying the Ordnung and trying to do right. Dat and Mamma had brought her up in the ways of the Lord, no doubt of that. Yet here she was perched on the steps of strangers, really, their grandchild forming beneath her frightened heart.

Ach, she'd had to tell Leah *something*. After all, Leah had been by her side to comfort her after Derry's unexpected letter had clear knocked the wind out of her. She hadn't breathed a word about expecting a baby, though. Didn't want to share that news just yet, not with anyone. Only Derry should know. She had told Leah she wouldn't be seeing her English beau any longer but guarded the letter and didn't offer to share it.

Unable to slip away from the house, she'd waited all week to walk down the road a half mile or so because she didn't dare risk trying to hitch up the driving horse to the family buggy. Not at this hour. And now that she was here, Sadie felt even worse about the things Derry had written her. And awful sad it was, finding out he wasn't home tonight. She had hoped he might've stayed home, sorrowfully pondering the many days and weeks of their love. But now his being gone made her wonder if he had ever loved her at all, to be out having himself a nice time while she was still crying over him—over what might've been.

Or, now that she thought on it, what could *still* be. Did she dare tell him what was brewing in her mind . . . in her heart?

Henry wondered now if he might've been too hasty with the young barefooted woman. Why *hadn't* he invited her inside, welcoming her with the usual gracious bedside manner he was known for? Yet he was a man of his own opinions, and he pushed back alarm at the thought of a tear-streaked Amish girl on their doorstep.

He walked back to the front room, ears alert to what might unfold. The hour was late. Robert and Derek would surely be home any minute, and his second son was quite adept at handling things, whatever the girl's issue might be. This was not his concern, nor Lorraine's, yet he stood to peer out the window as Robert's car pulled into the lane.

Derek spotted Sadie instantly, hunched over on the porch step, as if she could fool him and not be noticed. Nevertheless, she was there, brazenly waiting for him. "What's *she* doing here?" he snapped.

"Who?" Robert asked.

"Never mind." He leaped out of the car, mad as a threatened dog, and walked partway up the walk toward her. "Come with me, Sadie," he barked, not waiting for her to get up and follow. Marching around the side of the house, toward the entrance to the medical clinic where his father treated patients, he waited for her to catch up, arms folded across his chest. "What were you thinking, coming here?" he demanded.

She inched her way closer to him, yet keeping her distance. It was then that he noticed she was barefooted beneath her long blue dress, as she always was, and in the dark coolness of the night, with only the porch lamp to cast a spell of light, he was taken once again with her beauty. "Derry, I'm sorry to bother you, but I must tell ya something," she said softly.

They stood like two statues engulfed in amber shadows.

"My letter," he muttered. "Is this about the letter?"

"Jah." Her voice quavered. "And . . . something else, too."

"Look, Sadie, I'm sorry about what happened between us. I wasn't thinking—"

"No," she interrupted, "but *I* have been." Then she said softly, almost in a whisper, "Derry, I'd thought you'd want to know . . . I'm in the family way."

Stunned, he took a step back as Sadie's words echoed in his brain. "Are you sure?"

"I wouldn't have told you if I wasn't."

An uncanny silence hung in the air, separating them like a damask curtain. His words were measured. "What're you going to do?"

"This isn't just *my* concern, Derry. This is your baby, too." Quickly she hung her head—not in shame, he was certain. After a time she slowly lifted her eyes to him. "If you loved me half as much as you said all those times before, you could save yourself from goin' off to serve Uncle Sam, ya know."

He did not immediately grasp her meaning. Then he did. She wanted him to marry her, give her baby a name and a home. Any girl would want that. She must think he was looking for an exemption from military duty, and Sadie wasn't simply hinting. He could see by her posture she was giving it to him straight. "What a wonderful-gut excuse to stay home, jah?"

"But I *want* to join the army."

She fell silent again.

He tried to avoid her eyes. Those beautiful eyes that had taunted him from the first night. "Let's talk about *you*." He didn't want to sound crass, but what choice did he have? "My father might know of someone in Philly who could take care of this problem—and soon. I'd drive you there myself."

"No," she said. "What's done is done." She stepped forward, coming face-to-face with him. "This wee one inside me, *our* baby together, was created out of love. 'Least, I thought so. You should be ashamed, Derry Schwartz, thinkin' that I'd do away with my own flesh and blood." She was crying. "I don't know you anymore. Maybe I never did." Turning, she ran across the lawn, heading for the road.

"Wait . . . Sadie!" he called after her. "Let me take you home."

She stopped abruptly, hands on her slender hips. "I'd rather walk ten miles in the blackest midnight than let you drive me anywhere. You're the cruelest human being the Lord God ever made!" With that pronouncement of his moral fiber, she sped off into the night.

Derek stood watching her at the edge of the lawn. "Dad was right. Women *are* trouble," he whispered, then spat on the ground.

Chapter Sixteen

Leah remembered having placed a firm hand on Sadie's shoulder, hoping to talk sense to her, trying to stop her sister from going down the road to "talk to Derry, just this once."

"But . . . you've put the sins of the past behind, ain't so?" Leah had asked, aware of Sadie's glistening eyes. "Honestly, I don't mean to pry, but—"

"Then don't." Sadie had pushed away.

"Keep your vow to God" was all Leah could whisper before Sadie left their bedroom, rushing out into the night.

Now, alone in the room, Leah paced the floor, something she'd never done. Sadie was off somewhere talking to her former English beau . . . just why, she hadn't bothered to say. The letter that had brought such sad, sorrowful news days ago was buried deep in one of the dresser drawers—or Sadie's hope chest, maybe—Leah was awful sure, yet she wouldn't go searching for it. Would be wrong to read what Sadie had never offered to share.

But Leah wasn't about to take herself off to bed. Not till Sadie returned home, safe in their father's house again. She sat on the edge of the bed in her nightgown, praying silently and waiting for the tiptoed return of her baptized sister.

The biting smell of woodsmoke mingled with the autumn air as Sadie rushed home, indifferent to sharp pebbles tearing at her bare feet. She sometimes ran, sometimes walked on the two-lane highway that bordered the east side of the forest, where she and Derry had met on more occasions than she cared to count, the road that ran between Derry's home and her own. An owl hooted in the distance, the eerie sound coming from deep in the woods, though Sadie wasn't a bit scared to walk alone.

She thought of the toasty fire Aunt Lizzie surely had stoked all evening long, though at this hour the flames were no doubt reduced to smoldering embers, cooling now as she hurried toward home. Come to think of it, maybe Aunt Lizzie's place was the origin of the smoke that hung so heavily in the air, except that the little cabin was clear on the other side of the knoll. Just why was she thinking of her fun-loving maidel aunt on a night like this? Sadie knew how much Lizzie liked to walk in the woods. Sometimes even at night, especially when the moon was out. Aunt Lizzie said she could talk best to God at such times.

Sadie didn't know how she herself felt about the Lord God tonight. She'd built her whole future round Derry, only to have her hopes come crumbling down. She thought she might want to move to Hickory Hollow, live neighbors to some of her married cousins—Uncle Noah and Aunt Becky's grown children, maybe. Get away from not only the raised eyebrows that were sure to come, but the words of rebuke from Mamma, Dat, and eventually Preacher Yoder . . . all the way up to the bishop, if she didn't confess her terrible sin and come clean. Then, just as awful, she'd end up living alone, without the chance to marry. No Amish boy would want "secondhand goods." No more Sunday singings for her once she began to show, no more rides in an open buggy on a starry night, no more giggling at wedding feasts. Pairing up was a thing of the past. And tomboy Leah, of all things, would be the first of Abram's daughters to marry.

Sadie tied her prayer cap under her chin against the breeze, wondering what it would be like to live near her Hickory Hollow kinfolk. What had it been like for Lizzie, leaving all her friends and coming over here near Mamma? Especially when Lizzie had two sisters who were much closer in age than Mamma was, "and closer in spirit, too," Uncle Noah had said years back, one of the few times they'd visited Mamma's older brother and family. Of course, now it didn't seem to matter anymore. Lizzie was long settled in the Gobbler's Knob church community, a helper to Mamma, a caregiver for Dawdi Brenneman, and a woman of her own making. She'd never married, which often perplexed Sadie, and whenever the topic came up with either Leah or Mamma, one of them would say something like, "Some women seem content to live without a man." But Sadie didn't believe it, not for one minute. She'd noticed Aunt Lizzie at church picnics and whatnot, enjoying herself and everyone round her. Such a cheerful woman she was. Up until about five years or so ago, Sadie had wondered if Lizzie might not marry an older man—a widower, maybe—but no such opportunity had come along just yet.

Glancing over her shoulder at distant car lights coming fast, Sadie moved to the far left side of the road, near the grassy ditch where wild strawberry vines grew all summer long and lightning bugs could be seen flickering in June.

"I want to join the army. . . ."

Derry's words rang in her head. Thinking back to their dreadful conversation, she felt something snap way down inside her. No matter what Derry said or did from now on, she was going to cherish and care for their baby. The innocent child must be shielded from the murderous attitude of its own father.

Kicking at the road, she scraped her right foot but didn't care. *Der Derry Schwartz is en lidderlicher*—a despicable fellow—she thought. And the most frightening thing was she never would've guessed him to be anything but what she'd known of him these past months—kind and ever so loving . . . eager to see her as often as possible. What could've happened to change his mind about her? Had he found himself another girlfriend . . . in such a short time? Or was his decision to join up with the military the main reason? If that was true, why on earth would he refuse to write the letters he'd promised? Why?

A dozen questions or more gnawed at her peace. The car lights had caught up with her. She turned to see Derry waving his arm out the window. "Sadie! Stop right now and get in."

As soon as she knew who the driver was, she turned her head stiffly, still walking.

"Don't be stubborn," he was hollering at her. And now he'd stopped the car. She heard the door slam and his hard footsteps. Was he running after her to say he was ever so sorry, take her in his arms, tell her he didn't mean a word of what he'd said before? That they should be married right away, he'd changed his mind, decided not to go off with

Uncle Sam. He *loved* her, after all.

But no . . . his words rang out into the night. "Listen to me, Sadie!" She felt his hand on her shoulder now, turning her round to face him. "You can't go on like nothing's happened," he was saying. "You have to do something about the . . . baby."

"I'll do something. I'll be raising our child by myself," she answered, "and there ain't anything you can do 'bout it. Unless . . ." Looking past him, she saw his gray automobile sitting back there in the middle of the road, the door on the driver's side gaping wide just the way her life and her future felt to her—exposed for the world of the People to see and then condemn.

"Unless what?" He gripped her arms.

"Unless you change your mind."

"That's impossible," he said flatly. "Well, I guess there is adoption, but who's going to take a half-breed?"

She wondered if this might be the truest reason behind his rejection of their child. But she didn't think he'd be so uncouth as to put it into words. And such hurtful words they were. "Turn loose of me, Derry. I'm going home now."

He released her, though reluctantly, stepping back with defiance on his face. "Sadie Ebersol, I wish I'd never met you."

"Jah, well, I wish it more than you." She spun on her heels and began to run. She ran until her callused feet were numb to the sting of the hard pavement. She ran away from what might've been—all her wishes and dreams bound up in one horrible boy—and rushed toward her father's house, where she would do her best to hide her sin over the next months, sew her dresses and aprons ever wider, till she could no longer hide her secret. The People would then know the truth about her and her false covenant. They could either help her live as a maidel with a child, or they could reject her, cast her out—shun her. At this moment, she knew she was too stubborn to repent to a single soul.

Soon the rambling farmhouse came into view, and she quickened her pace, glad that Derry had chosen to turn round in the road and head back. She was sure she'd never see him again. She hoped so with all her might.

Leah heard Sadie coming up the stairs and stood in the doorway, waiting. "Gut, you're home at last," she whispered.

"I never want to see Derry again as long as I live."

Such a relief, thought Leah, but to Sadie she said, "I'm glad you're here, sister."

And then Sadie turned and looked at her, falling into her arms. Patting her sister ever so gently, Leah said no more, letting Sadie sob onto her shoulder, hoping her sister's cries were muffled enough to keep from waking Mamma.

Ida was put out with herself, having to get up several times in the night, rejecting the idea of the outhouse. She was thankful for the chamber bucket, especially here lately when her sleep was ever so deep. Like a rock, she felt, of a morning. Was this how her older sister-in-law, Becky Brenneman, felt come the change? She could talk right frankly with Becky face-to-face, she recalled. But it had been such a long time since Abram had agreed to drive all of them over there. "Too far to the Hollow," he'd said when she asked last week. "Not during harvest," he'd said just this evening. So she wouldn't be asking Abram again. Not till after the wedding season, but then it would be too cold, probably, too much snow on the road. Then his excuse would be the sleigh couldn't begin to hold all six of them. Seven, really, if Lizzie went, which she'd want to, Ida was awful sure.

Truth be known, Abram and Noah hadn't gotten along for the longest time. "We don't see eye to eye," Abram had often said. Which puzzled Ida when she thought of it, because there wasn't anyone else round the community who rubbed Abram the wrong way. He was a loyal and good friend to all the men in the church here. She sometimes wondered what peeved her husband about her elder brother. But, lying here in bed, she was grateful to have met and married such a man as Abram, who slept next to her breathing softly, not like many husbands, whose wives complained of their snoring. No, Abram's sleep was always placid. He could slumber through most anything, seemed to her. Even the mournful sounds coming from Sadie and Leah's bedroom just now.

What the world? she wondered. Sounded like Sadie crying, and when she leaned up to listen, jah, she was sure it was. Ach, she'd be ever so glad when all four girls were safely past their rumschpringe. To think that now Leah was coming into hers . . . and the twins not so far behind.

Dear Lord Jesus, help us through the comin' years. May we, each one, commit our ways to you, she began to pray.

When the sounds of sadness had ceased, she fell back into a stuporlike sleep where not a single dream invaded her serenity.

---◆---

In the morning, before Abram rose to pull on his work clothes and go out to get started with milking, the wind swerved round to the northwest side of the house; and in those early-morning hours he lay next to dear Ida, who was sleeping soundly and, he noticed, snoring to beat the band.

Listening to the droning, whistling sound of a pending rainstorm, he thought of his father-in-law, John Brenneman, over in the Dawdi Haus. It hadn't struck him before, but here lately, John was beginning to remind him of Noah, his wife's outspoken oldest brother. Not always, just once in a while, the retired farmer would speak his mind to the point where Abram wished he'd keep his comments to himself.

Take yesterday, for instance, when the two of them were out working in the barn. John was pitching hay to the animals and Abram redding up the place a bit—something Leah had been doing till she decided she liked women's work better. Anyway, Abram had mentioned this fact about Leah.

Well, John spoke up, saying, " 'Tis time the girl made her own decisions, ain't?"

Abram didn't rightly know what to make of it, not really. Same thing had happened back some days ago, when he'd got to talking in confidence with John about Leah and Smithy Gid—that he thought the two of them would make a wonderful-gut match, and didn't John agree?

Well, about all John had to say was, "Let Leah be. If ya ask me, she oughta be allowed to fall in love as she pleases, same as you and Ida did."

Truth was, Abram regretted ever asking John's opinion. The man just seemed too eager to let his voice be heard about things that didn't concern him. Abram sure didn't want a steady diet of John's yap. He and Ida were doing the man a favor having him move to their neck of the woods . . . looking after him the way they were. And Lizzie was helping out, too. All the girls, really. Jah, everyone seemed to be fussing over the man.

Just now, thinking on all this, Abram wondered if it was such a good idea to take John with him today. That is, if the rain blew away and things dried out some. He and Smithy, along with several other men from the church, had hoped to go down the road a piece and help harvest their neighbor's corn crop. Wasn't such a smart thing to tax the older man, but then again, if John found out and wasn't included in the work frolic, well, Abram would catch it later.

So the more he thought on it, the more he was leaning toward asking John to go along. If his father-in-law tired out, he could always go inside with some of the womenfolk and have himself some hot coffee or a catnap, or both.

Gideon Peachey was glad for the blustery winds, which had already started blowing away the dark rain clouds. He had his harmonica tucked away in his pocket and was headed in his open buggy over to help Dawdi Mathias Byler put a new roof on his old shed out behind the house.

On his way he happened to glance over his right shoulder at Abram's big farmhouse and the expanse of land surrounding it. And, lo and behold, if he didn't see Leah come out on the front porch and shake out a long braided runner. He wanted to wave but realized she wasn't looking his way anyhow, so what was the use? And hadn't that been the story of his life with Leah, at least as long as he could remember? She was always looking off in a different direction completely.

He could kick himself for confiding in his father about Leah's refusal at the recent singing. He'd only wanted to share his disappointment with someone was all. Of course,

Dat's reaction wasn't so encouraging, really. "Best take your-self over to Ebersols' and do something to get Leah's atten-tion," his father had said.

Do what sort of thing? he'd wondered, and why should he force the issue if Leah didn't feel the way he did about her?

So there she was beating rugs with a broom on a Saturday morning, and he'd missed the chance to wave her a greeting. But it wasn't his place to come between Leah and Jonas Mast. He'd seen the way they'd looked at each other over in the corner of the barn that night. Just wasn't the right thing to do, no matter what Dat said . . . Abram neither. It wasn't the way to win a girl's heart, Gideon didn't think, trying to vie for Leah's attention against her will. No, he'd let things play out between Leah and Jonas, let them decide if they were sweet on each other or not. So he'd wait his turn.

After about an hour or so, Abram knew he should've gone with his first hunch and left his father-in-law at home. Back where Ida and Lizzie could jump at his every beck and call. Wasn't so much that John needed attention this morning, he was just far too interested in Abram's conversation with Smithy, who said in passing that Gideon had been rebuffed by Leah.

"Well now, are you telling me Leah didn't ride home with Gideon?" asked Abram.

Smithy nodded his head hard. "That's what I'm a-sayin', all right."

John spoke up. "Did Gideon even ask her to?"

"Asked her right away," Smithy said. "But someone else got to her first."

"Did Leah ride home with *that* fella, then?" John asked.

"From what Gideon told me, jah, Leah did."

Abram didn't have to guess who that "someone else" was. The culprit was Jonas Mast. No doubt in his mind.

"The early bird gets the worm," announced John just then, having himself a good laugh.

Abram and Smithy didn't find it so amusing. And Abram tried to change the subject to the German shepherd pups Gideon was breeding for extra money, but John didn't show much interest.

"I'd say, if it was me, I'd set myself up with her long 'fore the next singing." John's eyes were beaming.

This irked Abram no end, but he held his tongue.

"Gid's not one to push himself off on folk, least of all girls," Smithy added. "There has to be a better way."

"Hoping the other fella sets his eye on 'nother girl, maybe?" John chuckled again.

"That other fella is none other than Peter Mast's son, Ida's cousin's eldest," Abram announced. There, he'd said it right out. See what they thought of *this* news.

"What're ya saying, Abram?" John's frown carved out deep lines on his already wrinkled brow. " 'S'nothing wrong with second cousins marryin'. Happens all the time."

Abram nodded. They all knew it wasn't something to bother disputing. However, here lately he'd heard of babies born with physical and mental problems, especially the off-spring of married first and second Amish cousins. "Does raise the chances of deformity and other problems, though."

"Puh! That rarely happens round here," John retorted.

Abram shrugged. John could say what he wanted. What he really cared deeply about was Leah, Gideon, and their future offspring. He wanted only the best for his gentle yet hardworking girl, nothing less. And that sure wasn't Jonas Mast. Not in his book. Besides, Gid Peachey needed a strong, sturdy wife—like Leah—to help him raise beef stock on the grazing land he was to inherit someday.

Chapter Seventeen

Jonas Mast worked alongside Derek Schwartz boxing up potatoes, preparing them for market. Katie and Rebekah, his sisters, would sell many of them at the roadside stand out front, but the bulk of the potatoes was headed for Central Market at Penn Square, in downtown Lancaster. Anna, the oldest of his sisters, was making lists with Mamma, getting ready for her wedding in a month. Anna had been too busy to help with selling potatoes and apples this year. But she and Nathaniel King were planning on living just down the road from the Mast orchard, so Jonas knew he and Dat could count on Nathaniel for help with cultivating and whatnot next year . . . making up for their loss of Derek Schwartz.

"We'll miss you round here, come next summer and the harvest," Jonas told his English friend.

Derek nodded. "I'll be long gone by then."

"Pop wishes you didn't hafta sign up for the military." Jonas didn't need to remind Derek of the People's disapproval of violence and war. The doctor's son surely knew or had heard of the Anabaptist stand against aggression and revenge.

"I'm glad to be leaving here," Derek said unexpectedly, surprising Jonas as they worked.

"Why's that?"

Derek shrugged. "It's time for me to see the world. Get a new perspective. You know how it is, small-town boy meets big-time world."

Jonas didn't identify with Derek's twaddle, and, truth be told, he didn't care about either seeing or meeting the wide world. "You'll still be round here for Christmas, though, jah?"

"I leave sometime before the New Year."

"Where to?"

"Won't know until I receive my orders."

Receiving orders . . . leaving home . . .

All this made Jonas uneasy, really. He had no interest in giving up his present life or leaving the community of the People behind. The one and only thing that would make him even consider moving away from his father's house was marrying Leah Ebersol. And after several months of courting her—by year's end, maybe—he was fairly sure she'd be in agreement with him about their future together. Wouldn't do to rush things, though. He'd take his time winning her, but he had a feeling it wouldn't take much, seeing that bright smile on her perty face all the way home from singing. Jah, Leah was the girl for him, and he'd known it since he was thirteen and even before that.

"Say, Jonas," Derek said as they loaded the last crate of potatoes into the market wagon. "I was wondering . . . would you happen to know of an Amish family who might want to . . . well, adopt a baby?"

"A baby?" Jonas wiped his brow. He found this mighty curious, coming from Derek, who didn't impress him as having an ounce of paternal concern. "Wouldn't know off-hand. Is this someone who's a patient of your father?"

Derek shook his head. "No . . . I just heard about a young girl who's in the family way."

"Well, then maybe you oughta ask your father, since he's in the business of family medicine and all. Maybe *he'd* know of a couple."

Jonas's response didn't seem to sit well with Derek. "Just forget it," Derek said quickly.

"Well, Mam's in the family way herself, so she'll have her hands full."

Derek shook his head. "I wasn't thinking of *your* mother."

"If it would help, I could ask her, though. She might know of a couple who could take in a baby . . . or folk who can't have any of their own."

"No . . . that's all right. Don't bother." And with that, Derek walked round the market wagon, said he needed a drink of water, and headed for the kitchen door.

Hannah had been dutifully following her twin around at school recess for quite a few days now, Mary Ruth having been convinced that Elias Stoltzfus wanted to visit with them. Of course, this was based on Elias's recent stop at their produce stand, Mary Ruth insisted. But they'd kept missing him, or he was involved in a baseball game or some activity with the other boys.

Watching for him today, Hannah spied him coming. He waved and ran over to say, "Hullo, Mary Ruth . . . and Hannah." He seemed happy to see both of them, yet Hannah felt like a third wheel and fell silent, which was how she preferred to be anyway round boys. She observed Mary Ruth's face brighten to a peach color and Elias, too, had a flushed face. Well, now, what was this? Were they embarrassed to talk together? Surely seemed so.

But, no, Elias was telling about his plans for fixing up an old pony cart his uncle was going to give him "here right quick," he said.

When the school bell rang and Elias dashed over to line up with the boys, Hannah whispered, "What was *that* all 'bout, Mary Ruth?"

"My guess is he's itchin' to have a way to get around. You know how Elias is when he drives his father's market wagon."

It was no secret that Elias Stoltzfus took a shining to anything that had some get up and go. His sisters all declared, up and down, if he was Mennonite he'd probably be out driving a fast car.

So the talk at afternoon recess—amongst the seventh-grade girls, anyways—was that Elias was going to have himself a pony cart.

"Maybe he'll hitch it up to his older brother Ezra," one of the girls said. That brought a big laugh.

Hannah could hardly wait to leave school and get home again. Who cared what Elias wanted with a secondhand pony cart? Truth be known, she was more interested in what *Ezra* had on his mind. Ach, but she was ever so shy. Too bashful to ever talk with a boy the way Mary Ruth could. All Hannah cared to do was busy herself with embroidery for the next few days. She wanted to give Anna Mast a special surprise. A blue cotton handkerchief with a white dove in the corner to carry in her pocket on the day she wed Nathaniel King.

Jah, Anna would be ever so pleased to receive such a gift, Hannah knew. She could hardly wait for that exciting day—

the Mast wedding. There she would see Ezra Stoltzfus yet again, if only secretly. Though, being fifteen and all, he surely had his eye on an older girl. More than likely, he did.

At half past nine Lizzie decided to walk down to Ida's for a bit. There she found both Leah and Ida in the kitchen, working shoulder to shoulder, companionably tending the wood stove. The cozy sight warmed her heart and she called out as she closed the back door behind her, "Yoo-hoo, any-body home?"

Leah and Ida looked up at the same time, smiles on their rosy faces. "Come in, come in, Lizzie," Ida said. "Nice to see ya, sister."

Lizzie felt special somehow, hearing Ida's usual warm greeting whenever she dropped by . . . as if Ida truly missed seeing her, even though it had been only a little over twelve hours since last evening's suppertime visit. Ida was a hospita-ble woman in every way, and Lizzie was mighty blessed to have such a dear big sister in her life. "Well, now, aren't the two of you lookin' chirpy," she said, making a beeline for the stove and sniffing at the kettles of homemade soup. "I take it you're feelin' better, Ida?"

"Oh my, ever so much better now." Ida's face lit up just then, and she turned back to the stove, where she busied her-self with two big pots of soup, chattering instructions to Leah a mile a minute in Pennsylvania Dutch.

Lizzie looked round. "Where *is* everybody this morning?"

Leah spoke up. "The twins are at school, and Sadie rode along with Miriam Peachey over to Strasburg to purchase some yard goods."

"Jah, we need to get busy sewin' new dresses. The girls are

growin' like weeds, and it ain't even summer anymore." Ida laughed softly at her own remark.

Leah had a twinkle in her eye. "Mamma thinks we grow more when it's hot out."

"Ach, 'tis an old wives' tale," Lizzie said. She had a taste of the soup from the wooden ladle Ida held out for her, Ida's hand cupped beneath to catch any drips. "Mm-m . . . 's'gut. Real tasty, I must say." She stood there, hoping for more. "Do I have this recipe somewheres?"

"Oh, I'm sure ya do. It's just vegetable-oyster soup and salsify, with celery leaves for extra flavor." Ida dipped the spoon into the black kettle yet again. "Here, this is your last nibble till we eat."

"I'm invited to stay for dinner?" She was chuckling now.

Leah nodded her head, looking at her. "You're always invited, Aunt Lizzie. You oughta know that by now."

She knew, all right. And it was so comforting, too. Ida's family loved her—*liked* her—enough to include her in their day-to-day life. What had started out awkward and strained early on had turned out to be all right. And for everyone involved. Mostly because Ida and Abram had been so kind back then to invite her to come live here in Gobbler's Knob.

"Leah, can you tell me all the vegetable ingredients?" she asked, thinking it would reinforce what Ida was trying to teach Leah.

Eager to recite—at least it seemed so—Leah faced Lizzie. "There's diced potatoes, onions, shredded cabbage, ripe tomatoes, some carrots, one big stalk of celery, four ears of cut corn . . ." She stopped to think, whispering what she'd already said, touching her fingers lightly, counting as she went. "Mustn't forget the string beans, green and red peppers, lima beans, rice, and barley. Oh, and parsley leaves if you don't want to use celery leaves."

Lizzie clapped at such a wonderful-gut recitation and told Leah so. "You're catchin' on fast . . . isn't she, Ida?"

"Well, I should say." Ida went and sat down for a moment on the wooden bench beside the long table across the room. "She's come a long way in a short time. Even Abram says so."

Lizzie had to smile at that. Hardworking Abram, dear man. He was the reason she'd moved over from Hickory Hollow after her rumschpringe . . . built her a cabin to live in with his bare hands. Jah, such a gut man Ida had married. Lord willing, if she ever had the chance someday, wouldn't it be awful nice to meet a man just like that? Seemed single men were few and far between these days, what with her approaching forty here in a couple of years. Probably would never marry, though. Still, she wondered why the Lord God kept putting the longing for a husband in her heart. What was the purpose, really, if she was simply to hope and dream, living out her life under the covering of Abram and his family?

"When are the girls gonna be sewing, then?" she asked Ida.

"Tomorrow afternoon, prob'ly. Care to help?"

Leah went and sat next to Ida on the bench, still beaming, proud of herself, no doubt. "Jah, you should come, Aunt Lizzie. The house'll be a mess with all the material laid out and whatnot."

"I'd be happy to help," she said. "And just when are you planning to make something for Anna's wedding gift?"

Leah clapped her hand over her mouth. "That's right,

Mamma. We oughta be thinking about what we want to give as a family."

"Best find out from Fannie what the couple needs." Ida was fanning herself with the tail of her long black apron.

"I'd say they'll be needin' everything," Lizzie added. "Most young marrieds do."

Leah rose and headed for the back door. "Dat's gonna wonder why I haven't fed the chickens yet."

"Well, run along, then. Tell your father, if you see him, we'll be eating dinner round eleven o'clock."

"Jah, I will."

"Such a wonderful-gut girl," Lizzie said as she and Ida sat there watching Leah slip out the back door and head to the chicken house.

Ida touched her on the elbow. "I'm glad we're alone, Lizzie . . . I have something personal to share with you."

"Oh?"

Pausing a bit, Ida put her hand over her heart. "I'm going to have a baby."

Lizzie clasped her sister's free hand. "Ach, you are?"

"Jah," Ida replied, looking a bit sheepish. "Think of it, at my age, and just when I thought . . ."

Lizzie's heart leaped up. "Oh, Ida, this is such a surprise— what gut news, really 'tis." She couldn't help it; tears sprang to her eyes. "I'm awful happy for you. Does Abram know?"

"Not just yet. I'll tell him tonight, then the girls tomorrow . . . when they're all busy cuttin' out dress patterns and whatnot. Will you come over after the twins get home from school, then?"

She was ever so delighted. A new baby in the family! "I'll be sure'n come, Ida." She released her sister's hand. "You can count on me to help, just as I did when Hannah and Mary Ruth surprised all of us by bein' twins!"

"Well, I can only hope this one's a singleton." Ida fanned her face harder. "Don't know that I could handle more than one baby at this stage of life."

"Won't Abram be happy? And the girls, too?"

"I have a feeling it's another daughter," Ida said, "though how would I know?"

"Five girls would be just fine with me."

Ida went on to tell her what Cousin Fannie had said about them needing a son to carry on the family name. "Puh, I said we'd leave it up to whatever the Good Lord saw fit to give us."

Lizzie nodded, glad to have shared this private moment with Ida. "That's a right good answer, I daresay. When's the baby expected?"

"Best as I can tell, middle May."

"A springtime baby . . . *des gut*." Lizzie got up and went to the back door, looking out the window. She could see her father helping Abram lead the horses and mules out to pasture, and over there, across the barnyard, Leah was scattering feed to the chickens. *We'll have us another little one to love . . . and lead to you, Lord*, she prayed silently.

———◆———

Ida sat at the kitchen table after Lizzie left to go out for a short walk. Enjoying the rare solitude of the house, she decided to write a letter to Becky Brenneman, her sister-in-law, clear over in Hickory Hollow. Wouldn't Becky be shocked with Ida's news, just as Lizzie had been? Ida could see the look of amazement on her sister's face just now. For goodness' sake, who would've thought this could happen, the twins being thirteen, and all? Why, it would be almost like raising her grandchild, except this baby would be her *child*— her and Abram's—in their twilight years.

Pen in hand, she began to write.

> *My dear sister Becky,*
>
> *It's been much too long since I've written. We've all been busy with vegetable gardens and canning and such . . . you too, probably. Dat is nicely settled in next door, and I do believe Abram enjoys having the extra set of hands to help out. (Leah's decided she wants to learn to cook, sew, and whatnot, which doesn't come as a surprise to me, really, since she's courting age now. I can hardly believe it . . . little Leah already sixteen.)*
>
> *Well, now, how about you and Noah? How do you like living in the Dawdi Haus yourself? Won't be too much longer, I expect, and Abram and I'll be doing the same thing here— after Dat passes on to Glory.*

She stopped writing just then, catching herself. There was no way in the world she and Abram would be moving over to their Dawdi Haus, even if her father should pass away within the next five to ten years. Not with a new baby coming on. What if she should give birth to a son? Being the baby of the family, and the only boy, *he* would end up farming this land, and a gut long time from now. Well, for pity's sake, this baby growing inside her just might upset the fruit basket, and wouldn't that be a perty sight? If the baby turned out to be yet another daughter, well, they'd still have to stay put and live on this side of the house, for the youngster's sake. There wasn't enough room in the Dawdi Haus for a growing family. A second family, at that!

She scratched out the last sentence of her letter, staring at the mess she'd made. *I'll start all over with a different letter to Becky,* she thought. Then, for no reason at all, tears sprang to her eyes, trickling down her face. She bowed her head and prayed for this precious new life within her—most truly unexpected.

Chapter Eighteen

The hours dragged on endlessly for Leah. Here it was only Thursday afternoon. She glanced at the farmland calendar hanging on the door that led to the cold cellar. *October twenty-first.* She had the rest of today and all day tomorrow to wait, then most of Saturday, before she'd see Jonas again. Nearly two and a half days!

She and her sisters set about laying out their homemade dress patterns and newly purchased yard goods across the long kitchen table. Leah thought of offering to do some of Mamma's chores later, as well as her own—get her mind off the upcoming secret meeting with Jonas this Saturday night. Mamma seemed to need more rest than ever before, and Leah sometimes wondered about what she'd overheard Aunt Lizzie say back that one time she'd listened into their conversation.

What had Mamma said? That she might be fast approaching the change of life? Well, Leah didn't know anything about that, really. Still, she could see the tired lines in her mother's face, the washed-out complexion. Wasn't like Mamma to look so wrung out.

"Hand me your scissors," Mary Ruth said to Hannah.

"What'sa matter with *yours?*" Hannah asked from across the table.

Mary Ruth looked down at the scissors in her hand. "Mine are awful dull."

"Well, take 'em out to the barn, to Dat," Leah suggested. "He'll sharpen 'em up for you."

Mamma came in the kitchen just then. "Girls . . . did I tell you, Aunt Lizzie's comin' over in a little bit to help us sew up your dresses?"

"Maybe Lizzie can take my place out at the produce stand later on, after Sadie's turn," Hannah said softly. "I'll do my *own* sewin'."

"But that's your job today, Hannah. Mustn't duck your duty." Mamma went to sit in the rocker.

Hannah wrinkled up her nose slightly, but said nothing more about her great reluctance to work at the roadside stand alone.

Mary Ruth piped up, eyes bright. "I wouldn't mind tending the stand till supper for Hannah. Really, I wouldn't, Mamma."

But their mother remained firm. "Ain't too many gourds or pumpkins left to sell, so I think Hannah can have her turn once more before the killing frost comes."

Aunt Lizzie came whistling up the back steps and into the house. "Good afternoon, everybody," she said. "What can I do to help?"

Mamma waved her hand, getting the girls' attention. "Before we do a speck of cuttin' and sewin', I have something to say. Somebody go out on the front porch and call Sadie in here real quick."

Mary Ruth scampered off to do Mamma's bidding.

Meanwhile, Leah turned and looked at her mamma. There was something different about the way she sat there, beaming now. What did she have to tell them on such a busy day?

Once Sadie was inside, Mamma said, "Girls, gather round."

They did so quickly. Sadie stood in the doorway, keeping an eye out for the road, no doubt. Leah and Hannah sat at Mamma's feet, and Mary Ruth leaned on Sadie's shoulder. "What is it, Mamma?" Mary Ruth asked.

Mamma rocked forward and back in the hickory rocker, then stopped. She folded her hands in her lap and looked up at them. "Ach, but I never thought I'd be saying such a thing. Not now . . ." She sighed audibly. "Well, girls, you're going to have yourselves a new little sister or brother."

At once Mary Ruth squealed, clapping her hand over her mouth. Sadie looked altogether startled, turning ashen. Hannah sat silently on the floor next to Leah, her face tilted in a question mark. But Leah felt great joy, a warmth filling her heart as she reached up for Mamma's hand and squeezed it. "Oh, Mamma, such wonderful news. What fun we'll have."

"How soon?" Sadie said rather glumly.

"Late spring . . . sometime in May, I think."

Hannah found her voice at last. "What's Dat have to say?"

Mamma nodded. "I told him last night, and he is . . . well, in shock I guess is the best way to put it."

"Surprised but happy?" Leah asked, glancing over at Aunt Lizzie, who looked as if the cat had gotten her tongue.

"It'll take some time getting used to," Mamma said, her eyes watering.

"Jah, seven more months," Mary Ruth said, trying her best to get Sadie to jig round the room with her, but Sadie wouldn't budge.

"We can take turns playing with our new sister," Hannah said.

"Who says it'll be a girl?" Leah spoke up. "Maybe Mamma and Dat will have a son."

"We'll see when the time comes," Mamma said wisely. "Now, don't we have some dresses to sew up today?"

Leah was truly glad for the news. Now she could think on something besides seeing Jonas again. Funny thing, though . . . Fannie Mast and Mamma both having babies. She wondered how long Mamma would be keeping her news quiet, just for the immediate family's ears. She didn't bother to ask. She was enjoying the prattle made by Mary Ruth and Aunt Lizzie. Hannah was her quiet self, but then so was Sadie. For some odd reason, her oldest sister was obviously silent. Could it be that all this fuss over a new baby coming bothered the firstborn of the family? But, no, Leah didn't think that could be. She'd never known Sadie to be the jealous sort. Maybe she was still wounded over whatever happened between her and that Derry fella. Jah, that was probably it.

Abram led the animals back from the pasture by himself. He'd spotted Lizzie up on the knoll, meandering down the mule road toward the barnyard. She was coming over to help with the girls' sewing bee, Ida had said last night after springing the news of a baby on him. And just before they retired for the night, yet. Did she think he'd be able to sleep after hearing such astonishing news? Well, he'd slept, all right, but only after mulling things over in his head for a gut hour or so.

With Smithy saying what he was about Leah turning down Gideon's offer at the last singing . . . well, Abram felt things were up in the air enough without the possibility of a son coming along way behind like this. A *real son.* Which was most likely what Ida would have, too. Wouldn't it be just like the Lord God heavenly Father to do such a thing, after all girls? Almost a practical joke, so to speak.

Removing his straw hat, he scratched his head. He wasn't sure he wanted to farm *that* much longer, not the way his arthritis had been acting up with every barometer change here lately. And his back ached some days like never before.

He turned and headed back to the barn, telling himself he ought not to worry so. What if the baby was another girl, after all? His main course of action, here and now, was to talk sense to Leah, get her to see that Smithy Gid was the best choice of a mate.

Still, he couldn't up and tell her not to see Jonas anymore, but he sure could try in a roundabout way. Jah, he sure could, and he would. First thing tomorrow, at the early-morning milking, when he and Leah could talk privately. Man to man, so to speak.

After the supper dishes were washed, dried, and put away, Ida sat down and wrote a short note to Fannie Mast, asking what Anna needed most in the way of handmade linens and such. Didn't take her long, though, and since she had plenty of space left on the lined writing tablet, she decided to share her news with Fannie, too.

P.S. I'd thought of telling you this the next time I visit there, but I don't know when that'll be, so I'm going to tell you now, and you can keep it under your hat for a while longer. Abram and I are expecting a baby come mid-to-late May. So your little one and ours will be ever so close in age. See what talking about babies in your kitchen did to me, Fannie? Ha, ha.

Let me know as soon as you can about Anna's needs. I'll look forward to hearing from you soon.

Lovingly, your cousin,

Ida

Rereading the letter, Ida knew she'd much rather be crocheting booties for her coming child than fussing over embroidering pillowcases and tablecloths or whatever it was that Fannie would say Anna needed. The reality of having a new baby was slowly sinking in . . . taking her over, really. Almost more than her joyful heart could hold. No more tears since yesterday. She wouldn't wish to turn back the clock, even if she could . . . no, she wouldn't think of going back to planning her and Abram's retirement years—the "slowing-down years," as Dat liked to say.

She hoped Abram might catch up with her delight here real quick, guessing it might take him longer than when she'd first told him about expecting their girls. He'd come round. Jah, in due time.

◆

The next morning Leah sat sleepily on the milking stool, wiping down Bessie's underparts before she got started with hand milking. Dat had come over to her and said he'd help with Rosie. So Leah knew something was up. But she promised herself—if Dat's eagerness to chat was over her lack of interest in Smithy Gid—she wouldn't mention a word about her plans to meet Jonas Mast tomorrow after dusk at the end of the lane. She felt she must guard their secret courtship now more than ever.

About the time she began milking Bessie, Dat sat down on his own stool nearby. She heard the tinny *ping-ping* of Rosie's rich milk against the sides of the pail.

"I know I ain't 'sposed to ask . . . but you won't mind, will you?" Dat said.

She smiled. "Just what're you sayin', Dat?"

"Well, now . . . I was just wondering how you liked your first singing, is all."

She shrugged a little, cautious to keep things to herself. " 'Twas all right, really."

"Didja see anybody you knew . . . from our church district, I mean?"

Dat wasn't doing such a good job of fishing for information, but she played along. "Jah, I knew some boys there."

Two milk pails being filled was the only sound in the barn at that moment. So just why was Dat asking her such questions when he knew she was already into rumschpringe? Was it Smithy Gid he was so interested in?

She wanted to help Dat out a bit. "Gid was at the singing with his sister." Then she added quickly, "Adah and I sat together at the long table all during the songs."

"Oh, didja now?"

"She and I stuck right close to each other for a long time." She wouldn't go so far as to say that Gid's sister had ended up riding home with a boy other than her brother. That was all she best be saying. Who a girl paired up with was supposed to be kept quiet. Besides, Dat knew better than to ask.

"Didja happen to talk to Smithy Gid at the singing, then?"

Dat's question startled her. "Dat . . . I—"

"Oversteppin' my bounds, I 'spose. You know, Leah, I have such high hopes for you and the Peachey boy."

She thought on that. "You've been sayin' this for as long as I can remember. But . . . truth is, I like someone else. Always have."

Dat snorted a bit from the underside of his cow.

"Does it matter that I'm awful happy?" she asked. "Happy as you and Mamma?"

Silence.

"Dat?"

"Leah, I just don't know . . ."

"Are you put out with me, then?"

Dat stopped milking and leaned back on his stool, catching her eye behind the cow. "Just try to be choosin' wisely, won'tcha?"

"Which means I don't have a choice at all, jah?"

"You've got your mamma's tongue!"

"Sorry, Dat."

"Well, then?"

"Best not talk about this anymore," she said softly.

Dat's dear face disappeared behind ol' Rosie.

Ach, her father was sorely hurt. She wished she could see

his face again, see around the cow, see just how disappointed he must be.

Finally Dat spoke. "Still, as long as you ain't a married woman, I won't stop hopin'."

Sighing, Leah didn't know what to say. Looked as though there was no way to change Dat's mind. Not just yet. But someday she would. She and Jonas Mast would.

Truth be known, Sadie was pleased that Mamma was in the family way. The news had jolted her at first, but now that she'd had time to think, she realized it was wonderful-gut timing. This way all the fuss would be made over Mamma and her midlife baby, not Sadie's sad and sinful situation. She could hide behind Mamma's skirt tail, so to speak.

Meanwhile, she was beginning to feel a tender bond with the little one inside her, though no life flutters had occurred just yet. She wanted to shield her baby from the likes of Derry Schwartz. Such hateful remarks he'd made. How a young man could be so unlike his father—the village doctor, a man who helped folk get well—was beyond her. Sadie recalled the smiling, polite faces of Derry's parents. Such nice folk. Why, they'd even invited her inside, though they'd never laid eyes on her before. She could scarcely believe it still, when she thought back to that dreadful night.

Now her turn at the produce stand was over. Gladly she left things to Hannah, who never truly complained, just made it known by the way her nose twitched, eyes blinking, too, that she didn't so much care for being out here alone with English customers. "Remember what Mamma said," Sadie called over her shoulder. "If ya sell out everything, that'll be it till next spring."

"I heard what she said" came Hannah's gloomy reply.

"Well, I'm goin' for a walk . . . over to Blackbird Pond, if anyone wants to know." This she said because the last time she'd upped and disappeared, both Dat and Mamma had given her a scolding. None of her sisters had been privy to it. She'd endured the severe tongue-lashing, though at the time she wouldn't have traded those stolen hours with Derry for anything. Now . . . she would do most everything differently if she could, starting with sneaking off Friday nights with Naomi Kauffman. The two of them had spelled trouble all along, and there was no telling what would happen to Naomi if *she* didn't hurry up and join church.

"Best go in and help Mamma cook," Hannah called back to her.

But Sadie had no intention of heading straight indoors, where she was expected. Taking her time, she took the road down to the Peacheys' long dirt lane, then turned and headed toward their farmhouse, aware of the sun on her back. There was a coolness in the breeze, the first sigh of autumn. She breathed deeply, swinging her arms as she made her way past the smithy's house, through the barnyard, and out into the pastureland toward the pond.

She didn't expect to find anyone out there this afternoon. Both Adah and Dorcas were indoors cooking food ahead for Sunday, no doubt, same as Mary Ruth, Leah, and Mamma. Smithy Gid, more than likely, was helping his father in the blacksmith shop in the barn. She didn't care so much about farm work, or shodding horses, either. Maybe that was the reason she'd gone off to Strasburg, flirting with English boys come Friday nights. For as long as she could remember, she'd had no interest in marrying a farmer. Clear back to grade school days. Being Amish, though, what other choice did she have?

The area surrounding Blackbird Pond was deserted, and she was glad. She sat down in the shade of the twisted willow, the ground beneath her lumpy and cold. She remembered playing in this spot more times than she could count when she and Leah were little, watching Smithy Gid dive into the pond, catching tadpoles with his bare hands.

Just now, staring at the murky water, she wondered what it was—if anything—she could hope for. Besides being the best mamma a child could have, there wasn't much else to look forward to in her future. She had truly lost her way in the dark woods. All her own doing, too.

Leaning her head down on her knees, she gritted her teeth, knowing she ought to be sorry for all that had gone wrong in her life. But she was more angry than repentant. She wanted nothing to do with Derry, would never again darken the door of that wretched lean-to where they'd spent their late-night hours. She wished the turkey hunters, next month, would go and tear the place down, such an old shanty it was, really. Thinking back to the vast woods made her shudder. What had Derry warned her about the dangers lurking there? Yet he'd said she could trust him. Why *had* she been so gullible? So completely foolish?

She wished she could cry and release some of the tension inside. Might make more room for her baby to grow. Then she realized how awful silly that was. Getting better rest at night and eating her fruits and vegetables would assure her of a healthy son or daughter. Knowing so little about what she ought to do between now and when the baby was to be birthed, she'd hurried to the Strasburg library this past

Wednesday and checked out a book on such things while Miriam Peachey chose dress material. Then, so Miriam wouldn't know where she'd gone after making her own purchase of yard goods for her sisters' dresses, Sadie had hidden the book away under the backseat of the buggy. Suddenly it dawned on her. She could observe Mamma—eat what she ate, do what she did to have a healthy child. Come to think of it, her baby and Mamma's would grow up like siblings. Now, wasn't that peculiar?

She stood and walked the whole length of the side of the pond, seeing Gid's German shepherd, Fritzi, bounding toward her. "Here, girl," she called, happy for some company now. When the dog caught up with her, she knelt and rubbed its neck on both sides, where Gideon said she loved to be stroked. "Are you supposed to be out here, away from your new pups?" she whispered. "Whatcha doin' so far from the whelping box?"

Docile-eyed Fritzi looked up at her as if to say, *I needed to run free for a bit.*

"Jah, that's all right. Come along with me." So Sadie strolled clear round the opposite side of the pond, Fritzi at her side, a silent companion.

Looking up at the sky, she wondered how almighty God might choose to punish her for her transgressions. There were times when she remembered the Scripture Dat often read from the book of Romans—"And we know that all things work together for good to them that love God, to them who are the called according to his purpose."

She hadn't been devoted to God the way she should've, not in the least, otherwise she wouldn't be in this sad predicament. Having been called "according to his purpose," she'd willfully sinned . . . even after her baptism. Preacher Yoder, if he knew, would counsel her to make things right, and mighty soon. Well, repenting to the preacher and the deacons was one thing. Their going home and sharing the news of her immorality with their wives so they could spread the shame-ful word through the community at upcoming quilting bees . . . well, that was another thing altogether. Such poten-tial gossip would not only hurt her chances of ever being courted again, but Leah's and the twins' reputations would be tainted, too. Yet once she became great with child, would it matter if she'd confessed to the brethren? The awful truth would be evident.

Oh, she hardly knew what to do these days. Didn't know what she believed in, either.

Chapter Nineteen

Jonas hurried the horse just a bit, eager to see Leah again. Her hazel eyes—the specks of gold in them—had brightened when he'd asked her, back on the night of their first singing, if he could come calling. "Jah, that'd be fine," she'd said, and he had walked back to the horse and open buggy with an extra spring in his heels.

Now, coming up over the hill, he spied Abram's flourishing acres of corn in the distance. Nearly half of it was harvested, he could see in the fading light. He might've offered to lend a hand if it wasn't that his own father needed him for the fall pruning of the apple orchard, some trees twenty feet high. The rigorous thinning process took hours of daily work, but it was best to press on and finish before the snow began to fly.

When he reached the spot where the long Ebersol lane met the road, he slowed the horse and pulled over onto the right shoulder. He glanced at the new dashboard, speedometer, and glove compartment he had installed just this week, hoping Leah would find his courting buggy to her liking and

not too fancy. Truth be told, he took more than a little pleasure in knowing just how fast his horse pulled the open carriage. And the glove compartment, well, it was right nice for
seeing Leah home from singings and whatnot, if she had any
particular need of it.

Jumping down from his shiny black buggy, he stood near
the horse, watching for Leah. Originally he had offered to
come by much later in the evening—after Abram's house was
dark—but she'd said she could easily meet him out here earlier, at the end of the lane. Being out late seemed to be of
concern to her—just why, he hadn't the slightest notion.
After all, tomorrow was the "off-Sunday," so courting couples
could sleep in a bit. Had Abram spoken to her about not staying out too long? Jonas wanted to start things out on the right
foot—wouldn't think of offending his dear girl's father, that
is, if Leah had even revealed just who it was she planned to
meet tonight. More than likely, she'd kept Jonas's name out
of any conversation altogether.

He whispered to his horse, looking out over the golden
serenity of the fall evening, his gaze wandering all the way
round Abram's rolling front lawn, then over to the adjoining
field. He'd heard the rumors about Abram's hopes of Leah and
Smithy Gid uniting in marriage someday, though he dismissed them as mere tittle-tattle. Abram was a reasonable
man. Surely he'd want Leah's say in the matter of a husband.

Tonight Jonas hoped to find out just how well he and
Leah got along together. He had a nice surprise in store for
her. They were going to drive over and visit his married
cousin on his mother's side. Later on, Anna and her soon-to-
be-husband were joining them there for pie and ice cream.

The gentle rustle of a breeze in the bushes made him

watch even more keenly for Leah, hoping she might appear at any minute. He started to walk down the lane to meet her halfway, and then there she was . . . he spied the white prayer cap atop her brown hair, and—if he wasn't mistaken—she wore a cheerful smile. "That you, Leah?" he called.

"Jah, 'tis. Hullo, Jonas."

He offered his hand as they walked across the road to the parked buggy. Giving her a slight boost, he waited till she was settled on the left side of the driver's seat, then, hurrying round to the other side, leaped into the carriage.

They rode down Georgetown Road a ways, talking all the while. He was struck yet again at how much he enjoyed the lively conversation. When there was a lull, he asked, "Does your dat know who you're out with tonight?"

"I didn't tell him."

He wanted to bring up the amount of time she expected them to be gone. "Didja want to return early, say before midnight?"

"Maybe closer to eleven," she replied. "Will that be all right with you?"

Jonas hated the thought of cutting their time short, because they wouldn't see each other again till next Sunday night at the singing, if Leah agreed to ride home with him again. "I'll have you back home early enough," he agreed.

When they got closer to his cousins' farm, he played a little game with Leah. "Can ya guess where we might be goin'?"

"To somebody's house?"

"Jah."

"Anyone I know?"

"You met 'em at the big family reunion several summers

back," he said, enjoying his clever pastime. "'Twas when Mamma's distant cousins from Hickory Hollow came, too."

"Oh, now I remember. Let's see." She paused to think. "Is it a newly married couple?"

"Tied the knot just two years ago." He was sure she'd know from this additional tidbit.

"I think I know. Must be Bennie and Amanda Zook."

"That's right, and there's something else exciting." He lowered his voice, sounding even more mysterious. "Another couple is coming, too. Can you guess?"

"A courtin' couple or married?"

He was impressed with how sharp she was. "Courtin', that's all I best say."

She began naming off one young girl and boy after another. "Becky Lapp and John Esh? Mary Ann Glick and Jesse Stoltzfus?"

"Wouldja like another hint?" he asked at last.

"Just one clue, but a *little* one, jah?"

He leaned closer, a gut excuse to do so. "Their married name will rhyme with 'sing.'"

She thought for only a few seconds, then said, "Now I know. We're meeting your sister, Anna, and her beau, Nathaniel King!"

This was the moment he'd been waiting for. He slipped his arm around her and drew her near. "You're correct, my dear Leah." And with that, he kissed her cheek.

The harvest moon, yellow and full, rose slowly over the eastern horizon. Leah pointed and said the sight of it nearly took her breath away. Jonas was ever so glad, for he'd hoped she might think so . . . have some wonderful-gut memories of this, their first night as a courting couple, something special to tell their grandchildren in years to come.

———————◆———————

The evening visit was filled with laughter, telling jokes and a few stories mixed in, but it was the chocolate-mocha pie and homemade vanilla ice cream that topped off the night. Both Leah and Anna decided it was the tastiest pie they'd ever had. Jonas was especially pleased to observe his sister and Leah getting along so agreeably.

At one point Nathaniel King whispered to him out of the girls' hearing that perhaps the two couples ought to have themselves a double wedding. Jonas was taken aback by the suggestion, though he assumed a casual attitude. "In less than three weeks? No, we've just started courtin'," he replied.

So the subject was dropped, since he was fairly sure the abrupt idea might scare off Leah. And if not her, then Abram, for sure and for certain. Jonas must prove himself over time, show himself to be deserving of Abram's daughter—his pick of the crop, far as Jonas could tell.

He took the long drive home, aware of the time, though it was only quarter of ten. Plenty of time for just the two of them. "Didja enjoy yourself?" he asked.

"Oh my, ever so much. Denki, Jonas."

"Anna and Nathaniel did, too, I think."

"Jah, they did. And I was glad to get better acquainted with your sister."

"Anna said to tell you it would be fun to do something else, the four of us . . . sometime."

"How does Nathaniel feel 'bout that?"

Jonas shook his head. "He's eager to have gut fellowship with us, too." Then he had the daring to ask her, right there and then, if she'd consent to riding home with him at the next singing.

"Why, sure, Jonas."

Right pleased with her response, he had to hold himself back a bit from moving too quickly, revealing the depths of his feelings for lovely Leah. After all, this was only their first time courting.

Enjoying the stillness, a trace of cinnamon in the fresh night air, he reached for Leah's hand and held it all the way home as they talked and laughed. Truly, they were so happy together!

Leah wished she'd never said a thing about Jonas having her home by eleven o'clock. Goodness' sakes, she was having the best time. And here they were, riding under a full moon, her hand in Jonas's, talking as comfortably as you please. She had built this night up in her mind, during the days between the last singing and now, yet how could she have known she'd feel almost sad to say good-bye?

Dat's cornfield was fast coming into view as the horse and buggy approached the Ebersol Cottage from the Peachey side. If only Dat could know how happy she was this night.

"I'll be countin' the days till I see ya again," said Jonas.

"A week and a day, jah?" She felt him squeeze her hand gently.

"My brothers and I will be workin' in the orchard 'tween now and then. Such a busy time it'll be."

"And I'll be helpin' Mamma finish up the canning and

doin' my outside chores for Dat, too." She didn't mention that her mother was in the family way, same as his mamma was. She just left that be. It was up to Mamma to share her news.

"We'll both be busy . . . so time'll fly, jah?" he said.

She nodded but didn't believe it for a second, knowing how the days had crawled along waiting for *this* night. And what if they both felt so strongly about missing each other? Just how many years would Jonas want to wait before they were married?

When it was time to say good-bye, he gave her a quick, awkward sort of hug. Oh, she wouldn't have minded letting him kiss her full on the lips, the way she felt just now . . . and the way he was looking at her, too. But she knew better. Mamma had taught her, *"Save your lip-kissin' for marriage."*

"God be with you, Leah." He held both her hands lightly now.

"And with you, Jonas." Though she said she could walk to the house on her own, he wouldn't hear of it.

Turning to tie up the horse, he then accompanied her down the lane that led to the barnyard. Yet another opportunity for Jonas to reach for her hand, and she had to smile, already having missed his tender touch.

Then, of all things, they got to talking again about how she had always worked outdoors with Dat, how that was just the way things had been. "I guess it happened 'cause Mamma and Dat were sorry they ever let Sadie go to high school, even though they could've gotten her a domestic permit when she turned fifteen." Leah had been hesitant to bring up her older sister tonight. She had no way of knowing just what rumors had been floating round . . . what Jonas might've heard of

Sadie's careless rumschpringe. "So when I finished eighth grade, Dat put his foot down . . . decided to keep me home, continue workin' outside with him."

Jonas stopped walking. "I'm so sorry, Leah. I wish you hadn't had to work that way . . . just to keep from goin' to school."

"I didn't mind, really. Dat and I get along just fine. And for the longest time, honestly, I didn't so much care for women's work . . . women's *talk*," she admitted.

"And now?" He was looking down at her, eyes searching hers in the moonlight.

"Oh, I don't know. I guess I never felt I fit in with the womenfolk. Wasn't like them, really." What she meant to say was that she didn't think she was as perty as the rest of them. But she dare not say such a thing. Jonas might think she was fishing for flattery.

"So you really *are* Abram's Leah?" whispered Jonas.

Her heart sank. "Where'd you ever hear that?"

"My sisters say it sometimes." He started walking again. "But I don't think it's right. To me, you're ever so perty. Maybe the pertiest girl I've ever known."

She wanted to say "no foolin'?" but she kept walking.

"Like a lovely bluebird, that's what you are," he said.

She could scarcely believe her ears. He had remembered her favorite bird from way back when! "I'd always thought of myself as a common brown wren."

"Well, if you're comparing yourself to Sadie, best not."

She swallowed hard, hoping he'd go no further.

"You've got it all over your older sister. You have such a gut heart."

"Well, that's awful nice of you, Jonas, but—"

"No, I *mean* it. You're *my* bluebird, Leah, and always will be."

His words startled her a bit. How could such a handsome boy be saying that *she* was perty? And besides, wasn't this too soon for him to offer such words of devotion?

But once Jonas was gone, and the clatter of carriage wheels on the road was but a memory, she was glad he'd spoken up like that. So they felt the same way about each other. After this many years, they still did.

At half past nine Sadie headed off to bed, not to sleep but to read her library book on pregnancy and childbirth. She had been careful to close the door securely, though there were no locks on any of the bedrooms—none in the house at all, not even the outside doors. So she sat in bed, the oil lamp propped up on a chair next to her, devouring every word, marveling at the information tucked away in one book. This, she thought, was a smart idea tonight, since Leah was gone with Jonas Mast—where she didn't know.

At ten-thirty she set the book aside, going to look out the window. No sign of Leah anywhere. At once she thought she might have to laugh, thinking that the tables were turned, her worrying over Leah this way.

Then, before creeping back to bed, she marked her place and hid the book deep in her hope chest, just as her secret was well hidden for now within her own body.

Yet she did not sleep, lying awake . . . waiting for the sound of footsteps on the stairs. And come along they would, fairly soon, she hoped. Leah had surely made it clear to Jonas that she wouldn't be staying out so late. Not on this, their first real courting night. Besides, Jonas would have a half-hour ride back once he brought Leah home. Because of the slightly longer distance between here and Grasshopper Level, Sadie wondered if Leah might not allow Smithy Gid to court her some, too, if for no other reason than for the sake of convenience. Most boys didn't care to drive too far to pick up a girl and take her home. She'd heard plenty of complaining about such things from some of her boy cousins, while waiting for the common meal after Preaching service. But no, Leah had her heart set on Jonas.

Sadie thought she just might go along with Leah to the next singing. Find out what was up. Wouldn't hurt none. Nobody at singing would have to know of her situation. Maybe, too, she'd find herself a nice boy. If she could get somebody to fall in love with her, then tell him her secret . . . well, if he consented to marry her even still, then her disgraceful state could come to an end. But who on earth would *that* boy be? Certainly not anyone she knew in their church district. No one she'd care to consider as a husband.

Putting out the lamp, she climbed out of bed and stood in the window looking down at the barnyard. So here *she* was, waiting for Leah to return, when she might've been out having some fun of her own on such a pleasant night. If only she hadn't been so foolish.

Chapter Twenty

The days passed quickly enough, just as Jonas said they would. Yet Leah often caught herself joyfully brooding over him, thinking ahead to the next wonderful-gut time, careful not to share too much with Sadie, who was ensnared in her own contemplation. The difference between them now was Sadie's tight-lipped response to most everything, while Leah could scarcely contain her happiness.

Mamma must've noticed, too, saying that Leah was nearly as *bapplich*—chatty—as Mary Ruth. This observation didn't seem to bother Mary Ruth at all, just made for livelier canning frolics in Mamma's big kitchen with Aunt Lizzie and Miriam and Adah Peachey.

Days grew shorter as the time neared for Anna Mast's wedding. One mid-November morning Leah awakened with the cold creeping in from outside, rousing her from deep slumber. Turning over, she saw that Sadie had pulled the heavy woolen quilts over to her side of the bed. Leah tugged at them, trying to get her fair share back, so she could at least sleep a bit longer before morning chores.

Here lately, though, Dat had said she didn't need to get up and come out in the cold for the first milking of the day. *Kind of him,* she thought, rolling over, her back against Sadie's.

Even after pulling her half of the quilts back over herself, Leah was still a bit shivery. But the weight of the heirloom quilts was always a comfort and a reminder of Mamma's love. Just as Jonas's wool throws kept her snug and warm in his open buggy each time they went riding.

At the last singing Sadie had surprised her by going along. They'd had such fun together, one of the first times recently—almost like their former days of childhood— though Sadie had latched on to her, hardly letting her talk with Jonas alone at all. And then, since Leah and Sadie had both ridden over with Smithy Gid and Adah, they had ended up riding back to Gobbler's Knob with Jonas, which was an interesting howdy-do.

Honestly, Leah had felt Sadie was spying on her and didn't appreciate it one bit. Jonas, on the other hand, took Sadie's presence in his stride, including her in their banter, paying nearly as much attention to Sadie as he had to *her.* Jah, Jonas had joked openly with Sadie, politely of course, who sat directly behind them in the second seat, clutching her own woolen lap robe. Such a peculiar thing, really—three in a courting buggy!

After that night, though, Sadie said she thought Leah ought to attend singings on her own. "Oh, why's that?" Leah had asked, sticking her neck out only for Sadie to wave her hand and say, "No reason. 'Tis just better for courtin' couples to be by themselves."

So now Sadie sat home nights while Leah entertained

Jonas in the kitchen, near the wood stove, after the family had gone upstairs to bed. And Leah was grateful that Jonas was not so much interested in the hops or hoedowns so frowned upon by the church yet attended by some of his "buddy groups." She felt he was ever mindful of the People's rules. The best beau, he was.

———————◆———————

Two nights prior to Anna Mast's nuptials, Dr. Schwartz's wife reminded her family of the Amish wedding "this coming Tuesday."

Amidst obnoxious groans from Derek, Lorraine rose and went to the kitchen, returning with a tray of dessert and hot coffee. "It's a rare opportunity," she said, eyeing her husband for support. "One we will enjoy . . . *all* of us."

Henry spoke up quickly. "Derek, it is important that you honor your employer at his daughter's marriage ceremony."

The boy muttered something unintelligible and stabbed a fork into his baked berry pudding. About then Robert spoke up and asked Henry's permission to drive the family car to a church meeting in nearby Quarryville. "When will yours be in running order again?" Henry asked.

"The mechanic said tomorrow. So if you wouldn't mind, Dad . . ."

"Sure." Henry pulled the car keys out of his trouser pocket. "When shall your mother and I expect you home?"

"Nine-thirty, if not earlier," Robert replied, to which Derek snorted loudly.

Henry's eyes locked with Derek's. This unspoken

exchange was registered, and the belligerent son sat up straighter, his spine now flat against the dining room chair.

From the entryway, Robert called good-bye and waved to them and turned toward the coat closet. Henry was filled with paternal pride at the sight of Robert, tall and honorable. *Such dire things he's seen and survived,* he thought, disconcerted but not surprised by his son's sudden interest in the ministry.

Though not a religious man, Henry believed in a Creator-God, one who had the power to grant life and take it away. A God who dwelt in the heavens somewhere, afar off. Only once in Henry's life had he ever prayed, and that was out of desperation, nothing more—when Robert had sent word by letter of the bloodshed on the battlefields of Europe. Never had he done so since, not even to offer a heartfelt thanks for Robert's safe return.

Just this morning his son had enthusiastically mentioned that he hoped to attend a nearby Mennonite church meeting. Robert had even gone so far as to inquire of his mother about Grandpa Schwartz's ministry and life, to which Lorraine had responded by promptly leaving the room, only to return with a tattered scrapbook. She said it had been in the family for many years, though Robert avowed he had never laid eyes on it. He had looked at the pictures with great interest, making note of his grandfather carrying a Bible in one photo.

Presently, Henry watched Robert open then close the front door behind him. The war had certainly turned their young ex-soldier inside out. What would it take to get Derek on better footing in general? The upcoming stint in the army? Henry was banking on it.

Derek was undeniably closed to any discussion, and Henry

was breaking no new ground. "What's bothering you, son?" he asked, truly frustrated.

"I can't wait to get out of here" was the surly reply.

"You're looking ahead to the service, I assume?"

"Not just that . . . leaving Lancaster behind forever."

The remark cut deep. *Why should our boy feel this way?* Henry wondered.

Lorraine kept her distance, pinching off leaves from the many African violets in the far end of the parlor. Occasionally she glanced at him kindly. Henry and his dear wife had certainly had their times with Derek and might have had similar difficulties with Robert had he not come home from Europe a changed man.

Not a father to pry into the private facets of his sons' lives, Henry had concealed the fact that he'd silently witnessed the heated exchange between the Amish girl and Derek in the yard some weeks ago. Though he had heard nothing of what was said, he worried that something was amiss, even at stake, between the two of them. Then when Derek had bolted after the girl—who had taken off on foot—revving up his car like a maniac and racing down the road after her, Henry felt grave concern.

Now Derek's words agitated him further. "Besides, I want nothing to do with this stinking life—yours and Mom's!" His son leaped up from the table.

"Just a minute, young man. I've worked all these years to establish our good family name. I'll not have you speak—"

"Save it, Dad!" With that, Derek brushed past him.

Stunned at this outburst, Henry looked at Lorraine, who sadly shook her head. She came and placed her hands on his shoulders. "Incorrigible," he heard her say.

Then Henry stood up and reached for his wife, enfolding her in his arms. "I'm sorry you must suffer our son's antagonism, dear," he said. "It makes me realize what I must have put my own parents through."

"Derek will grow up soon enough, just as we all do." With that, Lorraine rose on tiptoe to kiss and hug him tenderly.

Leah and Jonas had been out riding about a half hour or so, meandering round the county roads, taking their time getting Leah home. The most picturesque farmhouses had a way of rolling down across the meadows and settling back a ways from the road. Jonas surprised her by asking what sort of house she'd want to live in when she was married, and, of course, she said a house something like Dat's . . . "a house that's been in the family for generations, you know."

"Something real old, then?"

"Oh, jah."

Turned out, Jonas agreed. So they were getting awful close to the topic that mattered most to Leah, and she was mighty sure to her beau, too—the subject of marriage, just when they might tie the knot, and all.

But as Jonas talked, she realized they weren't going to be discussing that subject just now, probably. At least not tonight. He was more interested in his sister's wedding in just two days. "Anna's awful ferhoodled," he said, laughing. "Both Mam and Pop just look at each other sometimes—I've seen 'em—like they can't believe how harebrained she is."

"What sort of young bride will she be, then?" Leah ventured, hoping she wasn't stepping on anyone's toes.

"Oh, Anna will be right fine, just as any newly married woman is . . . given time." And here he reached around her and drew her near. "Just the way *you'll* be someday."

" 'Cept for one thing," she spoke up quickly.

"What's that?"

"I know my way round a barnyard better than most brides!"

This brought the heartiest laughter she'd ever heard from Jonas. And he made no attempt to disagree with her.

Chapter Twenty-One

The day of the Mast wedding dawned ever so bright. Sadie would have rather stayed home. But, of course, she didn't. The whole family—and Aunt Lizzie—piled into the family buggy and headed over to Grasshopper Level for the long day of festivities.

When they arrived at last, she and Leah walked up to a group of other girls their age waiting in the barnyard. They would remain there till they were given the signal to go inside for the service.

Naomi Kauffman and several other girls eyed her and smiled but stayed in their own little circle of fellowship. Sadie didn't let that bother her, though. What was troubling was seeing the Schwartz family drive up and get out of their car, the four of them walking up the lane toward the farm-house.

For a fleeting moment, while glimpsing Derry, she wondered if her baby would resemble the Schwartz side more than the Ebersols. And how awful would that be!

She quickly dismissed the niggling thought. Yet seeing

Derry, even from afar, was sure to spoil her time at Anna's wedding. She scarcely could wait to get home again. Why had she come at all?

Quickly, before Anna's wedding service ever began, Hannah sneaked up to the bride's bedroom, knocked on the door, and handed the embroidered dove hankie to Anna herself. Hannah stared at the special handkerchief in Anna's hand. A dove stitched all in white against a pale blue background.

"Oh, Hannah, this is so perty!" the bride said. "I'll be needing the dove of peace on *this* day, what with all the doin's, ya know."

Hannah caught the meaning. Anna was obviously a bundle of nerves. "But you mustn't be anxious," she spoke up, surprising herself. "This is the day you and Nathaniel have been waiting for, to become husband and wife. Such a wonderful-gut day 'tis."

Then, quite pleased with herself, she kissed Anna's cheek, wished her "Happy day," and scurried down the back steps and through the summer kitchen. Outside, in the midst of the swell of wedding guests, she looked for Mary Ruth, swinging her arms just a bit. Not only had she given Anna Mast something to treasure for always, she'd offered a kind word to an anxious bride. Even though she'd had to exert herself a bit to do so.

◆

After the main sermon, the bridal party—three young men and three young women—took their seats near the ministers' row in front. Then, toward the end of the three-hour meeting, in front of the bishop, Anna Mast agreed that she was indeed "ordained of God to be Nathaniel King's wedded wife." And Nathaniel was in agreement, too.

When they were pronounced husband and wife, plenty a tear was shed, especially after the words "till our dear God will again separate you from each other," pertaining to the duration of the couple's union under heaven. So solemn was this lifetime promise between two people.

Meanwhile, Sadie stuck close to Aunt Lizzie, steering clear of the likes of Derry Schwartz. Even so, the good doctor's gaze found her at one point, just as the fancy guests were preparing to leave before the wedding feast began. Sadie looked away quickly. Such embarrassment she felt, recalling how she'd made a fool of herself going over to the Schwartz home. Ach, she'd sat right down on their front porch steps, waiting to talk to their rat of a boy. She sometimes wondered what had gotten into her, going over there like that. But it had been the close of a final horrid chapter in her life. She hoped so, anyways, because she'd be paying dearly for her transgression once her secret was evident for all to see.

Now, though, she was being mighty careful to eat right—watching the sort of foods Mamma ate—and to get to bed at an early hour. Her body was in the beginning processes of making necessary changes, the baby growing ever so slowly at this point. All this was according to the helpful library book, which she had renewed one day here lately when she and Mamma drove to Strasburg for sewing notions and whatnot. She'd been allowed to keep the book for another three weeks and hoped by the time she had to relinquish it for good, such important things would be firmly fixed in her mind.

Gone were her actively sinful days, though she had never confessed her wickedness to a soul. Not even to Mamma. She'd pondered confiding in Leah, but what good would that do? Her sister couldn't redeem her. No one could. Unfortunately, her next younger sister was all caught up with Jonas, so dreamy eyed it was hard to get her attention during the day while she did her indoor chores. No, there was no need to spoil Leah's joy . . . not just now.

Mary Ruth was aware of Elias Stoltzfus's presence well before the wedding feast, especially when the young people were attempting to line up outside and some of the boys showed great timidity in pairing themselves up with a girl partner. Some were even grabbed and pulled to the door, where they had no choice but to stand beside a particular girl. Once they were in line, all struggling came to an end, and each youthful couple approached the wedding-supper table hand in hand, just as those in the bridal party did.

But Ezra Stoltzfus, who happened to be Hannah's partner, of all things, looked downright delighted to have managed to get in line, just so, to be precisely across from her twin. Mary Ruth couldn't help but think that somehow she and Hannah were *supposed* to be matched up with the Stoltzfus brothers for the wedding feast, recalling how spunky Elias had been about asking her if he could sit across the wedding table from her.

Thinking back on his unexpected visit at the produce stand, she felt her heart beat a little faster at what might become of their friendship. And at the years ahead, maybe. Then and there she decided to be the most cheerful wedding-feast partner to smiling Elias, who kept eyeing her in the lineup of girls, then quickly looking down his line of boys and bobbing his head, as if counting how many there were—and where he landed—making double sure he ended up being her partner.

Well, now, what a right fine day of days, thought Mary Ruth, overjoyed.

Abram felt he'd done a dance of sorts, trying his best to avoid Ida's brother, Noah Brenneman. Still, it seemed his brother-in-law was determined to confront him about the past. Yet another time.

The weathered farmer walked up to him after the feast. "You're avoiding me, Abram."

" 'Spect I am."

"Well, now that we've witnessed a blessed wedding and ate ourselves full, don'tcha think you could stand still for just a minute or two?"

"I'll see 'bout that." Abram wasn't surprised at the gray-bearded man's acute bluntness. Noah shot off his mouth this-away quite regularly; at least he had back years ago when the knotty problem between them had first reared its ugly head.

"Still holdin' a grudge, I see . . . after all these years," Noah said straight out.

"Jah, maybe so." Abram leaned on the well pump handle. "But you know the truth, same as me. What you had in mind for Lizzie . . .'twas awful wrong! That should be real plain to see now."

Noah stared him directly in the eye. "Maybe so, but I wanted to protect my family. I can't say the same for you, though. 'Tis a mighty big secret you're keeping, Abram. Mark my words. It'll blow up in your face one day."

"You leave that to Ida and me. That's our business."

"Don'tcha forget, Lizzie's *my* sister. What you and your family do affects all of us Brennemans." With that, Noah turned on his heel.

Abram shuddered. Noah's vicious remarks rang in his ears as Abram tuned out the frivolity, what with young people scampering round. He wished Noah would just keep to himself and his wife, Becky.

By gollies, he thought, *will we never see eye to eye?*

After supper that night the young people gathered in the Masts' big barn. There they had a singing of sorts, playing games till late.

Just before dusk, though, Leah and Adah Peachey left the games for a breather. They went for a quick walk by themselves, over in the high meadow behind the barn.

"I'm wore out," Adah said, reaching for Leah's hand as they made their way up the slope.

"A wedding day is always long. 'Tis understandable," Leah said.

"There's another reason I'm done in. My brother wants to know if you and Jonas are officially courtin'."

"And that's tiring you?" Leah said.

"Well, he keeps askin' . . . even though it's not his business to know."

"What do you say?"

"I tell him, 'open up your eyes . . . what do ya see happening at the local singings?' "

"Maybe he oughta go to a different singing," Leah suggested.

"I've told him that. Believe me." Adah sighed. "But it

does nothing. Gid's waitin' for you. He's stubborn thataway."

This puzzled her. "Why should Gid be marking time? He could be courtin' a girl of his own by now."

"Maybe so, but he cares for *you*, Leah."

The knowledge of this annoyed her. "Is this about some-thing, well . . . that our fathers are wanting?" Leah had to know.

"Gid's future has been placed in his own hands now," Adah said, then became ever so quiet.

This was news to Leah. "Since when?"

"Just here lately."

"Are you sure?"

Adah nodded her head, letting go of Leah's hand to reach down and pick a dried-up wild flower. Gathering a bunch of them, Adah stood up and rubbed them together between her hands, letting the breeze scatter dead pieces into the air. "Pop told Gid the other day that love can be fickle. 'Tis best not to hang too high a hope on it," whispered Adah almost mys-teriously. "My father told him to go ahead and court whoever he pleases."

Leah could hardly believe her ears.

Adah turned and gave her a strange little smile. "Why wouldn't you give my brother half a chance? I think you and Gid could've been a right gut pair is all I best say."

"I'm ever so sorry, Adah. Truly, I am." Leah wondered all the rest of the day if her father and the smithy had resigned themselves to her courtship with Jonas, which surely they knew from either Adah or Gid.

So most likely Dat knew about Jonas and had done abso-lutely nothing to stop them. Downright peculiar it was.

Chapter Twenty-Two

They attended one wedding after another all the rest of November and deep into the month of December. The ongoing weather could not have been more bitter—with snow-laden hills and dreary gray heavens, scattered with unsettled clouds. Wind and sleet visited them from the northeast, coming in with a vengeance from the Atlantic Ocean.

The forest behind the Ebersol Cottage seemed to grow darker with each passing day. Songbirds had long since flown south, and Ida especially missed hearing their cheerful warble as the babe within her grew. She looked ahead to spring with both a longing and a joy, and all who knew her said her face was simply "aglow" with radiance.

Though she was preoccupied with her coming child, she suspected something was terribly wrong with Sadie. But Ida would not allow her thoughts to stray down that path.

Leah was content to help her sisters and Mamma sew perty things for her own hope chest and others' and attend quilting bees and cookie frolics. Often she kept Aunt Lizzie company on the coldest afternoons, donning her snow boots and tromping up the hill to the cozy log cabin. Sometimes she would spend the night there by herself or with Sadie or Mary Ruth. Hannah never was one to care much for sleeping away from home, though. There at Aunt Lizzie's, they baked sweet breads and drank hot cocoa, or Lizzie's favorite hot drink, Postum. Leah enjoyed jotting down dozens of her aunt's recipes, asking for even more "for my own recipe files . . . come next autumn." That way Lizzie would know enough to quietly tell Mamma they'd need to sow a plentiful batch of celery next July for Leah's wedding feast in the fall. Lizzie's eyes lit up as the truth dawned on her, and she promised to keep Leah's plans quiet "till the time came."

Leah was ever so happy to entertain Jonas once each week all winter long, reading aloud to him from the book of Psalms and occasionally from *Martyrs' Mirror*—stories from seventeenth-century Christian martyrdom. Together they looked at colorful pictures in Jonas's book of birds, learning the voice and call of many different varieties.

One evening Jonas shared his keen interest in carpentry with Leah, telling her that some years ago he and his father had discussed the possibility of dividing up the Mast orchard and surrounding land if Jonas never had the opportunity to learn the trade of cabinetmaking. He and his bride could make their living growing apples and overseeing a truck farm, but Jonas wanted them to live close enough so Leah could be within walking distance to her sisters. Thus, living on Grasshopper Level wasn't an option, really.

They talked of joining Leah's church come next September, getting married early in November, settling down near the Ebersol Cottage, perhaps at first renting a little farm.

They discussed in whispered tones their future children and grandchildren, and at times played checkers into the wee hours.

Leah felt truly blessed to love and be loved in such a joyous way. She did sometimes worry, though, that she oughtn't to marry before Sadie, since that honor should go to the first daughter of their family. So she prayed that God would send along someone right quick for her older sister.

◆

Sadie, who was becoming more self-conscious about her body as January came and went, promised herself she would somehow change her outlook on life. Without offering repentance—by sheer willpower—she made an effort to become a more obedient daughter and loving sister . . . especially to Leah, who had put up with far more than she herself might have tolerated from a sibling back last summer.

On the Saturday nights that Jonas Mast came calling, Sadie stole next door to visit Dawdi John, who enjoyed telling her—sometimes the twins, too—the familiar stories of his growing-up years. "The olden days," he'd say . . . how he learned to cut wood as a boy and catch fish with his own dawdi, and about the day he asked Mammi Brenneman to "get hitched" with him. If he happened to light up his old pipe and smoke by the fireside, the smell of sweet tobacco made Sadie feel a bit light-headed, took the edge off her deepest fears. At such times she came mighty close to letting her secret slip out, knowing full well she could trust Dawdi, but she never quite let herself go that far.

Sooner or later, though, she knew she'd be telling Leah. Time was passing and she had fallen in love with her baby, felt it was surely a boy, though she wouldn't have known how to explain such a thing. Yet she believed her precious unborn child would be the first male to grow up in this house in many years. Thankfully, she had never heard again from Derry and assumed he had gone to the army, nearly finished with his basic training by now.

———————◆———————

Meanwhile, Mary Ruth poured herself into school studies, making the best grades she ever had through February. More and more she hungered for book learning, knowing full well how this might sit with Dat and Mamma when she finally had the nerve to tell them she wanted to attend high school. Then . . . college someday. Her twin was the only one who knew her true heart on this, and it pained her—the realization that one day their paths would surely have to part, knowing full well that Hannah intended to follow the Lord in holy baptism and join the Amish church.

Hannah had begun to write down her most personal thoughts in a journal every other day, starting back on New Year's Day. Some paragraphs—about certain boys—she could just imagine Mamma's eyebrows arching ever so high at what was being recorded. Her embroidered handkerchiefs had found a business outlet in a small gift shop in Strasburg. Hannah was saving her money toward helping Mary Ruth reach her secret goal of attending a teachers' college in the future. Yet the thought of living without her twin nearby was almost too painful to ponder.

Abram spent winter evenings reading the Bible in German and praying silent prayers with the family gathered near. Ida, who was putting on some extra pounds, sometimes complained that the wood stove put out too much heat for her liking. So they'd all get up and head to the front room, where the girls would shiver a little, all but Sadie, who seemed as comfortable in the cooler rooms as Ida.

If the topic of politics came up at all, which it sometimes did, he made a point of emphasizing to his family, especially his daughters, that he didn't have much use for America's new president. "Anyone who's bent on using such profanity, well . . . he ain't leadership material, not in my book."

But even more than Harry Truman's cussing, Abram was utterly annoyed by Jonas Mast's out-and-out determination to win Leah's hand. The smithy was none too keen on the idea, either, since Gideon hadn't shown the least interest in any other girl in the church yet. Leah was obviously Gid's one and only sweetheart girl, and he'd set his sights—and heart— on her, and nothing either Abram or the smithy thought about Jonas Mast made any difference. Far as Abram was concerned, his dear, dear girl was missing out on a gem of a boy while getting cozy with, even planning to wed, Ida's cousin's son. But if Leah loved him and he loved her, well . . . what was Abram to do? He couldn't demand his own way, could he? Why, no, he might push Leah away from his own heart, and then how could he live with himself?

Derek Schwartz never looked back once he'd packed his bags and headed for boot camp. His mother was teary eyed at the bus station, but his father appeared to be more serious than sad. Robert, not in attendance at Derek's farewell, had managed to beat his brother out of town, driving to Harrison-burg, Virginia, where he planned to find a part-time job and settle into an apartment, then begin second semester at Eastern Mennonite College. His father had been baffled at Robert's sudden interest in Anabaptist beliefs, in wanting to go into the ministry, too, but Mom had encouraged him to "follow your heart, Robert . . . wherever it may lead." It was typical of her, though he knew she hadn't taken too kindly to his brother's leaving home again.

Derek, on the other hand, figured it didn't matter as much what *he* did with his life. Mom would have turned irate— Dad, too—if either of them had known he was completely shirking his duty as a father-to-be, leaving naïve Sadie Eber-sol to cope with raising their grandchild on her own. But no turning back now. Hadn't he offered to help her end the unwanted pregnancy? And she had refused in no uncertain terms. So there was nothing more for him to say or do. He had been smart, too, not falling for her ridiculous idea of marriage.

◆

It was on the day that Englishers celebrate love—Valentine's Day—that Sadie decided she could keep her secret no longer. She and Leah were putting on their flannel night-gowns, and Sadie was straining to see the side view of herself in the small mirror at the dresser. "Leah, do you think I'm gaining weight?" she asked.

"How could that be? You're as thin as a rail."

"But, no, seriously, look at me," she insisted, wondering if her sister would notice any difference in her shape. "Am I bigger . . . anywhere?"

Leah shook her head, laughing softly. "What're you getting at, sister? You look the same as always."

Sitting on the edge of the bed, Sadie breathed in deeply. Now was the time. She simply must tell Leah about the precious babe inside her. What should she say, and how to say it? After all, Leah hadn't had nearly five months to become accustomed to the idea of a baby as she herself had. So she must be more guarded, careful to express the regret, even grief, she'd felt at her first knowing, back in mid-October. But now . . . *now* she was ever so eager to hold her tiny baby in her arms, cradle him, rock him, whisper "I love you" in his little ears. Yet she wondered how Leah would take such news.

Well, she'd never know if she didn't get the nerve to speak up, and in the next minute or so. Leah was heading for the oil lamp now, ready to snuff it out. . . .

"Sister," she said softly. "There's something I want to tell you."

Leah turned, a frown on her face at first. Then when Sadie motioned for her to sit beside her, she came quickly, eyes animated. "What is it?"

"Just listen, Leah. . . ."

"Have you met a boy, someone who wants to court you?" asked Leah.

Sadie wasn't taken aback at that remark. After all, it was a natural thing for a younger sister to be thinking such things, really . . . for Leah to feel awkward at being nearly engaged and here Sadie was almost nineteen and without a beau, or even the promise of one.

Reaching for Leah's hand, she clasped it tightly. "What I'm goin' to say will be so awful hard for you to take at first. It was truly that for me." She paused, stroking Leah's innocent hand. "I have done wickedness, *sinned* in the eyes of the Lord and this family. Oh, Leah, my sweet sister, how do I tell you that I . . . am with child?"

The room was still, the light from a winter moon on the snowy landscape bright enough to show clearly Leah's stunned expression. "Ach, Sadie . . . what're you saying?"

"Do you remember that English boy I told you 'bout last fall? Well, we . . . he and I . . ." She could not make herself speak the words.

"Oh, this is too awful!" Leah blurted.

Sadie shushed her sister gently. "Best not alert the whole family to this just yet," she said, but she understood Leah's shock. She reached out and gathered Leah near. "I'm sorry you hafta know this . . . that you have such an immoral sister as I am," she whispered.

For the longest time Leah seemed unable to speak, struck dumb with anguish, weeping softly into the pillow. "How could you do such a thing, Sadie?" she said at last.

Then they curled up together in their childhood bed, beneath ancient quilts sewn by the honorable and just women on both the Ebersol and Brenneman sides. And Sadie, sapped of strength, said no more, realizing anew this evil thing she'd done to bring such shame on herself . . . and her dear family.

Abram was awake and had just come back from the out-house, the light from the moon's reflection on the snow nearly blinding his tired eyes. Making his way up the stairs, he heard the sound of sniffling coming from the bedroom shared by Sadie and Leah.

Not pausing in the least, he headed straight to his and Ida's room, settling into bed next to his wife. He was awful sure it was Leah who was crying. Jah, it *was* Leah. But why?

He felt sudden wrenching guilt at what he'd gone and done just this afternoon, using a pay telephone in Strasburg to set a life-changing deed in motion. Of course, there was no way in the world Leah could know just yet, not *this* soon, that he'd placed a call to Fannie Mast's married cousin out in Ohio. Seemed easy enough when all was said and done. Jonas Mast would be getting a letter, being offered a job as a carpenter's apprentice in Holmes County.

If Leah ever found out what Abram had done, she'd be more than angry, beside herself with grief, which is how she sounded just now. But Fannie's cousin had vowed that no one would be told of his and Abram's quiet conversation this day.

So Abram let his thoughts drift toward sleep, knowing he'd stuck his neck out, more certain than ever of his choice of a mate for his most precious Leah.

It was pitch black in the haymow. Leah crept up the long ladder and hid herself away in the depths of the night while Sadie—expectant, *unmarried* mother—slept back in the house. As sisters, they had held each other till Leah slipped away, needing to be alone with her thoughts.

Fraught with worry, she sat there in the corner, where hay was stacked in even rectangular shapes, where only the sound of a mule's sighing broke the stillness. One of a half dozen barn cats found her and curled up in her lap.

It's all my fault—this horrid mess Sadie's in. I should've told on her while there was still time to save her purity. If only I'd known. . . .

Leah knew for sure . . . if she could simply turn back time, ach, she'd do it in a second—promptly run and tell Dat that her sister was in danger of hellfire.

Chapter Twenty-Three

March 1, 1947

It's not so hard to believe that I've been writing in my new diary for two full months now. Mamma sometimes will glance into my bedroom through my open door, looking at me with a peculiar grin and see me writing away so fast in my little book. She mustn't worry that I'm practicing my hand at being a writer, trying to develop individuality, so opposed by the bishop. That's best done with my embroidery, if I must reach for creativity at all. Mamma doesn't have to worry over me, not like she'll have to with Mary Ruth after eighth grade, come next year.

Won't be much longer and we'll see if Mamma's baby is our sister or brother. I must admit, I won't begin to know what to do with a little brother. After four girls in the house . . . just how would that be?

Mamma's constantly happy these days. Dat's the one out of sorts more than ever before. And Leah is, too. Honestly, I don't know what's gotten into my older sisters. The eldest is so pleasant to me—and to Mary Ruth. Sadie has made a change in

275

herself, I should say, now that she's through with rumschpringe. It's Leah who's so awful glum. Just how could they switch places like that?

But I'm thinking that Jonas will make Leah a right nice husband. He's over here visiting on Saturday nights, and I'm sure he's the boy bringing Leah home from the singings every other Sunday. He loves her a lot. I can see it in his eyes, before we get shooed out of the kitchen come nightfall. Mary Ruth and I hope Leah won't go getting married next autumn, like we suspect she might. Why? Well, it would be nice to have our happy little house snug with all four sisters staying put for a while yet. Of course, with a new little sibling coming along soon, things might just be a bit topsy-turvy anyways.

That's all for now.

Hannah Ebersol

Mary Ruth waited after school to chat with the teacher at the Georgetown School. "I'm wondering if I might get some extra assignments?" she asked. "I'm fascinated with mathematics."

"Well, let's see what I can do, Miss Ebersol." Flipping through her large math textbook, Miss Riehl found many pages of math problems. "Here . . . why don't you copy these down and work them at home?"

"Thank you ever so much!"

"I'll check your work when you're finished."

"I'll do them tonight," she promised.

"No need to hurry." The teacher sat down behind her desk.

"Oh, but there *is*." And Mary Ruth began to explain her goals for the future, pouring out her heart about her hope of becoming a schoolteacher someday. "But . . . please, will you keep this between us?"

Miss Riehl's face shone. She seemed to understand. "I'll help you all I can, Mary Ruth."

Saying thank-you yet again, Mary Ruth hurried to the door where Hannah was waiting. Together they walked to the small parking lot, watching for their ride.

"Well, didja do it?" Hannah asked, eyes smiling.

"You'll never believe how much extra work Miss Riehl gave me!"

"I'm so happy for you."

The girls exchanged tender glances. "I don't know how I'd manage sometimes if I didn't have you to share with," Mary Ruth told her twin.

Hannah nodded. "Will we always have each other?"

Mary Ruth heard her sister's sad desperation. The question came deep from Hannah's heart, from a girl who most likely would settle into the community of the People, never inquisitive about the outside world, while her twin sought to gain as much knowledge as her brain could hold.

◆

The day the Ohio letter arrived in the Mast mailbox, Jonas was driving down their lane in the enclosed family buggy, running an errand over to Bart. He'd thought of simply bypassing the mail, letting one of his sisters come fetch it for Mamma . . . but stopping, he hurried to see just what might be in store for the family on this snowy end-of-March day.

Flipping through the mail, he noticed several from Willow Street and one from Ninepoints, notes from girl cousins and friends of Rebekah and Katie, probably, since his sisters enjoyed writing letters the most. Except for Mamma, who'd been writing a lot here lately, she'd told him, to Ida Ebersol—his future mother-in-law. Mamma had said just recently that the two families were getting much closer "just since the last get-together back in August." Well, he couldn't agree more, especially if Mamma and Dat had any idea just how many trips a month he made over to Gobbler's Knob to see his Leah.

The envelope that made him stand straighter, take notice, was one addressed to him, the postmark being from Millersburg, Ohio. "Who lives clear out there?" he muttered to himself, hurrying back to the carriage to get out of the cold.

Once inside, he closed the buggy door and scanned the contents, which revealed, to his great surprise, an invitation from his mother's cousin, David Mellinger, an expert carpenter. And . . . of all things, Jonas was being asked to consider coming there and working for David "till your pop's apples are ready for picking early next fall."

Six months away from home?

Instantly, his first thoughts were of Leah, how much he'd miss her for that long a time. What might his leaving do to their plans to take the required baptism instruction before the fall wedding season? He hated to think of telling Leah of this opportunity. Not that it wasn't one of the best kinds of offers a young man his age could receive from a seasoned carpenter and all. The very thing he'd always dreamed of doing!

But this letter coming now . . . well, it was just so untimely. Still, he couldn't dismiss Cousin David's invitation. He mulled over the ins and outs of such an adventure all the rest of the day.

◆

Smithy Gid was well aware of the warm April morning "Sisters' Day" frolic happening at the house. Mam had invited all the Ebersol women, as well as their aunt Lizzie, over for a Saturday of making rag rugs. Adah and Dorcas had talked excitedly about the idea of doing such a thing for the past week, then last evening at the supper table had gently encouraged both him and Dat to "make yourselves scarce," the girls giggling too much at the remark for his liking.

But he'd followed their wishes, taking great pains not to go near the house after breakfast, tending to Fritzi and her second batch of pedigree pups, now three weeks old. He fed grain to the four Black Angus he and Dat were fattening for the butcher here in the next few weeks, then offered to help his father in the blacksmith shop. But Dat seemed preoccupied, saying he didn't need a hand. Not today, at least, which was downright peculiar, seeing as how Dat was *always* in need of something when it came to shoeing so many driving horses in the Plain community.

By Gid's calculations, his German shepherd pups were close to being weaned, in which case he could start contacting the folk who'd agreed to purchase at least five of the litter. The other two, well, he hadn't decided if he ought to advertise for them or not. He liked to amuse himself by thinking what Leah might do or say if he offered the gentlest one, with the pertiest markings, to her as a present, for no particular reason. He knew better than to step out of bounds with Leah Ebersol, but with word that Jonas Mast might possibly be heading out to Ohio for a time, working as a carpenter's apprentice . . . well, now, *this* news had surely come out of nowhere.

When he'd asked his father about it, the only thing said was "Don't know much of this, son. But . . . let's just see what comes of it." So it sounded like maybe Dat *did* know something, though Gid wasn't in the habit of questioning his father, even if only in his thoughts.

Leah felt ever so dismal. Her sister's words kept on ringing in her ears, even though now it had been nearly two months since Sadie's shocking revelation. She wished she'd never promised to keep quiet about Sadie and her English beau. Never!

Although Leah and Jonas shared most everything, Leah continued to keep her sister's secret from him. And from Dat and Mamma, too. Only once had she come close to sharing it with Aunt Lizzie, but she'd thought better of it, feeling it was Sadie's place to do so. Besides, there was nothing anyone could do.

Sadie would have to be the one to tell their parents, and perty soon, because she wouldn't be able to keep it from them forever. Leah had seen her sister's body slowly changing, especially in the soft glow of the oil lamp, when they dressed for bed at night.

Sighing, she laid down her scissors and left scraps of old fabric in a big basket on the floor. Excusing herself, she felt it was all right to go outside alone to the Peacheys' outhouse, though she might've asked Sadie or the twins to come along. It wasn't that she hoped to run into Gid on the way. She had no such thing in her mind, yet there he was over in the barn . . . stroking one of the new puppies in the whelping box. Quickly she turned her head and walked even more swiftly toward her destination.

Honestly, she felt almost sad for Gid these days—most all the time, really, clear back since her first singing that night in October. She wished he'd find himself a nice girl to court. After all, he was a right fine-looking fella himself, with a heart as pure as gold, Dat had always said. Far as she could tell, there had never been any reason to doubt it.

So when he called to her, after her return from the little house out near the barn, she turned and smiled, wondering what he had to say. "Leah, I've been thinking. . . ." Then he stopped and said no more, just held up a small dog with a reddish fawn coat with black overlay . . . sweet brown eyes and an almost curious smile. "Would you like to have him? He's yours for the taking."

"Oh, but I wouldn't think of—"

"No . . . no, I mean to say he's a gift. From one neighbor friend to another."

Gid's smile was so boyish just now. So eager to please her, he was. "I'm sure it's all right with your parents. Besides, I'm thinkin' you could use a gut watchdog over there."

With that, they both looked past the Peachey pastureland to the Ebersol Cottage, gazing on it from afar. Then Gid broke the silence. "If you're not so sure, why not ask your dat . . . see what *he* says?"

She couldn't argue with that. Then, reaching up, she touched the young pup in Gid's arms, and suddenly the dog began to lick her hand with his little pink tongue. "Oh, that tickles," she caught herself saying. "He's ever so cute."

"Well, now, I think he likes ya, Leah."

She had to laugh. "I think he does, too."

"I'd keep him for you. Then if or when you should decide to take him home, I'd be more 'n happy to bring him over."

"Aw, that's ever so nice of you. Denki." She hurried back to the house. A bright face like Gid's had cheered her up just a bit. She was sure his motives were honorable, though he would've had to be deaf not to have heard that Jonas was leaving for Ohio here right quick.

She'd been brave the night Jonas had shared this "rare opportunity" with her. Seeing his eyes light up at the makings of a dream come true, yet hearing the sadness in his voice, Leah knew she could not shed a tear in front of him. She had even wondered aloud if there was any way she might go along—maybe tend to an elderly relative or whatnot, so they could continue their courtship in person instead of by letter. Then, when the time came, they could return home and marry in the fall as planned.

She'd just have to trust the Good Lord—they both would—for the answers.

"I'll be back before the apple harvest next fall," he promised.

But when she'd shared this with Sadie, her sister said she ought not to count on such a pledge. "Best not to let him go at all," Sadie said. "If Jonas leaves, he might never return home. Remember Abe Yoder? He left poor Malinda for the lure of land in Ohio."

Sadie's words made Leah's heart ache. "I wouldn't think of speakin' up to Jonas like that. He has a right good head on his shoulders."

"Well, you might want to think twice 'bout keeping mum. At least tell him how much you'll miss him . . . let him know you'll pine for him."

Ach, she felt she knew her beloved, and if Jonas said he was going to come home before the harvest, then he would. For sure and for certain. And she'd told Sadie so. "You don't know my Jonas the way I do," she'd insisted.

By Leah's response and the heart-melting smile on her face, Smithy Gid was almost positive his gift offer—from his hand and heart to hers—had been an excellent idea, after all. So he wasn't one bit sorry about his impulsive deed, Jonas Mast aside. Leah was, after all, his longtime neighbor and childhood friend. If she chose to marry Jonas, well then, so be it.

Still, Gid had his hopes up that she might, at least, take the pick of Fritzi's litter and give the pup a home. Who knows, maybe a fond pet would be the start of something special between Leah and him. Then again, maybe not.

Chapter Twenty-Four

Abram was beside himself, downright befuddled. Jonas Mast had insisted on having a private meeting with him out in the barn after seeing Leah home rather early after the singing. The boy began by explaining some carefully thought out plans, it seemed . . . about his hopes to find a place for Leah to live and work near David Mellinger's home in Millersburg, Ohio. "I'm workin' on it and will have some answers in the next few days," Jonas said. "What would you think of that?"

Well, Abram wondered just what Jonas was afraid of—did Jonas honestly think Leah might start seeing someone else, maybe, if she stayed home on Gobbler's Knob? But no, when he quizzed the boy, Jonas said something about not wanting to go so long without seeing "my dear Leah."

"Well, then there's always letters, like anyone else in your situation," Abram advised. But deep down, he was shocked at Jonas's strong reluctance to leave Leah behind.

"I truly love her," Jonas confessed, eyes shining. "She's everything I live for. Leah's my dearest friend, too."

Nodding, Abram understood how a young man could be

smitten over Leah, sweet and gentle soul that she was. Still, he decided on the spot that his daughter was *not* going to Ohio. No matter what, she was staying put right here. Smithy Gid must have *his* chance to woo and possibly court Leah, too. Then, the way Abram saw things, his dear girl could make a choice between the two of them. And that was all he hoped to accomplish by Jonas's going away. Nothing more.

He tipped his straw hat as Jonas turned and left the barn, the boy full of hopes and dreams, obviously in love. It wasn't in Abram's thinking to wound him, no . . . not at all. But he knew in his heart of hearts he was altogether right about Smithy Gid and Leah. They must have their chance.

After the dishes were washed, dried, and put away that night, Sadie accompanied Dawdi John back to his side of the house, especially glad to go with him by herself. She hoped for yet another quiet evening with the wise older man.

Dawdi John was sure to give her a listening ear, and she was mighty glad to be here with him, away from the exciting talk next door, where Mamma, Leah, and the twins were still chattering about the Sisters' Day they'd enjoyed over at Miriam Peachey's. Leah was mostly interested in talking about a puppy dog Smithy Gid wanted to give her, "for the whole family, though," Leah was quick to say. "Go right on over there tomorrow and say you'll take the dog," Dat had said, wondering aloud why Leah had bothered to ask him, anyway.

So the whole family—the girls, especially—were beside themselves with glee, anticipating the arrival of Fritzi's perty little pup. Sadie could just hear it now—they'd be tossing round names for dogs for the next two hours or so till bedtime.

Once Dawdi was settled in his small front room, and Sadie had a nice fire blazing in the hearth, she asked him, "Dawdi, have you ever done something you were so ashamed of, you just couldn't bring yourself to confess to anyone?"

He regarded her curiously. "Well, now, I 'spect I have. We *all* have. There's nobody perfect, least that I know of."

She wasn't about to spill the beans on herself, lest Dat and Mamma would hear of her pregnancy secondhand. Of course, now, if she asked Dawdi to keep things in strictest confidence, he would. But wasn't that an awful burden to put on a man of his age, after all?

So she lost her courage and failed to share openly. He seemed to sense her need of comfort and amusement and recounted one story after another—mostly telling on himself as a youngster and into his teens.

Then his voice grew awful soft. "Listen here to me, Sadie. I want you to remember this saying as long as you live." He stopped talking to light his pipe, puffing on it just so to get the tobacco to ignite. When he was satisfied, pipe in hand, a thin puff of smoke spewed forth from his lips. "I care not to be judge of right and wrong in men," he said with a tender smile. "I've often lost the way myself and may get lost again."

Lost the way . . .

Well, she knew all about such things, dark and forbidden forest or no. Each time she had been with Derry Schwartz, she promised herself it would be the last, yet she longed to see him again and again. Such a feeble pact, one she hadn't been able to keep, loving him so.

But now part of her loathed him, and another part of her wondered how she could ever forget him, having conceived his baby. Could she ever truly release him from her heart?

"You know you're always welcome to talk to old Dawdi," her grandfather said, bringing her out of her musings.

"I'm awful glad of that," Sadie said, reaching for his wrinkled hand and holding it for a moment. But deep within, she knew this might be one of the last nights she'd have as an expectant mother. Very soon her baby would be nestled in her arms . . . and to think she'd kept it a secret so well from everyone, carefully sewing her dress seams thinner every time. Here lately, making her dress patterns a bit fuller through the waist was all she'd had to do.

◆

Off and on all day she'd had the strongest cramping, almost made her want to bend over, the pain was so bad at times. The library book she'd nearly memorized hadn't mentioned a thing about the baby coming this way—not when she was only at the end of her seventh month of pregnancy, far as she could tell.

When the light bleeding started, getting heavier as the day wore on, she panicked and wondered what was happening to her. Was she going to lose her baby?

"Leah," she began long after supper, when they were preparing to dress for bed, "something's happening too soon, I fear. . . ."

"What do you mean?" Leah asked.

"I think the baby might be coming early."

"Well, then, I say it's time to tell Mamma!"

"No, no, not just yet," Sadie replied in lowered tones. "I need a doctor first."

Leah squinted at her, a fearful look on her face. "I can hitch up the horse right quick and take you to the midwife."

But that would be much too far away, and she didn't think she could bear all the jostling in the buggy. The nearest doctor was Derry's father, Sadie knew, but his clinic was the *last* place she wanted to be. "What about Aunt Lizzie? Maybe she can help," Sadie said. "You could tell Mamma we're going there to spend the night . . . for fun."

"That would be a lie," Leah said.

"It's the best way for now."

Leah winced but then agreed. "Jah, I 'spose, but what will you do when the baby *does* come? You won't be able to hide the truth then. You're not thinking clearly, Sadie."

Her sister was right about all that, but Sadie had no energy to argue. "I need help," she whispered, feeling ever so faint. "Just please get me to Lizzie's."

"Can you walk all the way up there, do you think?"

"If you're with me, jah, I believe I can."

"Then go slip on your woolen shawl. It's a bit nippy out," Leah said. "I'll poke my head in and tell Mamma we're headed to Aunt Lizzie's overnight. She won't mind one bit— may not even suspect a thing."

Sadie still had no idea what on earth would happen after she did give birth, if that's what was about to happen tonight. *If* the baby lived . . . goodness' sake, this was much too early!

And, ach . . . Aunt Lizzie would suddenly know everything. No getting around it now. Still, come to think of it, maybe this way was for the best. Lizzie could help break the startling news to both Dat and Mamma when the time came, when Sadie was ready to bring her baby home.

She leaned hard on Leah, making her way up the long hill

to Lizzie's log house—step by painful step—ever so glad her
sister was near.

Lizzie bolted out of bed, hearing the pounding on the
back door. She hurried to see who was coming to visit her
after dark.

"For goodness' sake," she whispered, seeing Leah nearly
holding Sadie up, both girls' faces wet with tears. "*Dummle*—
hurry! Come in . . . come in."

She and Leah helped Sadie into the spare room. There
they got Sadie settled, limp and pale as she was. Sizing up the
situation, Lizzie could see that Sadie was definitely in the
family way, just as she'd suspected for some weeks now. "How
early is your baby, do you think?" she asked.

But Sadie wasn't responding except with occasional
moans, so Leah did her best to fill in the details. My, oh my,
Sadie needed help fast!

Lizzie hesitated to have anyone but an Amish midwife
come to her house. Yet there was so little time, and the closest one lived three miles away.

Dear Lord, please help me know what to do, she prayed.

Sadie's face was turning a chalky gray, and she was all
bunched up on the bed. Lizzie had no choice. An Englisher,
Dr. Schwartz, would have to deliver this baby.

Turning to Leah, she said, "We can't do this alone." Lizzie
gave directions to the medical clinic. "Run, fetch one of the
horses—forget hitchin' up the buggy." Then guiding Leah
into the doorway out of Sadie's hearing, she said, "You must
ride the horse to the doctor's home . . . ride for your sister's
and her baby's life!"

Frightened nearly to death, Leah ran all the way down the hill to the barn. She was glad that she, Smithy Gid, and Adah had once ridden bareback on their fathers' driving horses, years ago when they were but youngsters; otherwise, she wasn't so sure Aunt Lizzie's idea would've been such a wise thing. And, too, she knew it was not acceptable for horses to be used for such a purpose. But for an emergency— which by the look on Lizzie's face this surely was—she would obey her aunt and disregard the bishop's ruling about horse-back riding. If her dear sister died tonight, Leah could never forgive herself if she chose to follow the letter of the law.

So she rode, clinging to the horse's neck and mane, her waist-length braids flying through the dreary night. Up Georgetown Road, past the woods on the knoll, to the home and clinic of the doctor Lizzie had suggested.

Henry's drowsiness fell away remarkably fast with the arrival of the stranger at his door. Without much ado, the Amish girl, calling herself Leah Ebersol, described a desperate situation—her teenage sister was in premature labor a half mile away.

With no time to waste, he grabbed his coat and hat and rushed outside. Meanwhile, the girl had tied up her horse in their backyard, promising rather apologetically to return for it later.

The drive took only a few minutes, and the young woman sat in the front seat and gripped the door handle. In spite of her great anxiety, Leah offered clear directions as to where to turn to get to the "mule road that leads to my aunt's cabin."

Getting out of the car, Henry hurried up the steps to a little log house, following Leah, whose gentle yet frightened eyes and faltering voice exposed her innocence to the whole ordeal of childbirth. He intended to do his best to save the lives of both her sister and the coming baby.

Quickly she led him to the room where her sister was writhing in pain. He set to work, evaluating the situation, noting the intense struggle on the part of the young mother, whose face was covered with beads of perspiration.

He spoke calmly to her, introducing himself. "I've come to deliver your baby, miss. If you do as I say, things will go more smoothly. Do you understand?"

She looked up at him and nodded weakly. At that moment he recognized her as the same young woman who had come looking for Derek one autumn night, the one who had then quarreled with his son and fled on foot. Whom he had seen at the Mast wedding, in fact. He saw the glint of recognition in her tearful eyes. She said her name was Sadie Ebersol, that she was unmarried, and that her parents did not yet know of her pregnancy.

Could this be Derek's child I've come to deliver? Henry wondered, the thought filling his soul with anguish.

No time to ponder the possibility. Instead, drawing on his medical expertise, he moved ahead with the task at hand. In the hallway, he heard the younger sister, Leah, call to someone in the kitchen, followed by the muffle of footsteps and a teapot whistling loudly. He checked his watch, timing the contractions, helping Sadie know how to breathe.

Seemingly terrified, Sadie fought the birth spasms every step of the way. Considering the circumstances, he was concerned that this delivery might be unlike any he had performed in recent years.

When the baby finally did come, Sadie lifted her damp

head off the pillow, and in an exhausted whisper asked, "Do I have a son?"

"Yes, a boy, but . . ." Henry could not get him to cry even after repeated smacks on the behind.

He paused, holding the infant in his arms, his mind racing. "I'm terribly sorry, Sadie, but . . . your baby is blue," he whispered. "No breath in him."

At this news, the young woman began to weep inconsolably. She called out to her sister, who came rushing into the bedroom. "He's dead, my dear baby's dead!" Sadie sobbed.

In the midst of the commotion, an older woman appeared in the doorway. Henry's gaze held hers for an instant. Her soft hazel-brown eyes seemed vaguely familiar, but he couldn't quite place her. Perhaps she had been one of his patients or someone he'd met along the road at a vegetable-and-fruit stand.

"You'll handle things for my niece, then?" The woman joined Leah at Sadie's bedside, where the two attempted to console the grief-stricken mother.

He looked down at the shriveled baby in his hands, a lump in his throat. "I'll take care of the remains . . . for you."

"Oh, thank you, Doctor," Sadie's sister spoke up.

Moving toward the bed, he offered, "I would be happy to look in on you tomorrow, Sadie. Make sure you're feeling better."

"That's kind of you," the girls' aunt replied, "but I'll see to her myself."

Then, from beneath the long sleeve of her nightgown, Sadie slowly drew out a tiny white handkerchief with an embroidered butterfly on the corner. Her fingers trembled as she opened it and gently laid it over the baby's face. "Fly away, my little one . . . rest in peace," she whispered.

Henry quietly extended his condolences again and headed for the door, the tiny, dead boy wrapped securely in the warmth of his coat, the bloody face covered with Sadie's handkerchief.

◆

He placed the infant on the front seat of his car, keenly aware that he had most likely delivered his own stillborn grandson.

Mixed emotions swept over him, and he felt a sudden and inexplicable sense of loss. This was the little lad he would never have a chance to know, to play with, to watch grow into manhood. His own flesh and blood, though conceived in sin. His son's firstborn.

And yet . . . what would have happened if this boy *had* lived? Most assuredly Henry's reputation and that of his family would be tainted forever. If not destroyed.

He despised himself for his divided feelings and reached over and gently placed his hand on the dead babe's stomach. "Your mother's name is Sadie Ebersol," he said softly. The young Amishwoman's name would haunt him for years to come.

"And your father's name is . . ."

He thought of Derek. He and Lorraine had been excited by a recent letter, as they had not heard much since their boy's enlistment. Derek's note had been full of complaints about KP and acclimating to army life at Fort Benning, Georgia. He never inquired of either of them—of the home fires burning. And certainly not of the Amish girl he'd left behind. . . .

Lost in thought, Henry was aware of a faint whimper. Was it his imagination, or had the handkerchief over the infant's face fluttered slightly? And if so . . .

His hand still on the child's stomach, he felt the sudden rise and fall of the little chest. Then the infant's soft cry turned to a full-blown wail, as vigorous as any healthy newborn's.

What's this?

Evidently, he had accepted the child's death far too quickly. Medical journals documented rare cases such as this, infants who revived miraculously on their own.

Henry's pulse raced. Pushing the speed limit, he wasn't taking any chances. He must get Sadie's baby to the clinic— to an incubator. He tore into the driveway, then scooped up the infant, breathlessly carrying him inside.

Under the heat lamp, he washed its small face and body. Then he diapered him and wrapped the newborn preemie in a receiving blanket and settled him into an incubator. Even though the babe was breathing normally now, most likely he would be disabled either mentally or developmentally, having been deprived of oxygen at his birth—too tiny at the present to generate his own body heat. Later, he would even have to be taught to suckle for nourishment.

Henry hovered near, gazing into the now pink face of this child. Unmistakably evident—he recognized Derek's tuft of dark hair and the set of his eyes. This *was* his grandson!

Bewildered and torn, Henry took the soiled handkerchief—the one Sadie had placed over the infant's face—and rinsed it in cold water. Down the road, a grieving young mother wept in the night, totally unaware that her child was indeed alive.

He had the power to take her sorrow and replace it with joy, but in so doing he would bring shame to his own family's good name. Shame to her family's name, as well. What was he to do?

Back and forth he walked between the waiting room, his private office, and the infant nursery, muttering to himself, trying on every imaginable option. The right choice, of course, was to return the baby to its mother. Or he could simply arrange for an adoption, indeed saving Sadie's skin, who wanted to keep her Old Order Amish parents in the dark, for obvious reasons. Yet if he did so, he might never see his grandson again.

Long into the night Henry labored over a decision, rationalizing away all common sense.

◆

Leah felt weak with fatigue, drained of emotion. Still, she sat near Sadie in Aunt Lizzie's spare bed for several hours. She stroked Sadie's hair while she slept, exhausted from the pangs of childbirth, with nothing to show for her agonizing struggle.

Aunt Lizzie, asleep in the cane-backed chair nearby, had agreed that the girls should stay the night, as they often did. Leah was especially glad they'd cleared it with Mamma before ever leaving the house.

Meanwhile, Sadie rested fitfully, making sad, tearful sounds in her sleep. Leah didn't feel so well herself, though her wooziness came from spending half the night awake, either tending to Sadie after the doctor left or holding her and weeping along with her.

But then, once her sister fell into deeper slumber, Leah rose and walked back over to the clinic to leave the doctor's payment Lizzie had thrust in her hand. And she'd retrieved her horse at the same time, leading him back down the road to home long before dawn. Mindful of the bishop's decree, she'd hoped and prayed she might never have to break the church's rules for another emergency. Never again in her life.

Now, unable to rest or sit down, Leah walked the floor from one end of the cabin to the other, praying silently, asking God how this dreadful thing could have happened. But she felt she knew . . . would never tell her sister, though. The wretched sin of King David had been punished in a similar way. Why should Sadie's transgression be any different . . . or ignored by the Holy One? Surely, this was what the Lord God heavenly Father had allowed to befall her on this unbearable night. Divine chastisement.

Sadie had received just reward for disobedience. And Leah felt responsible for having kept quiet about her sister's sins.

Aunt Lizzie was more than a little reluctant about Sadie's plea not to tell Mamma. Truth was, Lizzie made an awful fuss, insisting that Mamma be told. Right then, Leah began siding with Sadie, begging Lizzie to leave things be. "What's done is done, and nothing good can ever come from Mamma and Dat knowing," she said.

At long last their aunt agreed never to utter a word of what had happened. Not unless Sadie spoke of it first.

So the three of them embraced the dark secret while a

heavy mist hung low to the ground outside, like a veil that would vanish at first light.

Soon as possible, Leah would have to tell Jonas that as much as she liked the idea of living in Ohio, being a mother's helper—while Jonas learned the carpentry trade in the Midwest—she simply couldn't see her way clear to leave Sadie. Not now. Sadly, she resigned herself to a courtship by mail. There was no other way.

Sisters came first, after all . . . even before a beau. Mamma had drilled this into all the girls, growing up. You stuck by family, no matter.

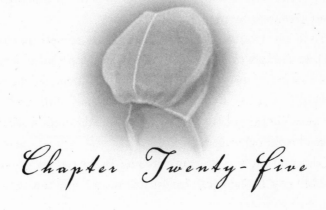

Chapter Twenty-Five

Faithfully, Leah looked after Sadie in the days that followed, once Aunt Lizzie gave the go-ahead for Sadie to return home. Every so often Leah noticed Mamma eyeing Sadie curiously as they worked together in the kitchen, yet their mother did not question the sudden overnight stay. Nor the paleness of Sadie's face and her gaunt figure.

Soon Mamma's attention turned to her coming child, and Sadie began to regain strength, resuming all her daily chores.

Best of all, the girls had a cheerful time making a place for their new sibling in one corner of Dat and Mamma's big bedroom. What a flurry of sewing and whatnot went on. Sadie joined in, too, making a lightweight baby afghan for the spring and summer months, when the new babe would still be tiny and in need of an occasional wrap.

Leah winced, looking over at Sadie crocheting up a storm one afternoon, wondering how her sister was doing emotionally. Surely the loss of the baby and the heartache had taken its toll. But Sadie shared nothing at all, neither in the privacy of their room, nor when they happened to be alone down-stairs, working together.

Sadie's ongoing silence worried Leah something awful. She felt strongly that if such a thing had happened to *her*, she would desperately need to confide in someone, share the wrenching sadness with a trusted sister or friend. But each time she made an attempt to open the door for such talk, Sadie abruptly changed the subject. It was ever so clear that her sister must be suffering terribly. But what to do? Leah wouldn't pry, for fear that might just push Sadie further away. Still, Leah couldn't imagine the loss Sadie must be feeling these days, especially now with all the talk of Mamma's baby coming soon.

A week later, nerves a-flutter, Leah hurried up the hill to visit with Aunt Lizzie, hoping to share some of the burden of concern. Lizzie met her at the door with a pained look in her perty eyes, though she did seem glad for the visit, serving up warm sugar cookies and cold milk. "Mm-m. You always have the best-tasting cookies," Leah said, settling down in the kitchen.

Lizzie's eyes brightened a bit. All of Leah's sisters made such remarks about their auntie's extraordinary baking talents. Mamma, too, would often say how nice and moist Lizzie's cookies were.

But soon Leah and Lizzie's talk turned to Sadie and how sick with worry both of them were. "My sister's too quiet all the time, scarcely ever speaks to any of us," Leah said, pouring out her heart. "I'm frightened, Aunt Lizzie. She's not herself, not one bit. And she takes off alone, walking out on the main road." Leah sighed. "What can we do to help her?"

Aunt Lizzie nodded, indicating that she, too, wished to

offer support somehow. "What's even more worrisome is your mamma's new baby comin' along in a few weeks now. How will *that* set with our Sadie?"

"Only the dear Lord knows. . . ." Leah felt there was little more to discuss. "But we can pray for God's help, ain't so, Auntie?"

"Jah, 'tis the very best we can do for now."

With that Leah felt a calm reassurance and thanked Lizzie for letting her bend an ear. "I best be getting home to help with supper." She kissed her aunt good-bye and hurried down the long hill toward the Ebersol Cottage.

———————◆———————

One morning, after Dat gave his okay on the German shepherd pup, the girls were taking turns coming up with names. "Let's think of one that's not so common," Leah said. She knew by the markings that this was a special dog indeed. The way Smithy Gid handled the pet when he brought him over told her just how important this pup was.

The whole family was ever so glad to have a little watch-dog in training nestled out in the barn in a box lined with sweet hay. And the girls each vied for the puppy's attention, taking turns feeding him milk from a bottle.

"I think he looks like a fuzzy peach," Mary Ruth spoke up. "Call him Peachy."

Hannah looked up, smiling, holding her sewing needle in midair. "You could name him Giddy Gid," to which they all broke out laughing. Even Mamma.

But none of the girls said why that was so funny. Still,

Leah caught it and hoped that by accepting Gideon's puppy dog she wasn't sending the wrong message. Surely not.

"You could name him *King*," said Mamma. "Since he's the only male round here besides Dat . . . so far."

"Jah, it's a wonderful-gut doggie name." So Leah took Mamma's suggestion, and King it was.

From time to time Sadie left the house and went walking down the narrow main road, beyond Dat's land and the adjoining acres belonging to Smithy Peachey. Sometimes ever farther . . . over toward the welding shop, a mile and a half from home, where she turned and headed past Naomi Kauffman's house. Of course, her friend Naomi was busy with her mamma and sisters, probably, so she wouldn't have seen Sadie wandering along, looking down in the mouth. Sadie didn't care how solemn she appeared these days. She was desperate for solitude, enduring her great loss in silence, for she dared not grieve openly. She made an effort to get outside every day or so, breathing in the fresh springtime air.

One afternoon she was out walking the same route, enjoying the fragrance of flowering trees and shrubs. The dogwoods were early this spring and so were the azaleas, the whole month of April having been much warmer than usual. She found it ever so amazing that this sliver of countryside was so pleasant, so out of the way, and yet speckled with interesting sights. And she'd never cared to notice before today that the road was winding in places, but best of all, it was free of summertime tourists who drove up and down Georgetown Road, hoping to catch a glimpse of a head covering or horse and buggy.

Oh, how she craved this time alone. Needed it desperately. Leah was getting on her nerves, asking questions and fishing to know how Sadie was coping—her arms empty and all. Of course, Leah was only trying to be kind, Sadie knew. Yet she resented her sister. Things had changed; tables were turned. She wished now for Leah's happy carefree life, since her own was in shambles. Too many church boys had heard—from Naomi, more than likely—that Sadie, too, had been awful wild during the years prior to church baptism. Such word, though whispered rumors, found its way to courting-age boys who might want to have a gut time for a while, but when it came to settling down and doing some serious courting, well, they much preferred someone innocent. Someone like Leah, who had *two* young men interested in her, of all things.

Sadie rejected Leah's repeated invitations to go to singings with her and Adah Peachey. If she went, she'd have to ride home with Jonas and Leah, which wasn't any fun for either of them, and certainly not for her. So Sadie had no one at all, not even her baby. God had taken away her precious infant son, allowing him to die before he could ever draw his first breath, before he could ever see the love in his young mamma's eyes. She wept bitter tears as she walked aimlessly along the road, feeling ever so light without her baby growing inside her, as if a wind might come up out of the north and simply blow her away.

Ach, how fair was it that Derry's life could just move forward, unfettered? Hers had come to a dead halt, beginning the night Derry suggested discarding their baby's life. She felt cut off from all that had previously meant anything to her, spending more time out on the road than round the house as the days grew longer, heading toward planting season. Soon they'd be knee-deep in vegetable gardens, including rows of celery to be served at Leah's wedding, and sowing early corn with Dat in the field. And soon a newborn baby would be living in the house, yearning for loving care, except Sadie wouldn't be its mamma.

The Lord God had dealt bitterly with her. Yet broken covenants required blood sacrifice. Dat's old German *Biewel* illustrated such truths, and Preacher Yoder was forever reminding them, especially the young people, what happened to people who broke their vows to God and the church.

Obey or die. . . .

She was reaping what she'd sown. Her world had completely collapsed. Losing her baby to death . . . it was the worst punishment any young woman could ever endure.

After lunch Hannah slipped off to her room and took out her writing notebook—her diary—while Mary Ruth sat at the kitchen table and wrote a letter back to her pen pal in Willow Street, and Mamma napped a bit.

April 23, 1947
Dear Diary,

I'm leery of putting my thoughts on paper today, lest they be read at some later time and be misunderstood. But I'd have to say (if asked) that Sadie is becoming ever so surly, distant to all of us. Even worse than a year ago. Mamma doesn't seem to know what to do about her, either. I can tell by the way our mother sighs and shrugs her shoulders. What with plowing and preparing the soil for planting, Dat isn't indoors all that much, except to eat, so he's not too aware of Sadie's behavior. If I didn't know better, I'd think she had been jilted by a beau, but just who that was or is none of us knows. And if Leah does, she ain't talking.

Putting down her pen, Hannah thought that even Leah's happiness seemed a bit tainted. But that was probably because Jonas Mast was leaving for Ohio very soon. Right perplexing it was, the similarity between Sadie and Leah these days.

And Hannah couldn't begin to understand what was causing such a feeling of calamity whenever Sadie walked into a room. She'd shared this with Mary Ruth privately, but her twin, not so sullen, had other things on her mind—excelling in mathematics, for one, saying that Miss Riehl was ever so proud of her accomplishments. Extra work completed and turned in for grading, too. Yet Mary Ruth seemed oblivious to the goings-on in the house. Ever typical, Hannah was the worried one, sensing the troubles of others.

Hannah was awful sure her twin was definitely on the path heading right out of Dat's house and away from the Amish community. If Mary Ruth kept up her thirst for learning, she most certainly would be. All the while, sisterly love prompted Hannah to sew more and more handkerchiefs, saving every nickel and dime toward making just such a dream come true for their someday schoolteacher.

While her girls assumed she was resting, Ida pulled a chair near the window, where the sun spilled in and the sky was dotted with high cloudiness. Sure enough, her little one began kicking and poking the moment Ida sat down. She smiled a bit, her gaze roaming over the barn roof, out past the windmill and toward the woods. It was then she noticed Sadie walking barefoot, up toward Lizzie's cabin. Ach, she'd been wondering a lot here lately, praying, too, for her eldest. Something just didn't sit right. Grouchy and aloof, Sadie had lost her smile; her confidence was all but gone. And, oddly enough, Lizzie seemed downright mum about it all.

And Ida had tried to talk with Sadie, too, on various occasions, but each time her daughter brushed her off, disinterested in any meaningful conversation, it seemed. No, everything was *hipperdiglipp*—slapdash—and almost hostile coming from Sadie these days.

Ida had voiced her concerns to Abram just last night. "What could be wrong with Sadie, do you think?" she had asked, fearing the worst.

"Now, what do you mean, dear?"

Well, if Abram hadn't noticed anything off-beam, then who was she to say anything and get him all stirred up? So she shrugged off the question and decided to look after her own needs for now. Though she wondered if Lizzie might know something and just wasn't saying. She'd seen Sadie out walking a lot this week, sometimes up the mule path between their barnyard and Lizzie's log cabin. Of course, she wouldn't press things with either Sadie or Lizzie. Time to think of the new little one, soon to be her babe-in-arms.

Aunt Lizzie's house was a one-level cabin that looked more like a perty cottage, one found in the pages of a magazine, at least inside it was. Set back amidst tall, budding trees and protected by flowering shrubs—lilac bushes and forsythia this time of year—the cozy place held a special, nearly sacred spot in Sadie's heart. Her darling baby had been born in Aunt Lizzie's spare room, yet the actual happenings that night were still so hazy in her mind.

"Come right in and make yourself to home," Lizzie said, meeting her at the back door.

"I shouldn't stay so long." But Sadie went in and sat down

right away, feeling awful weak suddenly.

"Well, why not catch your breath at least?" To this, Lizzie laughed softly. "You're here, Sadie. Might as well make it worthwhile. What can I get you to drink?"

"Oh, nothin' at all."

"Well, one look at you and I can see ya need something wet. What'll it be?"

Her aunt meant to coddle her, and she could certainly use some compassion today. Just as she'd needed Lizzie's listening ear the week after her baby son had been born, when she'd crept up here yearning to talk with someone. "All right then, I'll have what you like best . . . some Postum, maybe."

Aunt Lizzie must've seen right through her. "You never drink Postum, Sadie. How 'bout some nice cold lemonade instead?"

Too helpless to squabble, she nodded her head.

"I'll be right back. Now, don't go away, hear?" And with that Lizzie headed out to the kitchen.

Sadie shed her sweater and draped it over the back of the chair. From outside she heard the call of birds within the fox-tail grass, way out past the stone wall surrounding the cabin. Getting up, she went to stand in the window, staring out at a mass of red-winged blackbirds, tussling for their territory. Who'd win? Would the strongest, biggest birds claim their spot?

She let her eyes go misty, daydreaming. And just who had won between Derry and herself? The boy going off to Uncle Sam had, no question. He'd gotten what he'd set out for, then up and left her. But now she was all the wiser for it.

Lizzie hadn't meant to startle her niece as she returned carrying a tray with two glasses of lemonade and a plate of oatmeal cookies. "Here we are. We'll have us a nice chat . . . a snack, too."

They sipped their drinks silently for a time, then ever so slowly Sadie opened up and asked the question that continually weighed on her heart. "Tell me again . . . didja see my baby after. . . ?" Unable to continue, she put her head down, fighting back tears.

"Aw, Sadie dear." Aunt Lizzie came and placed her hand on Sadie's back, saying her name over again.

"I just wish I knew what he looked like." She wept into her hands.

Lizzie tried to console her, saying, "It's all right to cry, truly it is."

And Sadie did cry. She sobbed till Lizzie thought the girl's heart might nearly dry up and break.

Then sitting back, Sadie began to talk in sputters. "Oh, I wish . . . I might've at least held him . . . just for a moment . . . before the doctor took him away."

"Jah. Still, some things are best as is."

"I shouldn't have let Dr. Schwartz leave so quick, prob'ly."

"What else could you do?" Aunt Lizzie sat down nearby. She was ever so uneasy about her niece, who needed such care at the present time, both physically and emotionally.

"All this just pains me something awful," Sadie said.

"Still, it's no surprise to see you distraught over such a loss."

Sadie nodded. "There are nights when I dream of nothing else but my baby, Auntie . . . that I still have him safe inside me. Then the nightmare starts all over again. . . ."

"Well, maybe a little time away might help get you back

on your feet again. A change of scenery can help a lot some-times."

"But where could I go?" Sadie asked, sitting up a bit straighter.

"Most any place, really. Your mamma and I have cousins in Indiana and even up in New York State. Some kinfolk out in Ohio, too."

"How would I get there?"

"I have some money tucked away for emergencies. I could put you on a bus, maybe. How would that be?"

All this—every bit of it—seemed like music to Sadie's ears. And they spent the better part of an hour talking over the possibility of her living with a young family, cousins with a batch of children to look after, out in Millersburg, Ohio.

Lizzie made it clear that Sadie must go for only a short time, because to leave behind the church of her baptism for good would mean certain shunning. And so would being found out . . . about unrepentant sin. "What will your parents have to say about such a visit?" Lizzie asked. "Isn't it time you shared something—with your mamma at least?"

"No, I'd rather not just now. Maybe never . . ."

Oh, how Lizzie wished Sadie would openly share with her parents. Both Ida and Abram were right kind and caring folk, without a doubt. Was the dear girl afraid of being found out by the church elders? Well, if that were the case, Lizzie could attest to having seen the People rally round a wayward mem-ber. And once a wrongdoer repented, well, the arms of the community opened wide to welcome the church member right back into the fold.

Something was surely vexing Sadie. Perhaps it had to do with an unwillingness to repent. Truly, Lizzie wanted to ask why she didn't just offer her remorse privately to Preacher Yoder. But Lizzie kept her peace. Besides stubbornness, what on earth was holding the girl back? Was it the sin of pride, or was Sadie downright rebellious?

Then and there Sadie decided not to tell another soul about her plans to visit Ohio. She didn't know just how much longer she'd stay put here. Of course, with news that Jonas Mast was heading in the same direction, might be best to remain in Gobbler's Knob through the summer months till his return. That way, Leah wouldn't think she was running off after Jonas, for pity's sake. But if he *was* still in the area when she arrived, it sure would be nice to see at least one familiar face, though way off in Ohio.

So come next September, round the time Leah was to make her kneeling vow to God and the church, Sadie would simply slip off into the night . . . take herself away from Lancaster County for a while. And not a single Plain boy in Ohio would have any idea she'd disobeyed the Ordnung so totally. Nobody need know she'd allowed an English boy to court her, deceive her, and father her dead child. She'd be shunned, though, never truly welcomed back into her father's house if she stayed on. But what other choice was there?

Chapter Twenty-Six

The joyous birth of a daughter on May seventeenth had the Ebersol Cottage all abuzz with excitement. Aunt Lizzie rushed out of Mamma's bedroom to share the good news, letting the midwife have a chance to examine the pink, wailing newborn.

"It's a girl!" She passed the word to Hannah, who in turn, ran out to the garden rows, where Dat, Sadie, Leah, and Mary Ruth were planting pole snap beans, cucumbers, turnips, squash, and a variety of other vegetables.

"Well, looks like we're still just Abram's *daughters,*" Hannah called, grinning at Dat and her sisters.

Dat stood up and wiped his forehead, eyes wide. "A girl, is it?"

"Jah, 'tis."

At that Leah and Mary Ruth came and hugged her, jumping up and down with glee. Sadie kept working, though, and Hannah didn't quite understand that. But then, maybe their big sister had been secretly hoping for a brother. Who knows?

The first few days, Ida chose Sadie the most to help her with Lydiann, especially during the morning and afternoon. She felt sure things might improve a bit for Sadie once she held her cuddly baby sister in her arms. Jah, there was something real comforting about holding a wee one. So the first-born helped change and dress the baby of the family, walking the floor with her when she was a bit colicky of an afternoon.

After a full week of this, Sadie did seem to be settling down some. But not so much that she wanted to share with Ida. Not at all. *In due time, she will,* Ida decided.

Abram got a kick out of watching his new daughter make funny little face crinkles while she slept. He told Ida this was the pertiest baby he'd ever seen, which, if she remembered far enough back, he'd said the same of their other daughters when they were each brand-new.

Well, now they had five girls living under their roof, at least for now. Both Sadie and Leah would probably be wed here within the year, she guessed. Leah, for sure—to Jonas Mast. Lizzie had given her the word about the need for celery, thank goodness, so they'd best be planting some this summer, in mid-July.

Lo and behold, if Abram didn't have to worry over working the land after all, waiting so many years to hand over the farm to a son coming along behind. No, the Good Lord had taken care of that, seen fit to give them a daughter instead of a son. A right healthy girl at that.

So just whenever Dawdi John grew older and it was his time to go on home to heaven, she and Abram could simply move into the little Dawdi Haus with Lydiann—build on a bit, maybe—raise her over there, and let one of their sons-in-law tend to farming duties. Of course, by then both Hannah and Mary Ruth would be baptized church members and married, too, more than likely.

Thankfully, all things were working out wonderful-gut for those who love the Lord here on Gobbler's Knob. Seemed to be, anyways.

◆

Ida put a kettle on to boil, hankering for a cup of raspberry tea with a spoonful of honey. Never mind the late hour. All day she had been so busy with her little one, she hadn't had a chance to sit down and read her cousin Fannie's long letter, which had come in the afternoon mail.

Wanting something in hand while she read, she waited for the water to boil, then let the tea leaves steep five minutes. Once she poured the simmering tea into her cup, she settled down in Abram's favorite hickory rocker. Glad for the stillness of the house, she knew all too well that Lydiann would be crying for nourishment here perty soon.

So with her ear attuned to the upstairs bedroom, where Abram slept soundly and their infant daughter was tucked into a handmade wooden cradle in the corner of the room, she began to read.

My dear cousin Ida,

Greetings from Grasshopper Level, where Peter and I are the happy parents of twins . . . a girl and a boy. No doubt you've heard through the grapevine of our double blessing. They arrived full-term, though the boy is somewhat smaller and not nearly as hearty as the girl. We named them Jacob and

Amanda—Jake and Mandie for short. And such a joyous sight the two of them are! Jake has Peter's dark hair and jawline, and Mandie has light brown hair and blue eyes like our Jonas and some of the girls.

We're ever so thankful to the Good Lord and continue to trust Him to see us through the first months of little or no sleep, as you must surely know by now yourself. I'm so happy to hear that you've had a healthy baby girl. Just whenever you have a free minute, I'd like to know how it is for you and Abram having a new baby after all this time.

Then one of these days, maybe come late summer, our families can visit again and enjoy seeing all three of our young ones lined up in a row. Such a perty sight that'll be.

Well, I hear little Mandie fussing for the next feeding. She cries and then both she and Jake get fed. Now, how about that?

Give my best to Abram and all the girls. (Lizzie, too.)

> *My love to you,*
> *Cousin Fannie*

Ida sighed, folding the letter. It was awful nice to sit and soak up the quiet, sipping tea late at night, almost old enough to be a *Grossmudder*, and here she was starting all over as a new mamma, yet. What was the Lord God thinking, anyways?

Of course, she knew she'd just be on her knees that much more, raising Lydiann clear at the tail end of the family, asking for divine wisdom and help along the way. God would continue to be their joy and their strength. Each and every day. Jah, she could count on that and never take such gifts for granted.

Jonas had the use of one of his father's driving horses for the special occasion, this day Leah had dreaded to see arrive, yet she wouldn't have missed spending the afternoon hours with her beau. Not for the world. They'd taken to the road in Jonas's open buggy, diverting off from the main highway and heading toward White Oak Road, where the route curved round like a dusty ribbon under the hot sun.

One of the less-traveled paths, which they ended up following, shrank to a couple of furrows with a thin row of yellow dandelions running between, leading to a wide and open meadow. Thick green bushes, some thorny, others berry-laden, bedecked the roadside as they went. All the while Leah memorized the lush green acres and pungent farm smells around them, as well as the way the sunlight played on Jonas's light brown hair, listening intently as her dearest love shared his plans for their future.

"I'll return in late September or early October. For sure in time for apple picking." Jonas reached for her hand. "And I pray the time will pass quickly."

"Though I can't see how. . . ." Then she nodded, attempting to be brave. "But we'll both be ever so busy . . . so, jah, it oughta go fast."

"You should go ahead with your baptismal instruction, just as we'd planned. I'll do the same in Ohio."

"Ach, how will that all work out?" Leah had never heard of such a thing.

"I've already talked with my bishop. He's given me the okay, if I can find a conservative order in the Millersburg area."

Jonas slowed the horse as the buggy wheels *click-clacked* over a bridge made from old railroad ties, the creek rising and falling over giant stones beneath the old boards, some of them gaping too far apart for Leah's liking.

"I'll be countin' the days till I see you again," Jonas said, his voice husky now.

Oh no . . . don't say such things, she thought, having promised herself she wouldn't spoil the afternoon by shedding a tear. "We have all the rest of our lives, Lord willin', to enjoy our time together as husband and wife," she said.

He smiled at her then, his blue eyes alight with love. Leaning his head against hers briefly, he stopped the horse just as the road leveled out, past a slight incline. "Here's a good place to pick some wild flowers. Want to?"

Standing up quickly, she nodded. Jonas helped her out of the buggy to the grassy paddock, where flowing hills beckoned in every direction. "I'm planning a nice surprise for you," he said.

"Oh? What is it?"

"Well, now, it wouldn't be a surprise if I told you, would it?"

She was ever so inquisitive. "Just *when* will I know?"

He stood there, grinning at her to beat the band. "My dear girl, how will I get along without you by my side . . . even for such a few months?" Gently he pulled her near and brushed her cheek with a tender kiss. "You make it awful hard to keep a secret. Those big hazel eyes of yours."

She laughed softly as they strolled through the tall grass. "So . . . will you tell me, Jonas? Just what is it you have up your sleeve?"

"I'm going to try my hand at makin' you a big oak sideboard. What do you think of that?"

"Oh, such a wonderful-gut surprise! When will you have it finished, do you think?"

"When I return." He touched her face. "It'll be my wedding gift to you."

"I'll look forward to that day." She felt her throat close up and knew she couldn't have spoken more even if she'd wanted to.

"I love you, Leah." And with that, they spun round and round together. The whirling made her dizzy with delight, but she savored most the spot where she landed—in his strong arms. "Remember the day I hurt my ankle?" she said softly. "You picked me right up and carried me into your mamma's kitchen almost before I knew what you were doing!"

"Well, *someone* had to carry you, right?"

Aware of just how near she was to his heart, she laid her head against his white shirt and whispered back, "I love you, too, Jonas." And then she blushed. "Now, *I* have a secret. But I best not tell."

He reached over and cupped her face in his hands.

"Tell me or . . . well, I'll have to kiss you on the lips."

"If you do that, we'll spoil things."

Still, he held her face tenderly, moving closer. "What's your secret, Leah Ebersol?"

"Ach, must you be so impatient?"

"This minute . . . I must know, my dear one."

She breathed deeply, letting him cradle her in his arms once again. "I *always* loved you, Jonas. Even back when I was only ten. That's what."

He smiled down at her. "We both felt this way, didn't we? From the first time we met?"

"Jah—" she fought back tears—"and that we'd mean

much more to each other . . . go far beyond our childhood promises."

"And here we are, Leah."

"Did you ever think we'd be engaged, for sure and for certain?"

"I never doubted it," he said.

Then and there, she vowed their love must never become run-of-the-mill like other married couples. Theirs would be the strong and lasting kind, one that flourished well into old age, despite the strain of separation facing them now.

They walked hand in hand up to the crest of the hill, where they looked over grazing and cropland far below, watching butterflies drift up from the grasses. A single bluebird flew overhead, and Leah reached up happily.

"You're my bluebird . . . and always will be," her darling beau had said, back on their first night as a courting couple.

With Jonas by her side, she was right where she belonged— for always—certain no harm could befall two people so in love.

More From *NY Times* Bestselling Author Beverly Lewis

To find out more about Beverly and her books,
visit beverlylewis.com or find her on Facebook!

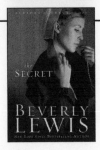

When Amelia Devries, thoroughly modern and equally disillusioned, takes a wrong turn during a rainstorm, she unexpectedly meets an Amishman—and a community—that might just change her life forever.

The Fiddler
HOME TO HICKORY HOLLOW

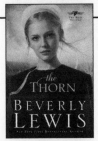

As two Amish sisters find themselves on the fringes of their Lancaster community, will they be forced to choose between their beloved People and true love?

THE ROSE TRILOGY: *The Thorn, The Judgment, The Mercy*

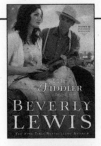

When her mother's secret threatens to destroy their peaceful Amish family, will Grace's search for the truth lead to more heartache or the love she longs for?

SEASONS OF GRACE: *The Secret, The Missing, The Telling*

More From *NY Times* Bestselling Author Beverly Lewis

To find out more about Beverly and her books,
visit beverlylewis.com or find her on Facebook!

The daughter of an Old Order Amish preacher, Annie Zook loves two forbidden things: art and Englisher Ben Martin. As Annie wrestles with her desires, a life-altering decision must be made. Will she follow her heart or stay true to her beloved Amish heritage?

ANNIE'S PEOPLE: *The Preacher's Daughter, The Englisher, The Brethren*

When their Amish community is pushed to the breaking point, Nellie and Caleb find themselves on opposing sides of an impossible divide. Can their love survive when their beliefs threaten to tear them apart?

THE COURTSHIP OF NELLIE FISHER: *The Parting, The Forbidden, The Longing*

A collection of inspiring prayers used by the Amish and Mennonites for over 300 years—compiled by America's favorite author of Amish fiction, Beverly Lewis.

Amish Prayers compiled by Beverly Lewis